Stories of Crime & Detection

Volume Three

This Way Out

James Ronald

Edited by Chris Verner

Moonstone Press

This edition published in 2024 by Moonstone Press
www.moonstonepress.co.uk

This Way Out originally published in 1938 by Rich & Cowan.
Diamonds of Death originally published in 1934 by Gramol.
Ruined by Water originally published in 1931 by The Daily Mail.

ISBN 978-1-899000-70-8
eISBN 978-1-899000-71-5

A CIP catalogue record for this book is available from the British Library
Text designed and typeset by Moonstone Press
Cover illustration by Jason Anscomb

Royalties from the sale of this book will be donated to MND Scotland, who fund ground-breaking MND (motor neurone disease) research and world-class clinical trials to combat an uncommon condition that affects the brain and nerves, and causes weakness that gets worse over time, eventually resulting in death.

Contents

INTRODUCTION

This third volume of *James Ronald, Stories of Crime and Detection* contains a novel, a novelette, and a short story.

The novel, *This Way Out* is a compelling thriller supercharged with suspense. The story takes place in London in 1902. It is concerned with a genteel middle-class Englishman, a clerk named Philip Marshall who is married to Cora, a harridan of a wife. Marshall meets a novelist, Simmons, who has not written for years. Marshall walks a very drunk Simmons home and during this walk they discuss the idea of the perfect murder. He meets young Mary Grey, who is unemployed and suffering from depression. Their deepening friendship, though physically innocent, is discovered by Philip's wife, who threatens him with exposure and scandal. He carefully plans her demise, and carries it out so that he can marry Mary. He appears to get away with it...

This Way Out was first published in the UK as a hardcover in July 1938 by Rich & Cowan, based at 37 Bedford Square, London WC1. This edition was followed by J.B. Lippincott, 1939 in the USA. In January 1940, the story appeared in *Cosmopolitan Magazine* Number 643. The book was made into an American film noir for Universal, *The Suspect*, released in 1944, starring Charles Laughton and directed by Richard Siodmak. To capitalise on the film, the book was reprinted in 1948 by Hodder and Stoughton, with a depiction of Charles Laughton on the dust wrapper.

The second story in this volume is a novelette, *Diamonds of Death*. It is a humorous mixed bag with American 'pulp fiction' overtones. It involves a stolen diamond necklace, murder and romance between amateur sleuth Bill and a beautiful girl:

> Out of the wreckage a girl ran toward him. An ermine evening wrap accentuated her tall, slim figure and emphasised the golden beauty of her bare head.
>
> Bill leaned out of the driving seat and she clutched his arm. He switched on his spotlight and shone it on her face. Her eyes were wide with horror. "Will you help me?" she gasped breathlessly. "You must help me!"
>
> For a moment Bill was silent. He was stunned into silence by her beauty. An odd feeling swept over him as he looked at her, an emotion no other girl had ever aroused in him. She had on too much make-up. She was fragrant with expensive perfume. Her wrap, falling open, revealed a shimmering white dress, cut daringly low. She was exactly the exotic, butterfly type of woman he had always faintly despised. But as he stared at her numbly, he realised that she was the first woman to come into his life who really mattered. Why, he could not have explained. She was beautiful, but the attraction was more than that. Character was expressed in her face, but even that did not explain the elusive emotion she evoked in him.

One of James Ronald's earliest works, *Diamonds of Death* was published by Gramol, Mystery Novels No. 17, 1934. It could be described as a companion story to *The Monocled Man* (Stories of Crime and Detection Volume Two). Not only is this story similar in length, it was also published by Gramol. The story is also about stolen diamonds, American gangsters, a gunfight on a rooftop, and a beautiful girl. It is a fast moving, tongue-in-cheek romp, not so much a serious crime and detection story, but nevertheless great fun to read.

The short story, *Ruined by Water* was published in *The Daily Mail*, UK, 22 September 1931. The story also appeared in several other newspapers, all under the pseudonym of Peter Gale, including: *The Australasian*, Melbourne, Victoria, Australia, 21 April 1934; *The Falkirk Herald* 27 February 1935, from which this text is transcribed; *The Linlithgowshire Gazette*, West Lothian, Scotland, 1 March 1935; *The Coatbridge Express*, Lanarkshire, Scotland, 27 July 1938; *The Saturday Evening Express*, Launceston, Tasmania, 17 June 1939; and no doubt others.

ABOUT THE AUTHOR

James Jack Ronald, to give his full name, was born 11 May 1905, in North Kelvinside, Glasgow, Scotland. He was the son of James Jack Ronald, a Chartered Public Accountant, and Katherine Hamilton Ronald. He was educated at Hillhead High School, Glasgow, established in 1885.

Until he was five, James Ronald says he was chubby, happy, and irresponsible; but in 1911, his sixth year, he was run over by an automobile causing a very real morbidity to creep in. For ten years following the accident he suffered recurrent dreams about a wheel that became larger and larger as it turned faster and faster. He was invalided over a long period during which, with his mother Catherine's encouragement, he enjoyed a prodigious amount of reading. He later claimed he owed his literary gift and resultant career to this near-fatal automobile accident, which caused him to change from a sunny little extrovert to a cloudy introvert.

When he was fourteen he wrote an account of the accident, setting down all the details in a somewhat light vein, not forgetting to note that the candy he had purchased with such delight on that foggy morning was found sticking to the wheels of the car as he was being carried off. The piece won him first prize for composition and congratulations from the masters at the school and even the headmaster wished him well, but that did not prevent corporal punishment for his appalling handwriting. He was called into the headmaster's office, but kept waiting so that everybody knew that he, James Ronald, was going to receive a beating from the headmaster. This injustice obviously affected him very deeply, because it remained with him all his life, and crops up in interview after interview:

> After all, I taught myself to read before going to school and could see no reason for accepting a beating because they failed to teach me how to write, so I bolted.

In a spirit of rebellion against repeated punishments for bad handwriting for compositions for which he invariably got an 'A', Ronald came home from school one day announcing he would never return. It was time to leave. His mother Catherine was understandably distressed, concerned her elder son leaving school at such a young age would diminish his career prospects. Aware of the scarcity of jobs just then in Glasgow, she told him he could only stay away from school if he remained active in some useful employment, making it clear she would not condone an idler in the family.

Within three days James Ronald was an errand boy for the *Glasgow Evening News*, a paper into which he had smuggled a poem some months earlier. But there was 'no writing, nothing editorial' in his set up and he thoroughly disliked it and lost the job. He found another post immediately with the *Glasgow Sunday Mail* and kept this one until he printed his own rival paper on the office mimeograph. He broke the machine and, failing to cover his tracks by leaving a sheet in the copier, he was fired. Then came a dozen jobs, including one with an art dealer for whom he gilded statues and washed windows. His mother told him, 'It is no disgrace to wash windows, James, but it is a disgrace to wash them like that.'

By the age of seventeen, James Ronald had run through all prospective employers in Glasgow, including every newspaper.

He felt the need of open space—'a lot of it'—and after various and sundry abortive departures, finally won grudging permission to seek his fortune in the New World.

For some reason, Chicago stuck in the mind of the young Ronald as a magic word. He became determined to travel to the United States of America. The main method of crossing the Atlantic Ocean in the 1920s was by steamship and ocean liner. The passengers aboard the *SS Saturnia* included seventeen-year-old James Ronald, who arrived at his destination on 6 December 1922, at the Port of Québec, an inland port located in Québec, Canada. From there he continued his journey across the Great Lakes to Chicago, Illinois, United States. He managed to survive in Chicago; the fastest-growing city in world history, with a flourishing economy approaching three million people, attracting huge numbers of new immigrants from Eastern and Central Europe. Ronald stayed in Chicago for five years, wanting to write, but unable to afford the time because he was forced to earn money to live. He was taken on and fired from a variety of jobs with monotonous regularity. Like his experiences in Glasgow, he exhausted all potential employers, dabbling in some forty jobs ranging from short-order cook and dishwasher to muslin salesman; from dance promoter and theatre manager to washing dishes again in a Greek restaurant. He edited ten trade journals at one time for a Chicago publisher; and gave new life to a women's religious magazine. A chain-smoker, he confessed slyly to have worked for the Anti-Cigarette League, his excuse being 'a man must eat don't you know'—at that time eating being the only philosophy he could afford to practise. It was in the Windy City that he learned about life.

Working in the U.S as 'a visitor' to avoid immigration may have caught up with Ronald because, in 1927, he returned to Britain on a more permanent basis, and secured a well-paid job with an English newspaper chain, and a promise of future advancement. However, during his first holiday in the job, a car accident disrupted this promising career trajectory. Whilst driving a small open two-seater Rover 8, Ronald was struck by a two-ton truck and thrown out against the radiator of another vehicle. Left with a broken hip and temporarily crippled (and without the newly acquired job), he settled down to write.

Ronald's writing developed in three stages. First, he hammered out serializations and short stories which were syndicated in newspapers, both at home and abroad; and a number were also published in obscure pulp magazines. Some stories then became lost and forgotten and this has unfortunately contributed to a lack of recognition for an impressive body of work. These early narratives were very difficult to track down, but searching has provided me with an enjoyable and rewarding task—a treasure hunt for lost tales. This was not made any easier because many of these stories were published under pseudonyms; Peter Gale, Mark Ellison, Kenneth Streeter, Alan Napier, and even women; Cynthia Priestley and Norah Banning—in addition to known pseudonyms Michael Crombie and Kirk Wales. Those I have discovered have all been gathered together for republication in this series.

A second writing stage followed; the full-length mystery stories which have made him so popular with Golden Age of Detection aficionados. They are out-of-print, elusive to find, and first editions are very expensive.

Finally, late in life, James Ronald embarked on his Dickensian-style life drama novels. He received enthusiastic praise for his ingenuity, freshness, and sharp sense of humour by many critics and writers of the time, such as August Derleth. Orville Prescott, the main book reviewer for *The New York Times* for 24 years, called James Ronald 'a born novelist', and that he 'has in full measure the two basic drives which inspire a writer of fiction–the urge to create characters and to tell stories about them. Mr. Ronald does both naturally, directly and well.' His work received praise and has been compared to William de Morgan, H. G. Wells, Rudyard Kipling, J. M. Barrie, and Somerset Maugham.

James Ronald is a writer who has not gained the long-term recognition he deserves. His work has received high praise for his ingenuity, freshness, and sharp sense of humour by many critics and writers of the time and current enthusiasts, highlighting him as one of the leading storytellers of the day, yet barely anything has been republished since his death in 1972. I hope the reader will enjoy these imaginative and entertainingly written stories as much as I have collecting them.

Chris Verner
Berkhamsted, Buckinghamshire, UK
April 2023

THIS WAY OUT

Chapter 1

They were telling stories at the other end of the bar and Philip wanted to join them but Simmons had a firm grip of his sleeve. Simmons was talking volubly, the words tripping over his tongue and breaking off their final letters. He was telling Philip about a book he intended to write and gradually leading up to asking for the loan of a pound. For years he had been telling people about this book as often as he could grip a sleeve and edge the wearer into a corner. As a prelude to borrowing money it had worked fairly well at first—for it seemed stingy to refuse a small loan to a man about to make a fortune out of serial, film, and book rights—but now few habitués of 'The Hole in the Wall' would listen to him.

Before he was thirty Simmons had written three novels of promise but now he was thirty-five and for years had not written a line. He still described himself as a novelist and was hurt if anyone suggested he should look for a job. At seven every evening he swaggered into the saloon bar of 'The Hole in the Wall' with a shilling or so in his pocket and after closing time he wavered out again with a skinful of beer and most of his shilling. He never paid for more than his first drink of the evening; the rest grudgingly was supplied by habitués of the pub. Frequently the regulars vowed to leave him out when they ordered a round but when they came to pay, invariably they found that Simmons's pint of bitter had included itself in the order.

For the third time the barman said wearily: "Time, gentlemen, please."

"Two pints of bitter," said Simmons, pushing an empty tankard across the bar. As a matter of form, he went through the motions of fumbling for money before he said to Philip:

"You'll have to pay, old boy. I'm broke."

"Sorry, sir. It's after time."

"But I ordered them five minutes ago. You heard me, didn't you, Marshall, old boy?"

"No," said Philip.

The barman moved on. "Come along, gentlemen. Drink up, please. It's after time."

Simmons hammered with his tankard on the bar. "How the hell can I drink up when I haven't anything to drink?"

"Let's go," said Philip, taking his arm. "It's late."

"Damned if I do," retorted Simmons, hammering louder than before. "I ordered drinks ten—fifteen minutes ago and I'm going to stand here till I get them if I have to stand here all night."

The landlord, a phlegmatic man with immense shoulders, came out of his den behind the bar and stood looking at Simmons. The sprinkling of customers who were finishing drinks craned their necks, hoping to see Simmons bodily thrown out. The landlord was capable of doing it. An ex-prize-fighter, he was built like a champion, but he had not gone far in the ring because he had a weak stomach. He liked to talk about his stomach, and he liked Philip Marshall because Philip was the only one of his regular customers who showed any interest in it. He was equal to handling twelve of Simmons, weak stomach or no weak stomach.

In silence, the regulars waited for something to happen. But nothing happened. Nothing, at least, worth watching. For a moment the landlord stared at Simmons and then looked down in mild surprise at the hammering tankard. Simmons stopped pounding the bar. He put down the tankard. The landlord raised a flap in the counter and followed his departing customers to the door.

"Good night, gentlemen. See you tomorrow."

And the devil of it was, reflected Philip, he probably would. He would see them all tomorrow, Philip included. At the age of forty-six, Philip had become a pub-haunter, a regular, one of the coterie that nightly trooped out of the 'Hole in the Wall' a few minutes after closing time. Most of the others had the same reason as he for lingering as long as possible in the place; it was so much pleasanter than home.

Fresh air struck Simmons like a physical blow and sent him reeling diagonally against the wall. Philip followed without haste and took his arm.

"I'm going to be sick."

"You'll be all right in a moment."

"I tell you; I'm going to be sick. I ought to know." Simmons was right. In wracking spasms, he rid himself of all he had consumed, and then Philip guided him home through slumbering streets. Simmons ran on garrulously about his book. It was going to be a mystery novel but ordinary thrillers could no more be compared to it than a pimple can be compared to Mount Everest. The trouble with most mystery novels, he said, was that they were too involved. The murders were done with revolvers hidden in clocks or fountain pens or radios. That was all rot. The perfect murder must be so simple that no one would suspect it to be murder.

An arranged accident was the perfect murder.

"You hate a man and you want to kill him but you don't want to hang. All right, what do you do? You make friends with him; you take him up to town for a night out. You stand him a slap-up dinner with plenty to drink and you go on throwing drinks into him until he can hardly walk. You're a little drunk yourself and you pretend to be drunker than you are. You come home by Tube when the platforms are crowded with theatregoers returning to the suburbs. Everyone is jostling to get in place for a train that's coming in and in the crush you push against your poor old pal and he falls on to the line. Too bad. Too bad." Simmons clicked his teeth sadly.

"Or, you buy a revol—a revol—you buy a gun and show it to your pals in the local boozer. One evening you show it to this special pal and the damned thing goes off. Everyone knows a thing like that's always liable to happen when you play with firearms. At the inquest the coroner ticks you off for being so bloody careless and hopes this will be a lesson to you. You haven't a licence for the gun, so they fine you fifty quid or send you to gaol for three months. But they don't hang you. It was an accident and no one can prove it wasn't."

"This is your gate," said Philip, stifling a yawn.

"Let go my arm till I find my key."

Philip obeyed. Simmons reeled across the garden path and fell into a rosebush. He rolled out, cursing, and picking at thorns in the seat of his trousers. Philip went forward to help him up but Simmons butted him away with his head. "Let me alone. You pushed me."

On his hands and knees Simmons crawled up the front steps to the door. Grasping the handle, he drew himself up and put a thumb on the bell-button. He kept it there and the bell shrilled through the house until a light appeared in an upper window.

Simmons looked over his shoulder and giggled. "My dear little wife, God bless her, damn her," he said, falling off the steps into Philip's arms.

A light went on in the hall and a woman in pyjamas opened the door. She cast a look of utter loathing at Simmons, lying giggling in Philip's arms, then she opened the door wider and stood back.

"Bring him in."

In the hall Simmons struggled upright and pulled himself

out of Philip's grasp. He wobbled over to his wife with both arms extravagantly outstretched.

Without heat she raised her hand and slapped his face. He staggered back and fell against a standard lamp, slid down it, and lay in a heap at the base. The shade fell off and settled over his head.

The woman stood looking at him dispassionately. At first sight Philip had taken her to be about forty but now he realized that she was fully ten years younger. She had the pale aloof face of one who is dead, who had suffered greatly before dying, and upon whom has settled the chilling calm of the dead. Her features were lovely. She must have been very beautiful, Philip thought, before she died.

"And I slave my life away to support *that,*" she said.

She looked at Philip. I suppose I ought to thank you. You're the only pub-crawling pal who's bothered to see him home. Not that I should care if he never came home but when he wanders about drunk, he gets into trouble and that costs money I can't afford. A month ago, he went for a joy-ride in a car he found outside a pub and made a complete wreck of it."

Philip did not reply. It was no good saying anything. She did not want sympathy. She had gone beyond the stage at which sympathy might have helped.

"You don't look Gilbert's type," she went on dryly. "You look like a respectable little man with a steady job. A managing clerk, or something like that."

"You're a good judge of character."

"Why do you bother with him? You haven't got to. You're not married to him. He's nothing to you. How can you put up with him?"

"I don't know exactly. I lead a lonely life. I—"

"You must be damned hard up for a friend if that drunken scrounger is the best you can do."

"I am damned hard up for a friend. But it isn't only that. When I was younger, I wanted to write and—well, he's the only author I've ever known."

The woman laughed. It was not a pleasant sound. "That's funny. That's very, very funny. You stand him drinks for the same reason that I married him. He was the only author *I'd* ever known. I thought it would be something to be the wife of a novelist. Well, it *is* something, by God it is. A few days after the wedding he broke the news that he wouldn't have any money until he finished his next book. To keep the wolf from the door while he finished it, I got my old job back. I'm still waiting for him to finish it. I've waited five years."

"You ought to kick him out."

"Don't tell me what I ought to do," she retorted. "I know what I ought to do, a damned sight better than you can tell me. If you knew so much you wouldn't have to rely for company on a thing like that"—she jerked a contemptuous finger at her husband, sprawling on the floor with a lamp-shade over his head like a snuffer on a candle. "Why don't you marry, if you're so lonely? You're not so very old. In the middle forties, I suppose. Lots of girls would jump at a nice little man like you."

"I am married."

"Oh. Married—and lonely. I thought only women were lonely after marriage. So, you got stuck too, eh?"

"Yes," said Philip. "I got stuck, too."

"Not so badly as me, I'd be willing to bet."

"You'd lose."

"My God, she must be a terror."

"She is."

For an instant her face became softer. "Poor little man. You don't look as though you deserved it." She shrugged her shoulders. "Oh, hell! I'm going to bed before we start crying on each other's shoulders."

"What about him?" asked Philip, indicating Simmons, who had started to snore.

"Nobody asked him to lie there."

"He'll be stiff when he wakes."

"I hope so," she replied, mounting the stairs.

Chapter 2

Going home down a quiet street lined with trees, Philip saw a familiar figure approaching. He halted under a lamppost and waited. The figure came nearer, the yellow glow of the street lamp fell on a solemn young face, a hatless head with a shock of curling brown hair.

"Hello, John," said Philip, a pathetic eagerness in his voice.

The young man started. He smiled. "Hello, Dad." They shook hands and stood awkwardly looking at each other. The boy was a head taller than Philip and built like an athlete. Although so big he looked very young, far younger than his twenty-three years. He had the fine features of a youth in a Greek sculpture. Philip never saw him without a feeling of wonder that such a youth could be a son of his. It was quite impossible to think of him as a son of Cora's.

Years ago, Philip had overheard a scrap of conversation between two boys at the annual sports of the secondary school at which John had been a pupil. One of them had indicated Philip and his wife as the parents of the school champion athlete and the other expressed amazement:

"Those two? They can't be."

"They are. I've seen him with them."

"That little tick of a man and that hay-bag of a woman? No wonder he keeps them dark."

Many a man would have resented a son so much his physical superior but Philip's love for John was too great to allow of envy or resentment. "You're looking well. A little pale, perhaps, overdoing your studies?"

"I don't think so, Dad. I do a couple of hours every evening, of course. Don't want to be a clerk all my life."

"Of course not," said Philip quietly.

John gripped his father's arm. "I didn't mean..."

"That's all right. What are you doing in the neighbourhood? Not changed your digs?"

"No, I'm still living out on the Great West Road. I've been visiting a friend."

There was an uncomfortable silence.

"I've been missing you rather badly," said Philip at last.

"I know. I've been missing you, Dad. But I had to go, you know that."

"Yes, you had to go."

John ran his fingers through his hair. "I couldn't stand the atmosphere at home any longer. Those continual rows! —I look back on them as one long nightmare." He glanced hesitantly at Philip. "How is Mother?"

"Pretty much the same."

"Now I'm gone you'll come in for all of it."

"That can't be helped. What are the digs like?"

"Oh, they're fine," said John, a shade too quickly. He avoided Philip's eye.

"The last time we ran into each other you told me your landlady has a daughter about your age."

"Yes."

"That doesn't tell me anything. What's she like?"

"Oh, I don't know. Quite a decent sort. But girls are...funny. I never know quite what to make of her."

"I'd like to see something of you. Do you suppose I could come round to your digs for a chat some evening?"

Another awkward silence, and then: "I'd rather you didn't, Dad. I wouldn't know how to explain you. You see, well, I didn't want to go into a lot of explanations, so I told Mrs. Lemon I was an orphan."

"I see."

"Don't look like that, Dad. I know wiping you out sounds pretty cold-blooded, but I only did it because I didn't want to tell her why I couldn't live at home."

"That's all right. Well, can't we meet some evening and go for a walk or drop into a pub for a glass of beer and a talk?"

"That would be great, Dad. I don't know just when it will be for, I don't get much time these days, but I'll give you a ring at the office some time and we'll fix up something. I'm pretty busy studying in the evenings and I've joined a rowing club and then Gladys—that's Mrs. Lemon's daughter—Gladys and I go to the movies every so often, so I…don't get much time."

John shifted his weight from one foot to the other.

"It's getting late," he said.

Philip sighed. "Yes, it's getting late. Well... We'll run into each other again some evening, I expect."

"I hope so, Dad."

They shook hands. Philip stood under the street lamp and watched his son swinging briskly away from him. There was a dryness in his throat as he turned the corner into the street in which he lived. Two rows of little brick houses, all built from the same plans, identical with each other almost to a brick. In front of each house a pocket-handkerchief garden, surrounded by a hedge. Some of the hedges were neatly trimmed but the one in front of Philip's house was tall and ragged. It was a long time since Philip had done any gardening. Cora had grumbled about the cost of seeds and tools; about the dirt he brought in; about the results of his efforts, which were never quite as good those achieved by his neighbours. So, Philip had given up the garden and now Cora grumbled about its neglected state. In twenty-five years of married life, Cora had never run short of things to grumble about.

She was waiting up for him. She always waited for him and rolled her eyes at the clock when he came in. Her wispy, greying hair was in curl-papers. It stuck out all over her head like a star-fish. She had undressed down to corsets and knickers and put on a soiled flowered kimono. There were bones missing from the corsets; she had loosened them and she bulged in the most unexpected places. The kimono—or perhaps the way she sat—left her legs uncovered to the thighs. They were fat and shapeless, like two pork sausages. Cora's eyes were sullen, her mouth was peevish. Philip averted his gaze. He could not bear to look at her.

On her lap lay a darning basket and a heap of socks but Philip knew that if he looked under the cushion flattened behind her broad back, he would find *Peg's Paper* or *Film Weekly* and a sticky bag of chocolate creams. The darning basket was only a stage property, to help her sustain the role of a hard-working, long-suffering housewife. Every night she had the heap of socks lying at hand, ready to be snatched up when she heard him coming. They were always the same socks and the heap never became any smaller.

The room was a jumble of shabby furniture. There was a drawing-room at the rear of the ground floor but it was kept locked for Cora grumbled that an extra room in use would mean additional work. The single electric light bulb, covered by a paper shade, which hung from the centre of the ceiling was not strong enough to enable one to see clearly the dirt that lurked in the corners, but one knew it was there. By day there was little additional light in the room, for Cora kept the windows closely curtained; but one was still aware of the dirt.

"This is a nice time to come home night after night. I suppose you'll say you've been working late at the office but you can't fool me with that story, Mr. Philip Marshall. No employer keeps his clerks until eleven and twelve every night. If he did, you'd get overtime and I've yet to see a penny of it."

Philip's supper was spread on a corner of the table. The end of a loaf of bread. A scrap of butter in a greasy dish. The remains of a leg of mutton which had done duty for five days and now wore an air of defiance. A few dejected pickles on a saucer. A pot of lukewarm tea. Pushing aside the mutton, Philip buttered a crust of bread and spread the evening paper at his elbow.

"Don't imagine that I don't know where you spend your evenings. You've been seen. Mr. Greener saw you. You're in 'The Hole in the Wall' every night, guzzling beer. It's not good enough. I won't have it. If you have money for beer, you can give me more for the housekeeping."

Cora did not look directly at him while she ranted on. She looked at a point in mid-air above his head. It was years since they had looked at each other squarely. Philip had a feeling that if they ever did something would break.

"I'd like a bath," he said, his eyes on his paper. "Is there any hot water?"

"You know perfectly well there's no hot water. I've more to do than stoke fires all day on the off-chance you're wanting a bath. Not to mention burning coal at forty-eight shillings a ton. It's as much as I can do to manage hot water once a week. If you want baths oftener than that, my lord, you'd better take up your abode at the Ritz."

"We ought to have a geyser."

"And who'd pay for it, may I ask?"

"I would. You can hire one for a few shillings a quarter and they don't burn much gas."

"Indeed. Well, you listen to me, Mister Philip Marshall: if you can pay for a geyser, you can give me more money. There isn't a woman in the street who has less to manage on than I have. Five pounds a week for everything! I'd like to see Mrs. Greener's face if her husband expected her to make do with that. But then"—she infused into her voice a mocking purr that made Philip long to wring her neck— "Mrs. Greener's husband wasn't content to be a clerk all his life. In a few years Mrs. Greener will be riding in her own car and I—I'll still be a domestic drudge, scrimping and saving to make ends meet. If you were a man, you'd ask for a rise and see that you got it."

Philip smiled inwardly. He did not tell her that he had asked for a rise twice within the past two years—and got it each time. He had not the smallest intention of allowing her more money. Heaven knew what she did with the sum he already allowed her. She didn't spend it on the house; they had not had so much as a new pair of curtains for years. She didn't spend it on food—or, if she did, she was robbed, for Philip could not remember one decent meal in his own home.

"You're not even handy about the house. I told you weeks ago about the broken step at the top of the stairs but you haven't done anything about it. I suppose you're waiting for me to trip on it and break my neck."

Philip kept his eyes on his paper and let her rave on and on and on. But he was not reading. It was impossible to read with that barbed tongue dinning in his ears. His mind framed replies to the thing she was saying but he did not utter them. She liked him to talk back, so that she could make a scene and bawl at the top of her voice. It annoyed her when he held his tongue.

"It beats me why I ever married you. I had plenty of other chances. If I had married Dick Burbage, I need never have soiled my fingers. But no, I had to marry you. I've given you the best years of my life and what have I got in return? A life of drudgery, that's what. You stay out until all hours of the night.

I might be a widow for all I see of you. I believe you hate me. You do. You hate me. You needn't deny it."

"I wasn't going to deny it," said Philip quietly.

Cora stared and her face became purple with anger. "You brute. Oh, you beast."

Philip rose and left the room. Her voice, shrill with rage, followed him up the stairs. He groped his way up, for the hall, the stairs, and the upper landing were in darkness. It was typical of Cora that she could not bear to buy light bulbs. When one burned out, she replaced it from another part of the house. At the moment there was a light in Philip's bedroom, one he had bought a few days before, but he knew the next time a bulb fused Cora would replace it without hesitation from his socket.

The bed was unmade. Philip had been in a hurry that morning, and had left for the office without making it. Only after a series of arguments with Cora had he achieved a bedroom of his own. Cora's sense of the fitting had been outraged by the thought of husband and wife sleeping apart.

"You don't care how much work you make!" she had stormed when Philip had pointed out that sleep was the only purpose for which they had shared a bed for many years and that sleep would be more comfortable for both of them if they were separated. "How many pairs of hands do you think I have? I've more to do already than I can manage. I've no time to make extra beds and tidy extra rooms."

"If that's all that's worrying you," Philip had retorted, "I'll keep the room in order myself."

Cora had held him to his word. Since he took possession of the room, she had never entered it, except to appropriate his light bulbs and pry into his belongings for evidence of infidelity. Cora put great emphasis on fidelity. That was the buoy to which she clung when, in a marital argument, she found herself floundering out of her depth. "I'm a good wife. I've always been faithful to you..."

Philip no longer considered faithfulness the most important factor in marriage, as he had done in his youth. He would not care greatly if Cora gave herself—curl-papers, kimono and all—to the milkman, the coalman, to Tom, Dick, or Harry; if only she would be pleasant about the house.

Chapter 3

Tr-r-ing… Tr-r-ing… Philip burrowed into the pillow and clung to the skirts of fleeing sleep. A moment more to dream, another brief period of escape from reality. But the red tin imp on his bedside table would not be denied. Across its face was printed: RotoRex—The Reliable Alarm, and the red tin imp was as good as its word. Tr-r-ring… Tr-r-ring… It screamed in his ear, insistently, imperatively: 'Half-past seven. Time to get up.' Fumbling about the table-top, Philip knocked the little red clock over the edge. It rolled across the floor ringing with undiminished vigour, with shrill defiance. He rose and wrung its neck.

Barefooted, in faded cotton pyjamas, shrunk in the wash, which exposed two bony ankles, he tiptoed to the door and opened it softly. With relief he listened to the familiar sounds that came from Cora's room. Gr-r-raw—whee. Gr-r-raw—whee. Gr-r-raw—whee. That was Cora snoring. She snored in a bass and soprano duet. Thank heaven the red tin imp had not disturbed her. To waken Cora early in the morning was the surest way to start the day badly.

He stood at his open window and breathed deeply forty times, spreading his arms as he inhaled, letting them drop to his sides as he exhaled. That was a good idea, his favourite newspaper had informed him. He sprinkled his thinning hair with a much-advertised tonic and kneaded the scalp with his fingers. With the aid of two mirrors, he inspected his bald spot and shook his head over it. He was beginning to lose faith in this hair tonic. For three months he had been using it night morning and the bald spot—which at first was the size of a shilling—should now be covered with thick, glossy hair. Instead, it had grown to the size of a florin.

After a close shave he stripped to the waist and washed himself vigorously in cold water. Rubbing himself down with a coarse towel, he felt warmly alive. Nothing like cold water, he reflected, to wake a chap up in the morning. It was a reflection that occurred to him daily. For years he had been toying with the idea of starting the day with a cold bath but there was the danger that the running water might waken Cora—and besides a whole tubful of cold water looks so very cold.

In a neat blue suit, he stood before his dressing-table mirror, tweaked the knot of his tie, brushed down a stray hair. The receding tide of his hair had given him a high forehead, lending a touch of distinction to a face otherwise insignificant. Staring back at him from the mirror it was so familiarly his own that it did not occur to him that it might have belonged to any one of a million other men; but he would not have recognized it as his own if it had sat opposite him in a Tube train, attached to another body. It was one of those plain, utilitarian faces with no outstanding features which accompany the bodies of so many middle-class Englishmen in the middle forties. Even the clipped moustache was from stock.

The bed had been airing while he washed and dressed. Now he made it with brisk efficiency. Shoes in hand, he crept downstairs, collected morning paper and milk from the mat, and stole into the kitchen. He put the kettle on and polished his shoes while he waited for it to boil.

The kitchen cupboard was musty with the smell of stale food. One of Cora's pet economies was hoarding bits of this and scraps of that in saucers and cracked cups. Some of the leftovers had fuzzy white beards. There were some eggs in a bowl. Philip broke one into a cup and hastily covered his nose. As he threw it out, he noticed that the shell was stamped: PRODUCE OF CHINA.

He breakfasted on toast and tea, skimming the morning

paper while he ate. There was nothing to read in it, for it was one of those illustrated dailies that cater for Coras, but he looked at the pictures. At twenty-five past eight he brushed his ancient bowler until it looked almost youthful, put it on at a sober but not forbidding angle, took his rolled umbrella from the hall-stand, and left the house.

It was with a sense of relief that he closed the door quietly and started down the garden path.

*

At ten Cora woke with a dark brown taste in her mouth. In a drowsy stupor she lay staring at a crack in the ceiling. She dozed off, woke with a start, dozed off, woke with a start. It was almost eleven when she sat up in bed and began to scratch her back. In the act of scratching, she lapsed into a sort of hypnotic trance and sat staring at nothing for several minutes, her mouth hanging open, her eyes glassy.

She struggled out of bed and took off her nightdress. Beneath it she wore her underwear, partly for warmth, partly to simplify dressing in the morning. Feminine garments of every description, all slightly soiled, lay on chairs about the room and the wardrobe bulged open.

Yawning and scratching, Cora buckled on her corsets, pulled a petticoat over her head, slipped into the flowered kimono. From the rail at the foot of the bed she took the stockings she had worn the previous day. There was a large hole in the toe of one, so she threw them aside and reached for another pair.

Removing the curl-papers, she ran a comb through her hair and put it down threaded with dead hairs. It was time she had a shampoo and a perm, she reflected listlessly. She dabbed her face and neck with a powder puff, coating some parts thickly and leaving others untouched. She slapped the puff back into the bowl, spilling powder on the dressing-table top.

Waddling down the stairs, she went into the kitchen and wrinkled her nose at the food in the cupboard. No, she didn't feel like breakfast this morning. She didn't even feel equal to making tea. The charwoman would arrive presently; she'd make tea and Cora would have a cup with her. In a crumpled paper bag on the mantle-piece Cora found some chocolate peppermints which had escaped her memory since she placed them there a few days before. She popped two of them into her mouth and sucked unenthusiastically.

At a quarter-past eleven the back door bell rang. Opening the door, Cora admitted a little wisp of a woman with a pinched red nose, dressed in shabby black and carrying a leather shopping bag which bulged with God knows what. A sour smell came in with her. Had she been a house instead of a bundle of stringy flesh and chalky bone one would have said that her drains were bad.

"Late again," snapped Cora.

Mrs. Meggs opened her beady little eyes wide in simulated surprise. "Am I, Mum? I did me best to 'urry. But me varicose veins is that bad this mornin' it was all I cud do to 'obble along. If it 'ad bin anyone else but you I was comin' to I'd 'ave stopped in bed but I wouldn't let *you* down, Mum, not for nothink, not if I was dyin', I wouldn't."

While she took off her rusty coat and hung it behind the door, removed her shapeless hat and speared it with long pins, she cast sly glances at Cora. "You don't look up to much yourself this mornin', Mum."

"It's not to be wondered at," said Cora bitterly. "I waited up half the night for Mr. Marshall to come home and when I did get to bed, I couldn't sleep a wink. I was awake all night.

How I managed to struggle up to get Mr. Marshall's breakfast I really don't know."

"Poor dear! You'd think Mr. Marshall would be more considerate. But men is ungrateful critters. I'll be bound 'e didn't lose any sleep. I can sympathize with you, me dear. I bin through it all in me time an' me 'eart goes out to you. You sit there an' rest an' I'll make you a nice 'ot cup of tea an' you'll feel better d'rectly."

"I don't think I could swallow it," said Cora weakly, "but I'll try."

"That's me brave little dear."

Half an hour passed pleasantly while they sat over a pot of tea, discussing the shortcomings of Philip Marshall. Cora let herself go and poured all her grievances, real and imaginary, into the willing ears of Mrs. Meggs, who kept nodding her head and clicking her tongue and remarking suitably at timely intervals. It was almost twelve when Cora glanced at the clock and jumped up with a cry.

"Good heavens, I'll be late. I'm meeting Mrs. Greener at the A.B.C. at twelve. Don't forget to give the kitchen floor a good scrubbing and you might blacken the grate. It looks a positive disgrace."

"Leave it to me, Mum. I'll 'ave the 'ouse shinin' like a noo pin."

"Well, be a bit more thorough than you were last time. After you'd gone, I could have written my name in the dust on the dining-room furniture."

"Eddication's a wonderful thing," retorted Meggs sourly—under her breath.

Cora was late for her appointment but so was Mrs. Greener, so they met in the doorway of the A.B.C. They ordered French pastries and white coffee and had a delightful time discussing their husbands.

"So, I said to him, 'Leo it's no good grousing. It's the coat

I've always wanted and whatever you say I shan't send it back, so you can pay up and look pleasant. If you think fifty pounds is too much to spend on your wife, I can soon find someone who doesn't!'"

"Fifty pounds for a coat," breathed Cora, a stifling with envy. "It's as much as I can do to spend five."

"Then you're a fool, my dear. Do as I do. Buy what you want and let your husband worry about the bills."

"But he couldn't pay. He hasn't the money."

"Then let him get it. Any man can earn money if he has to. Where d'you suppose Leo would be today if I hadn't kept him on his toes? At an office desk like Mr. Marshall, earning five pounds a week."

"Mr. Marshall earns six," said Cora stiffly.

"I spend more than that on hats and stockings. It's a man's business to earn money and his wife's business to spend it. If a woman takes care of her end, her husband will be forced to take care of his. It's a question of supply and demand. The more you demand the more they've got to supply. Of course,"—from beneath long, mascaraed eyelashes Mrs. Greener glanced contemptuously at Cora—"you don't sleep with Mr. Marshall, do you? That makes a difference. You lose your hold on a man when you let him manage without you, if you know what I mean." She smoothed her large thighs complacently. "Now Leo needs me, he's one of those hungry men, wants me all the time—and that's where I've got him."

"That's what *you* say," thought Cora, but to my mind it's the other way about. That plump body of yours is like a flame, and your Leo is burned-out grey ash. I know who the hungry one is in your family, my girl. I can guess why you're always willing to let vacuum-cleaner and refrigerator salesmen give you demonstrations.

"Heaven knows I tell Philip often enough that he ought to be earning more money," she said peevishly. "It isn't my fault he's a failure. I often wonder why I let him inveigle me into marrying him. If I had my time over again—"

For an hour they gossiped and consumed pastries, washed down with richly sweetened coffee. They talked at each other, trying to rouse envy with one sentence and flick a raw spot with another. They disliked, despised, and distrusted each other, which, with women of the type, is as much as to say that they were the best of friends.

At last, Mrs. Greener glanced at her watch and gathered up gloves and bag. "I'll have to fly. I've a washing-machine salesman coming to give me a demonstration. Bye, bye, dear. See you tomorrow."

They kissed fondly. Mrs. Greener hurried paying the bill for both as she went out. Paying the bill was not a generous impulse on her part, it was one of her ways of rubbing in the difference in their financial positions. Washing-machine salesman, indeed! Cora thought, munching a final pastry. A nice demonstration that'll be.

She lingered a little longer, then eased herself up with a grunt and waddled out. She boarded a bus and took a penny ticket. Opposite a super cinema she alighted. Before crossing the road, she went into a delicatessen and bought a plump leg of chicken and a slice of York ham for her evening meal. No need to buy anything for Philip. There was still some meat on Sunday's leg of mutton.

Settling comfortably in a stall, she fumbled in her bag for chocolate peppermints. Leaning back, with her eyes on the screen, she surrendered to the bliss of imagining herself in the arms of Frederic March.

Chapter 4

At five to six Miss Jenner covered her typewriter and began to apply a fresh make-up. The junior clerk lit a cigarette and polished his shoes on an office towel. The office-boy licked stamps for dear life, slapping them on the envelopes every way but right side up. Each kept an eye on the clock as though afraid goblins would get them if they were not out of the office when the hands stood at six.

Philip worked on steadily. He liked to clear his desk every night, no matter how long it took him. He did not blame the others for hurrying away. They were young. They had absorbing outside interests. To them the office was only a necessary evil; to him it was the larger part of life. The others regarded him with affectionate amusement as a dry old stick but a decent sort. Although in charge of the small staff of Sturgis & Matthews, Importers of Irish Linen, he never put on airs. He kept them in line without losing his temper and stood up for them to the boss when they made mistakes. He was not above licking stamps to help the office-boy get away on time, even if he had a couple of hours' work to do after the boy had gone.

A bell rang twice. "Damn the man!" cried Miss Jenner, glaring at the clock. "It's always the same. Trust him to think of another letter at the last possible moment." She dropped lipstick and compact into her handbag, snapped it shut and picked up pencil and notebook. "Eric swore he wouldn't wait for me if I was late again."

Five minutes later she came out of the inner room, slapped the notebook down on her desk, and wrenched the cover off her typewriter. Philip was writing busily, but the others had gone.

"Two of 'em," she hissed, flipping open the notebook. "And

he's sorry but they're important and will I please get them out before I go. You're to sign them. For two pins I'd go back and tell him to—"

"Leave your notebook beside the machine," said Philip, without looking up. "I'll do them for you."

Miss Jenner turned eagerly. "Oh, would you?" She stood looking at him for a moment, then she shook her head. "No. Fair's fair. I'll do 'em myself. They won't take me a minute really. All the same, it *is* a bit thick."

"What about your young man? If he's told you he won't wait—"

"Oh, he'll wait. He talks like that but I can manage him."

Above the rattle of the keys she said, over her shoulder: "Oh, I forgot. He wants you."

Philip rose and went into the inner room. Henry Sturgis was standing by the window, practising golf swings with a steel-shafted driver. "Hello, Marshall. Busy?"

"Not very, sir. Just running through the letters that came in the late post."

"Sit down. I want to talk to you."

Philip sat down. His employer dropped into a padded leather chair behind his desk and balanced the club on knees. He opened a silver box and pushed it toward Philip.

"Cigarette?"

"Thanks."

Sturgis lay back and blew a smoke ring. "Marshall, my brother-in-law has a chance to go in with a firm that makes motorboats. He's keen on the idea. There isn't enough for him in this business, he's been hankering after a change for a long time. But to put the deal through he needs every penny of his capital. As you know, he owns a quarter share in this business. He wants to sell it. I can't afford to buy him out at present, so we're looking round for someone who can.

"Now you've been with me for years. You know the business inside out, probably better than I do. Frankly, my brother-in-law hasn't been of much use to the firm lately, he's had too many other bees in his bonnet. You and I have been running things between us, you on the inside, I on the outside. As a system of management, it's worked very well. I'm not anxious to change it. Marshall, how would you like to be a partner in Sturgis & Matthews?"

"There's nothing I'd like better."

"I thought so. Could you raise two thousand pounds?"

Philip almost laughed. He could not have raised as many shillings.

"No, sir," he replied promptly.

"Could you raise half that amount? If you could find a thousand in cash, we might be able to arrange the rest through my bank."

"I couldn't raise a hundred, sir. I've about fifty pounds in a savings account and I wouldn't know where to lay hands on another penny."

"That's a pity. You'd have suited me down to the ground. Oh, well, if it can't be done it can't. But think it over. There's no great hurry. I'll keep the offer open as long as I can. Talk it over with your wife. Two heads are better than one. She may be able to think of something."

"I'll see what can be done," replied Philip politely.

"Good. Well, I'm off. See you in the morning."

"Good night, sir."

"'Night."

Philip went back to his desk and went on opening envelopes. He put the offer out of his mind. There was not the slightest likelihood that he would be able to accept it. He knew of no one he could approach for the loan of even five pounds with the smallest degree of optimism. When John was born, he had tried to borrow twenty pounds from his nearest relative who was so outraged by the suggestion that they had been estranged ever since. It was disheartening to have the chance of his lifetime dangled in front of his eyes and be unable to grasp it but he wasted no time in brooding about it.

It was long after closing time before his work was finished and even then, he was in no hurry to go. At this hour he could feel that the office belonged to him.

It was a feeling that made his life bearable. He replaced on its rail a towel that someone had thrown on the floor, closed a filing-cabinet that gaped open, adjusted a typewriter cover which was neither on nor off; these things offended his eye like blemishes on the face of a loved one. He removed his grey office jacket and hung it on its peg—by the tab—washed his face and hands, donned his blue jacket, his neat fawn coat, his sober bowler, took his rolled umbrella from the stand, and switched off the lights.

A last look round in the dim half-light of the dusk, the rosy glow of the dying fire. The room was so peaceful he felt reluctant to leave it. There was not another sole in the building; there might not have been another soul in the world. In the dark he walked across the room and stood at the window looking out.

He saw a quiet square of grey Regency houses, a plot of green grass bounded by wrought-iron railings, some tall spreading trees, a bench beneath one of the trees, a naked iron boy in the centre pouring nothing out of a jug into a cup. Deserted pavements, empty roadway, darkened windows. Like anthills on fire the offices had emptied on the stroke of six and the old houses had settled back to doze and mutter, after the fashion of the old, until morning.

Dozing, they sighed, their timbers grumbled. They had seen

better days. They had not always been rushed into at 9 a.m., rushed out of at 6 p.m., left lonely through dusk, dark, and dawn. Time was when prosperous city merchants were proud to live in them, when children's voices echoed through the upper rooms, when good dinners were eaten and good wines drunk beneath their ornamented ceilings, when servants gossiped and grumbled in their basements, when dusk saw the square ablaze with lights, when the hooves of sleek horses and the wheels of smart carriages beat lively rhythms on the cobbles at the hour when gentlemen were wont to dine.

Gone. All gone. Now the houses were divided and sub-divided with matchboard and glass and the names of business firms were painted on their pretentious doorways and no one lived in them, no one died in them, except furtive caretakers with moist noses. Shabby the fabric of the old houses, sooty the trees, threadbare the green carpet in the middle of the square, faded the street lights that encircled it like a necklace of amber beads. Only one thing was new and bright and it was blatant and red; a telephone box at a corner.

While Philip looked down from the window a woman came out of the telephone box.

At first, he thought she was drunk. She clung to the door of the box as though afraid to let go. In the subdued light, with the width of the street between them, he could not tell whether she was young or old. All he could see was a thin, crumpled figure in a dark coat and small dark hat, with neat silk-stockinged legs. At least, from a distance the legs looked neat, but Philip, who had a healthy interest in feminine legs, knew from experience that in this matter distance was often deceptive.

The legs were not as steady as they ought to have been, for she wavered slightly as she went into the railed enclosure in the middle of the square and walked along to the solitary bench. She let herself drop down on it with the sagging abandon of defeat. The drooping lines of her body suggested age and weariness. A flutter of white told Philip that she had produced a handkerchief and was holding it to her face. From her attitude he knew that she was crying as certainly as though he could hear her sobs and see her tears.

The sight was profoundly touching; the empty square; the brooding old houses; the murky lights; the lonely woman weeping, her only companion the naked iron boy. Philip, who normally would have run a mile from a woman in tears, felt an irresistible impulse to go and comfort her. It was impossible for him to stand there watching her in a spirit of detachment. He went downstairs and out of the building, shaking the door after he shut it to make sure that it was locked.

He paused at the top of the flight of stone steps that led to the street and wondered if he were about to make a fool of himself. Nothing ever frightened him so much as the thought of making a fool of himself. Had there been one other human being in the square besides himself and the weeping woman he would have gone his own way; even a prowling mongrel would have made her solitude less utter. It was her loneliness as much as her misery that made him go steadily across the street into the enclosure.

When he approached the woman the sound of her weeping brought a lump to his throat. A child alone and afraid in the dark cries the way she was crying. She was huddled on one end of the bench with her hands to her face. He could see little more of her than he had seen from the window but the curve of her back was youthful.

"Is something wrong?" asked Philip, in a small, reluctant voice. "Can I help?"

A voice speaking at her elbow when she thought she was

alone made the woman start. A startled white face looked up at him and then was hurriedly averted. With a gulp she said quickly, breathlessly, in a tone of embarrassment: "No. No. There's nothing wrong. I'm perfectly all right."

But the effort of speech made her start sobbing more bitterly than before. Philip did not know what to do, what to say. He felt like turning on his heel and walking quickly away but something inside him made him stay and try again.

"I don't want to pry into your affairs and I'm not trying to pick you up. It's obvious that you're in some kind of trouble. You needn't tell me what it is but if there's anything I can do—"

Without looking up she said fiercely, brokenly: "You can go away. You can leave me alone."

"I'm sorry," he replied, turning away.

"Don't go," she said.

Philip halted and waited for her to say something more but minutes passed before she spoke. She was dabbing her eyes with the handkerchief, fighting back the sobs that were still struggling in her throat.

"I didn't mean to be rude," she said at last.

"That's all right. I asked for a snub. But…I saw you from my office window...You were in such distress...I couldn't go my way and leave you like that."

"I know. You were only trying to be kind. But you startled me. The square was so silent and empty, I didn't think anyone was near."

"It *is* quiet, isn't it? Just over there Holborn bustles with life but here we're all alone, the last inhabitants of a deserted village."

Swiftly she turned on him an odd half-frightened glance. Philip laughed, and tried to make the laugh sound confident and natural. "You're wondering if, after all, I'm one of those middle-aged men you read about in the papers. Don't worry. I'm not."

She did not speak, only drew the collar of her coat more closely about her neck—for it was chilly—and staring straight in front of her at the naked iron boy who placidly poured nothing out of a jug into a cup in the middle of the grass. Again, Philip shifted his weight from one foot to the other.

"Feeling better?" he asked, for something to say. It was a silly remark, he felt, after he had made it.

"Yes, I'm all right. It was nothing. I was acting like a fool. If you thought there was a dramatic reason for my sorrow, you're in for a disappointment. I've nothing to cry about, really"—but the tone in which she said this was bitter. "It was only… only that I'm lonely. Quite suddenly I realized that I was in for my seventh lonely evening in a week and I simply couldn't bear it any longer. So, I broke down and cried.

"I expect," she added, almost savagely, "I expect that sounds too silly for words."

"No, I don't think it's silly."

Philip was remembering a night when he himself had broken down and wept for sheer loneliness. It was just after John, finding home unbearable, had walked out of it for good, and Philip, alone in a darkened room, thinking about his son, had started to cry and been unable to stop. It was the first and last time in his adult life that he had shed tears, for the experience had been so shattering he could never let it happen again.

"No, I don't think it's silly. I've been through it myself."

"You!" she said scornfully. "What can you know about loneliness? You're a man. You can go where you like and do what you like. You needn't wait, evening after evening, in a cold bed-sitting room, listening for a knock that never comes, longing for someone to ask you to come out somewhere—anywhere—and knowing all the time that no one will. You can make friends; a man can always make friends. A girl can't, not if she lives on thirty-six shillings a week in a grubby boarding house and has no one to care whether she lives or dies. It's easy for you to talk. If you're lonely you can get married, you don't have to wait until you're asked. Or if you don't want to marry you can go to a public-house and mix with other men and drink and talk and have a good time. But where can I go? I'm not pretty. I'm not clever. There's nothing about me that would make people want to know me."

"That's a very sad story," said Philip briskly. He felt that if he spoke sympathetically, she would burst into tears again. "But you haven't a monopoly of loneliness. You can be married and lonely—and I've spent some of the loneliest hours of my life in a crowded bar. I could tell you a sad story about myself if heaping my troubles on yours would do any good, but it wouldn't. And we're not the only ones. There are thousands of people walking the streets of London who could add their sad stories to ours."

He hesitated, then added: "Here's a suggestion. We're in the same boat, so why shouldn't we row together for an hour or two? Let's go somewhere for a bite to eat and a chat."

She turned her white face to him again. She was younger than he had thought. In the early twenties, about the same age as John. For a while she sat looking at him. He could see what she was thinking.

"Don't be a damned fool," he said. "I'm not going to seduce you. I couldn't, in a public restaurant, if I wanted to."

"Then you're just asking me out of pity, because you're sorry for me?" With the perversity of her sex, she was on the point of resenting being pitied.

"Yes," he said. "I'm sorry as hell for both of us. Well, will you come, or won't you?"

The girl rose and straightened her back. "I will. And thanks very much."

"My name, by the way, is Marshall. Philip Marshall."

"Mine's Mary Grey. But what about your wife?" she asked, as they walked to the entrance of the garden. "Won't she be expecting you?"

"I'm not married," said Philip.

Chapter 5

Waiting in the entrance for Mary Grey to return from the ladies' room, Philip said to himself: Why did I tell her I'm not married? That's the sort of shabby lie a man tells a girl when he's out for an affair with her. But there's nothing like that in my mind, so why did I lie? Although it was the first time he had disowned Cora the lie had slipped out as glibly as if he uttered it every day. Perhaps it was that the thought of his wife was an unpleasant one and when you are trying to comfort someone you steer clear of unpleasant topics. Even so, he needn't have lied. He could have admitted to Cora without going into details about her, he could have said: "No, my wife won't be expecting me, I'm never in until late." That would have been sufficient answer to her question. Why lie? Oh, hell, what did it matter? In an hour or so Mary Grey and he would part, go their separate ways and never see each other again.

The entrance hall was in the best tradition of the public lavatory school of architecture, the school which inspires the design of most large popular restaurants and super cinemas. There were a great many too smart, too slick young men standing about waiting for their girlfriends to return from the rest rooms. A tall girl in a fur coat gave Philip a tentative smile and said:

"Hello dearie," in a low tone.

Philip said apologetically: "I'm waiting for a friend," and she walked on.

Minutes passed. No Mary Grey. She's thought better of it, she's remembered mother's advice, she's left by another door. Well, what do I care? She's only a girl I found crying on a bench and tried to comfort. A mousy sort of girl, not pretty, not clever, not attractive. She could be everything that's desirable in a woman and I still would have no other desire but to comfort her, for I've long since outgrown the hunger for women, thank God. Living with Cora has cured me of that. Let her go if she wants to. It was she who was weeping with loneliness, not I. I'll eat my steak alone and drink a glass of beer and go home early for more beer at 'The Hole in the Wall.'

Nevertheless, he was disappointed. Oh, the girl herself meant nothing to him, but she was young and it was a long time since he had had someone young to talk to. Talking to her might have eased the ache that was always in his heart, the pain of frustration because John didn't need him as he needed John.

When he was making up his mind (for the third time) that she was gone and that he had better go too, Mary Grey came up the stairs. She had made good use of her time; the havoc tears had wrought with her face was repaired. She had done something to her clothes as well, they did not look smart, they were too shabby, but they sat upon her more confidently. Raising his hat, Philip went to meet her and she gave him a shy smile.

"I hope I wasn't too long."

"No, not too long."

They went into a crowded, many-mirrored room in which a string band was playing pseudo-Viennese music. They weaved their way, interminably it seemed, between occupied tables on the heels of a dark-skinned waiter who suddenly halted and, with the flourish of a conjurer producing a complacent rabbit, presented them with a table for two in a corner. He offered them a menu. Mary Grey ran a dubious eye over it, concentrating on the price column. "I think, perhaps, a poached egg on toast—"

"Two thick steaks," said Philip. "On the rare side. Fried potatoes. Cauliflower. Rolls and butter. Some green salad, if it's crisp."

Mary Grey's eyes brightened like a child's at a party. Poor

kid, thought Philip, for the first time feeling a personal warmth toward her. She's half-starved. On thirty-six shillings a week her life must be one long round of poached eggs on toast.

"And to drink, sir?" murmured the waiter approvingly.

"Beer. A pint of Löwenbräu München for me, a half-pint for the lady."

A stifled, protesting sound came from Mary Grey but Philip ignored it. When the waiter had gone, Mary said: "I don't like beer."

"You'll like this beer. Even if you don't, it'll do you good."

"I'm sorry I was rude to you when you spoke to me in the square."

"You've said that already. Please forget it. I have. In any case, I asked for it. To be allowed to share a sorrow is a privilege only a close friend has the right to claim. We'll share our happiness with anyone. When we're happy we love to see our smiles reflected on the faces of everyone we pass, but when we're miserable we want to crawl into a corner and weep alone."

"Yes, that's how I felt."

"I almost left you to it. It's a natural instinct in man to run from a woman in tears. But something stronger than fear of embarrassment, something—I don't quite know what—made me speak to you. I had to do it. I couldn't help myself."

"It wasn't because I was a girl and—and young? That would be the average man's reason." She said it bitterly.

"When I saw you from the window," said Philip simply, "I thought you were quite old. Something about you, the way you stood, perhaps, suggested age and weariness."

While they ate, they exchanged hardly a word. Mary Grey cleaned her plate. She drank her beer to the drop.

"That was good," she said, laying down knife and fork with a sigh. "You mustn't think I always eat like that. I usually remember my table manners. But—a steak. And what a steak! It seems years since I saw one. When it's eggs, eggs, eggs, day after day you forget what appetite is. If you were shocked by the way I wolfed it, remember you brought it on yourself."

"It must be rotten trying to keep body and soul together on thirty-odd shillings a week," said Philip uncomfortably.

"I'm not going to tell you how rotten it is. That will be a poor reward for your kindness. But it isn't fun."

"You're all alone in London?"

"Quite alone."

"But surely you have relations somewhere?"

"Only one maiden aunt, as far as I know. She's at Lytham. That's in Lancashire, near Blackpool. I could live with her if I wanted to. I did, for a few months, after my father died. But we don't get on very well. She's trying to live with.

"Heaven knows how Father came to have a sister like her, for he was the jolliest man I ever knew. I suppose it was never being married that soured her; there's a sourness about most elderly spinsters. Am I making her sound like a beast? She isn't really. It was just that she nagged a lot and wouldn't trust me to behave myself when her back was turned. Because I was an only child, she was sure that I'd been spoiled and felt it her duty to take me severely in hand. If I went out of an evening, I had to be in by half-past nine and had to account for every moment that I'd been gone." Mary laughed, and Philip was disturbed by the bitterness that again infused her tone. "No one had told her that you can trust a plain girl anywhere.

"I was twelve when Mother died. I remember crying a lot at the time but I didn't really feel it as much as I did years later when Dad died—I was always more Dad's girl than Mother's. For a while we had a woman come in to do the housework but when I was fifteen, I took it over. It was fun, keeping house for

Dad. I've always liked cooking and work you do for someone you love is a pleasure. Dad was sweet. He was only an assistant master in a council school in the Midlands and he didn't earn much but we were always having good times. Religiously every week we'd put aside money to pay the rates or the gas bill and then when we'd got enough Dad would look at me and I'd look at him and he'd wink and we'd go off on the spree with it instead.

"He used to bring some of the older boys and girls from the school up to the house of an evening and we'd play games and pound out tunes on the rickety old piano and sing songs and make a lot of noise, and I'd serve sandwiches and lemonade and think I was the perfect hostess and—oh, everything was lovely. Other evenings we'd sit by the fire and I'd darn Dad's socks and munch toffee and he'd read aloud and smoke his pipe. On Saturdays and Sundays, we'd go tramp across the moors with our lunch in our pockets. We always took a book along. Dad was a great reader. And a very happy man. I've never known a happier nature. He knew he'd never be anything much in the world. He knew he'd never have any money. But he was content with what he had and he knew the secret of getting every ounce of happiness out of just living. He used to say: 'Work for hands and brain—but not too much—books to read, good food, a snug bed, a warm fire, a pipe, and someone to love, what more could a man ask than that?'

"When he died, I thought I'd never be happy again. I never *have* been happy since. After the lovely life I had with Dad you can imagine what living with Aunt Ada was like. She was stiff. Angular. Cold. I couldn't love her—and I'd learned from Dad that life is nothing without someone to love. I stuck it for a few months and then I couldn't bear it any longer. Everything Dad owned had fetched a little over fifty pounds. That was mine, and I came to London and lived on it while I learned shorthand

and typing. When I was fairly proficient—I've never been more than that—it was easy to find a job, although less easy to live on the salary. At first it wasn't too bad. I had plenty of clothes. They weren't fashionable but they served. I had dreams which helped me bear with reality. But clothes wear out, dreams fade.

"At that point I made some friends through a girl I knew. They weren't the sort I'd have chosen if I'd been able to choose—all they thought of was drinking and dancing and making love of a sort and generally imitating the people you read about in gossip columns— but when you're starving for companionship you grab what you can get. I never fitted in with them and I don't think they ever more than tolerated me. And then something happened and I dropped out of that set and they were all content to let me go and—and— well, that's about all. I'll be crying again if I don't stop talking."

She gave Philip a tremulous smile. "I don't know why I've inflicted all this on you, except that it's been a long time since I've had anyone real to talk to and it's been lovely to talk and talk and talk. You don't know how much better I feel."

"It's been interesting," said Philip quietly. "I wish I'd known your father. He sounds delightful."

"He was," she said, and her eyes were misty. She moved her shoulders as though to shake a burden from them. "But I've done all the talking. That isn't fair. Aren't you going to tell me your story?"

A shadow fell across Philip's face. "My story isn't very interesting."

"Oh, yes, it is. I can tell. It's written on your face."

"I hope not," said Philip fervently.

Long ago the waiter had placed the bill (face down on a plate) at Philip's elbow and now he was hovering near with a look of straining patience. The etiquette of popular restaurants dictated that having eaten and drunk and sat for long enough to let the meal settle, it was time to go.

"What now?" asked Philip as they came out to the street. "It's early yet. Shall we go to a movie? Or are you in the mood for a variety show?"

"It's nice of you," said Mary Grey, "but if you don't mind, I think I'll go home. It's been lovely but now I'm tired."

"Then I'll see you to your bus or the Underground or whatever it is you take."

"Underground. I live at Ravenscourt Park."

"Then we go the same way home. My station's a couple of stops farther."

In the train they were silent but there was nothing comfortable about the silence, it was warm and friendly. Once or twice, they looked at each other and smiled, the restful unchallenging smile that passes between tried and intimate friends. At Ravenscourt Park Philip left the train with Mary. As they walked side by side down a residential street which led to the one in which Mary lived, he said abruptly:

"At what time will you be lunching tomorrow?"

"Half-past one."

Philip's regular time was an hour earlier but that could be adjusted. "Meet me at the Tottenham Court Road Underground?"

Mary hesitated but only for a moment. "If you'll let me pay for my own lunch."

"Very well."

At the gate of the large gloomy house in which she had her bed-sitting room they paused under a sadly drooping yew and looked at each other. Mary leaned forward and kissed him on the mouth.

An incredibly precious moment, and then she was gone.

Philip had forgotten that soft lips could be so sweet.

Chapter 6

When noon approached the following day Philip discovered that he was looking forward with eagerness to his luncheon date with Mary. He knew what his public-house acquaintances would think of that. Nudging one another, they would wink knowingly. Many would envy him. None would be able to conceive more than just one reason for a middle-aged man's interest in a young girl. And they would be wrong. Dead wrong. Philip was sure of that. Having submitted himself to a mental cross-examination, he was quite certain that companionship was all he wanted from Mary; the sort of companionship he might have had from his son.

At luncheon they were both a little shy at first but soon they warmed to each other's hungry desire for friendship. The food grew cold, the clock stole a march on them, while they talked. It was amazing how much these two normally silent folks found to talk about. Through each other they discovered things about themselves they had not known before. That night they went to a movie and for the next two weeks they shared almost all the time that was not occupied in work or sleep.

One wet Sunday afternoon they visited the National Gallery and stood tongue-tied before the paintings. In front of one Mary ventured, in a solemn-hushed voice: "I don't like it. All that purple."

Philip replied: "It must be good, or it wouldn't be here."

They found one or two paintings they liked enormously without knowing why. And then a young man in a canary-coloured pullover paused with a girl before the one they liked best and spoiled it for them by using to describe it in a lot of words they had not heard before. As driftwood is pulled by the wash of a boat, they were drawn unwillingly after him by a sort of morbid fascination. Listening to his shrill, positive voice, they soon did not know whether they were standing on heads or feet. A rather untidy, white-haired old gentleman saw their predicament and took them in tow. He explained one or two paintings quite simply and what had been obscure before became clear and wonderful, almost as though the old gentleman had lent them his colour-keen eyes. Afterwards, he took them to tea at a Corner House and drew Donald Duck on a menu card and told them he loved the talkies but his wife wouldn't let him go often as she considered his favourite gangster pictures bad for his blood-pressure. They found out later that the old gentleman was a past-President of the Royal Academy.

Mary would not let Philip pay for her meals and although she earned very little, she steadfastly refused his offers of help. When they were out together, he did most of the paying because she had so little money but Mary contrived that the expeditions were inexpensive. They went for long walks. They fed the deer in Richmond Park. They feasted on beauty at Kew.

A lovely fortnight they spent together and then, inspired by the vague dread of becoming what his public house acquaintances would take him to be, Philip put Mary off two days in succession.

He telephoned John and tried to arrange a meeting but John was evasive. All too plainly, he wanted no part of his father. In early family rows he had been on Philip's side but the rows had gone on so long that at last he was on no side but his own.

When he put down the telephone receiver after a conversation with John that was all doubt and hesitation and embarrassment, Philip picked it up again and rang Mary at her office and arranged another meeting. They took up again where they had left off two days before.

With Mary he found a quiet happiness and the soul-easing peace of understanding. There was nothing beautiful about the girl; only the youth in her saved her from being plain. She was not clever; she had only an alertness of mind and an eager, absorbing interest in the things about her. Philip knew that their friendship was giving him a new lease on life. Even his wife had noticed how much happier he was—and duly resented it:

"You're up to something, Philip Marshall. You've the smug look of the cat that swallowed the canary."

On a fine Saturday afternoon Philip hired a car and drove Mary to the country, overruling her protests at such extravagance. (It cost little more than formerly he would have handed over the bar of 'The Hole in the Wall' in the course of a couple of evenings.) Mary brought a picnic lunch. On top of a hill, eighty miles from London, she read aloud to him. Only a good book can stand reading aloud, but a taste in literature was her principal inheritance from her father.

The sun was warm but kind, and before them colour and beauty stretched to the distant rim of the earth. Beauty of gnarled old trees with young green headdresses, of sprouting corn, of lush, grassy slopes, of slumbering white farm-houses, of darting birds. The flaming colours of scattered jewels, tender hues of young growth, harsh shades of rugged age.

Mary stopped reading. There were tears in her eyes. "There's something I must tell you. I don't know how to start."

"If it makes you look like that I'd rather not hear it."

"You've been so kind to me. I can't live a lie with you."

"We took each other on trust. There's a lot I haven't told you about myself."

"This is something you've a right to know. It may make you hate me."

"I can't imagine anything that would do that."

"You don't know," she cried, with a desperate intonation that startled him. "You don't know."

He felt a tingle of apprehension. Suddenly, he had an unreasoning fear of hearing what she had to say. Putting out a hand, he laid it gently on one of hers.

"We're happy as we are. Days like this have been rare in my life. Let's not spoil anything." Jumping up, he pointed to the far horizon. "Look over there. That distant silver streak is the sea. Let's go to it."

"Is there time?" she asked doubtfully.

"There's time for anything today. Race you to the car?"

They tore downhill pell-mell, arriving at the bottom out of breath and laughing.

At the sea they hired costumes and went in bathing. Neither could swim more than a few clumsy strokes but that did not matter. They had fun splashing each other, playing at being children again.

On the way home they fell silent, and then, in a small voice, Mary said: "I've had a row with my landlady. She wants me leave."

Philip laughed. "Is that all you were trying to tell me!"

No," she answered soberly, "that was something much more important."

"What was the row about? Why does she want you to go?"

It was so long before Mary answered that he turned his head and stared questioningly at her. In the dusk, her face had grown suddenly old. She stared straight in front of her.

"The row was about...about my stopping out late at night. She made a scene. It was terrible. The other lodgers were listening at their doors. She said she knew what girls got up to when they stopped out late. She said I'd get her house a bad name."

"Nasty-minded old beast," declared Philip violently. "You

shan't go back there tonight, except to collect the things you'll need immediately. You can spend the night at a hotel and find a new place in the morning."

"No, Philip. I can't afford a hotel and I shan't let you pay. It won't hurt me to spend another night under her roof. She's said all she has to say. Since the row she hasn't spoken to me. Only sniffed."

"Then I'll call for you in the morning and we'll find another room."

"Don't come to the house," said Mary quickly. "She might start on you."

"That'll be fine. There are things I'd like to tell her."

"It would be silly to start a fuss." Her voice was firm.

"Meet me at the Underground, Philip. Please."

"Oh, all right," he grudgingly agreed.

They met at eleven the following morning—church bells were tolling—and spent two hours looking at one cheerless room after another. Hard beds with springs in unexpected places. Dust and fluff under the beds. Sheets grey with age and inadequate laundering. Wallpapers that hurt the eye. Sepia photographs of unbelievable human beings, the males with preposterous facial growths, the females with incredible busts. Picture rails felted with dust. Narrow strips of threadbare carpet on worn linoleum. Mirrors that lent an ordinary face the grotesque fascination of a freak. Wardrobes that wobbled when you opened them, threatened to fall upon you when you shut them. Corners best left uninspected. Landladies with hands clasped in resignation, eyes flat with suspicion, who didn't know what you wanted, they were sure, for the money.

To each, Mary said falteringly: "Well… I'll let you know if I decide to take it."

None of the landladies was fooled. They had heard that one

before. As a matter of form, they responded grudgingly: "Well, you better make up your mind. I've had other inquiries."

Lunching at 'The Star and Garter' at Kew Bridge, Philip said, in a tone of annoyance: "They were all utterly impossible. How on earth people expect to let rooms like that—"

"They *do* let them. And, impossible or not, I'll have to take one and move in today."

"If only they'd regard letting rooms as a business and make a workmanlike job of it."

"Landladies," said Mary, with wisdom spawned by experience, "are neither born nor made. They are thrown up by domestic upheavals. A man dies or loses his job and a woman is forced to be the provider. She resents the necessity. She doesn't want you to think she's used to this sort of thing. So, she does it as badly as possible. It's a way of showing her pride."

After luncheon they set out wearily again. In a quiet side street, they knocked on the door of a house advertised in the local paper and were so taken aback by the superlative ugliness of the middle-aged woman who answered that they almost fell off the front steps. She had the face of a gargoyle. The features were large and humorously misshapen as though a sculptor in gleeful mood had played pranks with a lump of putty. They gaped at her, too startled to speak. It was rude, it made them scarlet with embarrassment, but they simply could not help it. The woman did not seem to mind. She even grinned.

"It's a shock at first, ain't it? You can imagine what a trial it used to be to me. But I got over it and so will you, if you take the trouble to get acquainted. They say beauty's only skin-deep, but having myself skinned to find out is too much bother. You've called about the vacant room, I expect. You'll find it more agreeable to look at. It's a bit small for two, though."

"I—I only want it for myself," stammered Mary.

"Oh," said the gargoyle, looking sharply from one to the other. "Not married? My mistake. I thought at first you was. I should have noticed you hadn't a ring. Well, don't stand there. Come in, come in."

The room she showed them was not particularly well furnished but it was spotlessly clean and the wallpaper was not too vociferous. The gargoyle plumped her ample proportions on the bed and bounced up and down, giving a convincing demonstration of its springiness.

"Try it yourself," she urged. "Go on. Don't be shy. Try it. There! You couldn't ask for better than that, could you?"

Bouncing on the bed beside the big woman, feeling a little foolish, Mary admitted that she couldn't, indeed, ask for anything better than that.

"I can do you bed and breakfast and a bite of something at night," said the gargoyle, "for seventeen shillings a week. That's cheap but I'm a first-rate shopper. The tradesmen know me. They know better than put something over on me—I'd like to see 'em try. You'll find the food plain but plentiful. I'm a fair cook but don't expect any frills, for you won't get 'em."

Mary looked at Philip. Philip looked at Mary. They found themselves smiling. Mary took out her purse and counted the first seventeen shillings into the woman's huge red hand.

"That's that, then. I was opening a bottle of Guinness when you knocked. What say we make it three, to seal the bargain?"

"I'm afraid I don't drink," said Mary.

"Taking a drop of the right stuff to buck you up isn't drinking," said the gargoyle, beaming. The beam made her uglier than even before but also more human and immensely likeable. "You'll keep me company, won't you, Mister Whatever-your-name-is," she added, to Philip. When he hesitated, she gave him a nudge in the ribs that almost knocked him downstairs. "Of course, you will. Do you good."

Talking all the way, she led them down to her bright, cheery kitchen. "I'm a single woman myself. You won't wonder at that. It's the goods in the fancy wrappings that get taken off the shelf. I might have had some luck if I'd ever met a man as ugly as myself, but I never have. In a way that's a blessing, when you think what the kids'd look like. Sit down, sit down. You don't mind the fire, do you? I like a fire myself, even on a hot day. It makes the place look a bit more homely. Smoke your pipe if you feel like it, Mister Whatever-your-name-is. Liberty Hall, this is."

Still talking, she handed Philip a glass of rich dark stout with a creamy head and put on the kettle to make Mary a cup of tea.

"Don't run away with the idea that I've been neglected, though. A woman's got to be worse than just ugly before men'll leave her entirely alone. They've made do with me more than once until something better came along. Why, only the other night a man picked me up. A skinny little runt in a raincoat with a moustache like chopped hay. It was dark and he came sidling up and said: 'Hello, Girlie. What about a drink?' To me, mind you. Can you imagine it? Well, I'm always on for a lark so I said I didn't know as I minded just one. I told you it was dark, didn't I? We didn't get a good look at each other until we'd gone about a hundred yards and was coming to a lamp-post. Then he stopped dead in his tracks and stared at my face. He gave one gasp and ran like a hare."

Throwing back her head, opening wide her large mouth, she gave out gusts of hearty laughter. For a split-second Philip and Mary struggled to be polite and then they too, surrendered to mirth.

"I can see we're going to be friends," said the gargoyle, at last, wiping her eyes. "A bit of a joke is meat and drink to me."

When they were leaving, to fetch Mary's things from her former abode, the gargoyle gripped Philip's sleeve and pulled him back. Mary had gone on and was opening the front door. Philip and the gargoyle were hidden from her by a bend in the passage.

"Before you say so, I'll admit it is none of my business—but you're going to do right by that girl, aren't you?"

Without the faintest idea what she was talking about, Philip nodded his head in disconcerted embarrassment.

"That's all I want to know. She's a good girl, I can see that with half an eye. And I'm not denying that you look like a decent little man. Play fair with her."

She let him go. Philip paused, waiting for something—he didn't quite know what—and she gave him a push that propelled him along the passage and almost to the front door.

"You'll want to be off, now, dear," she said, beaming at Mary. "Here's a key. I'll expect you when I see you."

Out of earshot of the gargoyle, they started to laugh again.

"A scream, isn't she?" said Philip. "But you'll be safe in her hands."

They were still smiling reminiscently when they turned into the street in which Mary had lived until that day. A hundred yards from the house Mary stopped and looked at Philip. Her lips trembled.

"Philip, do you mind... I mean... Well, I'd rather you waited for me here."

"What nonsense. I shan't let you come out of that house like a servant girl in disgrace, lugging your own cases."

"But I think it would be better—"

"Well, I don't. If it's your landlady you're afraid of, I'm ready for her."

"Philip, please."

"Come along, Mary."

They felt eyes on them as they approached the house. Fitting her key in the lock, Mary's hand shook. They went into the hall.

"Wait for me here," breathed Mary nervously. "I shan't be a minute. I did most of my packing last night."

Without waiting for a reply, she darted upstairs. Philip took off his hat and stood just inside the front door. Hearing a creak behind him, he looked round and saw a sour-faced woman peering from a room to the left of the hall. She sniffed. It was the father and mother of all nasal noises.

"So, you're the man. Married, too, by the look of you. Old enough to be her father. A nice thing. (Sniff.) Well, you can tell your fine lady friend from me that if she ain't out of my house in an hour there'll be trouble."

Livid with anger, Philip stepped forward. "I'm afraid I didn't hear you correctly. Have you something to say?"

Malignantly, she glared through the aperture at him. Rabbit-like, her nose went up and down. Sniff. Sniff. Sniff.

"To the likes of you," she snapped, "no."

Pulling in her head, she slammed the door.

Mary came running down with a suitcase in her hand. Her face was white. "What did she say? What did she tell you?"

"Nothing." Philip's mouth was a thin line. He took the suitcase from her. "You're shaking. There's nothing to be scared of, my dear. Fetch the rest of your things and we'll get out of this damned house."

"Damned house yourself, you lecherous little viper," cried a shrill voice from the other side of the door that had slammed.

Mary fetched two more pieces of luggage quickly and they went out of the place, leaving the door-key on a hall table. From behind a curtained window, the acid eyes of the landlady burned into their backs as they went down the garden path.

They walked away in silence. Mary looked as though she were bleeding internally. Philip did not try to comfort her. The incident, he felt, was best ignored. As they walked along, he called Mary's attention to a garden gay with flowers and she looked grateful for the casualness of his tone.

But during the week that followed, Mary was far from being the good companion he had found her. Their meetings were weighted with heavy silence. Often, she withdrew into herself, shutting him out, locking the door. Philip knew he was losing something very precious, and there was nothing he could do about it. Frustrated, he grew angry, then sullen, and the breach between them widened.

One evening, walking by the river at Richmond, Mary started to cry. All Philip's efforts to comfort her were unavailing. It seemed as though she would never stop. She wouldn't tell him what was wrong. She said nothing at all. She only wept, wept, wept. It was late and the towpath was all but deserted, but Philip imagined there were eyes all round him, gloating over his discomfiture. Losing patience at last, he turned on his heel and walked away from her.

In a pub in the town, he downed three whiskies in succession and told himself that women were all alike, there was no making them out, they were illogical, unreasonable and damned annoying. But all the time he knew that Mary was not like that, that he ought to be patient and find out what was wrong and end, if he could, the misery that was eating her alive. He started to go home. Jumped on a bus. Jumped off again. There was a pain in his side. For no reason he could fathom, he knew something was wrong, and that something terrible was going to happen if he didn't hurry, hurry, hurry...

He ran back to where he had left Mary but she gone. He raced along the towpath like a madman, staring into the faces of those he passed. Almost out of his mind with anxiety, he found her. Mary was kneeling on a parapet, gazing down, as though hypnotized, at the sluggish yellow water. And Philip knew, as if a loud voice were shouting in his ear, that in another moment she would be over the wall, into the river.

With a frantic cry— "*Mary*!"—he threw himself forward and pulled her back. And then they were in each other's arms, sobbing helplessly, like two frightened children.

"We can't go on, Philip," Mary wept. "We can't be friends any longer. If you only knew… I'm no good. No good, I tell you. I'll bring you nothing but unhappiness. One day you'll be sorry you ever took pity on me."

"But, Mary, I need you. I can't live without you. You're everything to me. We can't part now. I need you too much. You need me. We must be together always."

Torn by doubt, she looked up at him, her brimming eyes searching his face. "Don't say that, Philip, unless you're sure."

"Of course, I'm sure. Certainly, I'm sure. My God, you're all I've got."

"I've never known anyone as fine as you," she said, wonderingly. "I'll try to be worthy of you. I'll try—oh, so terribly hard—to make you a good wife."

Wife? The night upended itself and threw the stars in his face. He blinked at her. Wife? He had said nothing about marriage. Or, had he? Ruefully, he comprehended that what he had said had implied it. Few men put their proposals into so many matter-of-fact words. Mary was smiling up at him, smiling through her tears, a light shining in her eyes. This was a nice mess into which he had plunged himself.

Chapter 7

Walking home, he began to think more lucidly and the position seemed less hopeless than at first. True, he could not marry Mary as long as he was married to Cora, but need he go on being married to Cora? Their existence together was a mockery of everything for which marriage ought to stand.

Marriage ought to be a mating, spiritual, mental, physical, but his spirit and Cora's had always rebelled against each other, their minds had clashed at every angle, even the physical part of their union had died an early death. The thought of sexual intercourse with Cora was to Philip as revolting as some bestial act. He could not understand those husbands and wives who go on using each other's bodies when love, respect, understanding are gone and there is nothing left but flesh to hold them together. No matter what the parsons said, married life under those conditions was indecent and beastly, and an illegitimate union based on love was beautiful, clean, honest by comparison.

No, there was nothing left between Cora and him. Not even sex, that shabby anchor. Their son had grown up and left them. All the feeling they had for each other was an active dislike.

If Cora would look facts in the face, she was bound to agree that they would be better apart. But would she? There was the rub. To look facts in the face was foreign to her nature. She preferred to look round them or ignore them altogether. Under the existing conditions she could not possibly be happy, but she might prefer not to be happy as long as she could go on making Philip miserable.

Cora was waiting up for him, her flabby body, released from the restraint of corsets, spreading over the sofa like a monstrous growth. And she was ready for him. Her peevish mouth was angrily set, her sullen eyes were bitter. For an hour she had been brooding over her imaginary wrongs and preparing barbs for the tongue-lashing she was going to give him.

Although she had no more need of Philip than he of her, periodically she liked to play the role of the dutiful wife scorned and neglected by a brute of a husband. At the movies that afternoon she had seen her favourite actress in just such a part. The plight of that lovely creature—with whom she completely identified herself—had made her moist mouth work convulsively, her eyes swim with tears. Emotion had given her a headache. For that, Philip must pay.

"Do you see the time?" she demanded furiously as soon as Philip entered the living-room. "Where have you been until this hour of the night? Don't tell me you've been at 'The Hole in the Wall', it's been shut for an hour and a half. Besides, you haven't been there for a long time. Mr. Greener told his wife he hadn't seen you there for ages. You've found another way of amusing yourself. You're up to something, but I'll find out what it is. You won't go on pulling the wool over my eyes much longer."

Philip tried not to look at her. Now more than ever his stomach turned at sight of the ungainly body; the curl-papered head; the fat morose face. It was no easier to look with pleasure at the scraps of food which had been left for him on a grubby cloth spread at one end of the table. He pushed the food aside and sat down at the table, staring into the crumbling fire, marshalling his thoughts.

"Not good enough for you?" hissed Cora. "We it's the best you'll get until you allow me some more money. How many wives would have any food waiting for you at this time of the night?"

This was his life. This fat, untidy woman; that barbed tongue which never tired of ranting; this drab, uncared for room; those bits and pieces of stale and ill-cooked food. This was his life—no, by God, it wasn't. Not any longer. Not after tonight.

When she saw that her words were not finding a way through his thoughts, Cora's voice grew shriller, determined to batter into his brain and make him squirm.

"Oh, shut up," he cried suddenly. "For heaven's sake, shut up."

The outburst was a victory for Cora. It was what she wanted, evidence that she was stinging him. "How dare you talk to me as if I were a slave? I believe that's what you think I am. An unpaid servant, to wait on you hand and foot. A domestic drudge, not your wife at all. Night after night I'm left to sit here—"

"Let's forget all that for a moment," said Philip wearily. "I want to talk to you."

Cora stared at him. It was a long time since he had wanted to talk to her. "What's wrong? Something's wrong, I can see it in your face. Don't lie to me, Philip Marshall. What is it?" Her eyes narrowed; her mouth became pinched. "You've lost your job?"

"No, my job's safe enough. And there's nothing wrong, except what's been wrong for years. It's time we took stock of our lives and gave some intelligent consideration to what we've done with them."

"I can't make head or tail of all this. What are you driving at?"

"Cora, you're not happy with me."

"Well, what do you ever do to make me happy? I never see you except last thing at night."

"When we spent our evenings and Saturday afternoons and all-day Sunday together, we weren't any happier. We've never been happy together, that's the long and short of it. We're not suited to each other, never were. Let's be honest with ourselves for once and admit it."

Cora was puzzled and when she was puzzled, she always hedged. "I don't know what you're talking about."

"I'll put it this way; do you care in the least for me? I'm not asking if you love me, I know you don't. I only ask if you have the smallest spark of feeling for me?"

"I'm your wife, aren't I?"

Philip sighed. "Yes, you're my wife. But that doesn't answer my question."

A vague fear stirred in Cora's muddled brain. Where was all this leading? There was something strange about Philip. He had never talked like this before. The scene she had planned had suddenly wrenched the reins out of her hands and was galloping off with her, to the Lord knew where.

"What do you expect me to say? I can't understand you, Philip Marshall, talking this way. It isn't decent."

"Not decent to ask you to be straight with me? Cora, we've been married almost a quarter of a century. Surely just once we can be honest with each other?"

"There's something behind all this. You're leading up to something."

"We should never have married each other, Cora. Marriage should make two beings stronger; it's made us weaker. There's something fine about a marriage that is a blending of two minds, two bodies, to one purpose. Ours was never like that. We started off on the wrong foot. We weren't in love. You know that. We never had anything to offer one another. We've always been out of step with each other."

"I've been a good wife to you, Philip Marshall. I've always been faithful to you. I sometimes think that's more than you can say."

"Perhaps it is—but what does that matter?"

Here Cora was on familiar ground. Sex was a subject she knew something about. She had given it a lot of thought.

"What does it matter?" she cried. "You sit there boasting that you've been unfaithful to me—revelling in your filthy lusts—and have the impertinence to say what does it matter. Faithfulness is the most important thing in married life, any one knows that. Read your Bible. Supposing I had affairs with other men—how would you like that?"

"I shouldn't mind. Considering how we've felt about each other for years, it would be silly for me to care what you did with your body. We've made a disgusting mess of our married life and you can't redeem it by saying you've never slept with anyone but me. That's making sex the soul foundation of marriage—and sex is a damned poor foundation for anything."

"May God forgive you, Philip Marshall, for daring to talk like this to your wife. Have you no sense of decency? What would people think if they heard you? Sex and bodies and sleeping with people. It's disgusting."

"There's been no respect, no companionship, no love, no loyalty in our marriage; only a mutual antagonism that has grown and grown until now, if we told the truth, we'd admit that we hate the sight of each other."

"So that's what all this has been leading up to? You hate the sight of me, do you? I wonder you've the audacity to look your wife in the face and say a thing like that."

"Oh, come off it, Cora. You're not indignant, only puzzled. You're very fond of giving me what you call home truths; well, let's have a few home truths now."

"I'll give you all the home truths you want and more," she screamed, livid with rage. "I hate you; do you hear? I hate you. I detest your silly face, the airs you put on, everything about you. So now you know. Put that in your pipe and smoke it. Why I ever married you I don't know. If I'd listened to—"

"You don't know why you married me. And I'm damned if I

know why I married you. You hate me. I dislike you. We can't bear the sight of each other and we both know it. We can't even pretend to feel differently; we've gone too far for that. So, what are we doing living together as husband and wife?"

"But we *are* husband and wife," said Cora stupidly.

"Yes, but that doesn't mean that we've got to be locked in this prison cell of ours for ever. You spoke about decency. Is it decent for us to live together, feeling as we do? We're miserable together, let's separate and try to find happiness apart."

"So that's it. You want to leave me. After all these years of—"

"After all these years of hell, Cora, I want to leave you. Is that surprising? Or have you got so used to hell that you wouldn't feel at home elsewhere? Do you want us to go on this way for the rest of our lives? We're not old, we've got years ahead of us, why should we poison them with hatred and misery? We're not chained together. We can get a divorce. You hate the sight of me; surely to get rid of me would be something gained? You've always loathed housekeeping, well, here's your chance to be done with it. You like Eastbourne. You once said you'd like to live there. Well, you can. You can go there and live in a boarding-house. I'll allow you four pounds a week. On that you can live in comfort—more comfortably than you do now. By divorcing me you've everything to gain and nothing to lose."

"Oho," said Cora, and her eyes glittered. "You will allow me four pounds a week out of an income of six. And how do you propose to live on two? At last, I'm finding things out. You've been lying to me about your pay. You earn more than six pounds a week, a lot more."

"If you must know, I earn nine. But that's neither here nor there, the point is—"

"Neither here nor there? You've been lying to me, cheating me, as good as stealing from me; robbing your own wife, making her scrimp and scrape to make ends meet and you think you can pass it off like that."

"All right. Perhaps I've been doing all you say. You've never given me value for what money I did allow you, but let that pass. We've something more important than money to consider. Cora, you must see—"

"I see that you're a two-faced wicked liar. You've lied to me about the money you earn and I dare say you've lied about a lot of other things. You don't want a divorce for nothing. There's another woman in this."

For a while Philip was silent. Usually, his silence would have provoked another outburst from Cora but now her voice, too, was stilled. She was watching his face intently and the tip of her tongue crept out and licked her lips.

"All right," said Philip with a sigh. "I'll tell you the truth. There is another woman. I love her and I want to marry her."

"Well, you shan't! You're married to me and you're going to go on being married to me. I shan't set you free so that you can give your name to some shameless whore."

White to the lips, Philip said: "I could kill you for that."

"What else is she? A woman who gives herself to a married man, who deliberately breaks up another woman's home."

"She hasn't given herself to me. So far, we've been no more than friends, we've hardly thought of anything else. And she doesn't know I'm married."

"Then she soon will. I'll find her. I'll teach her a lesson. I'll brand her in public for what she is. I'll shout it from the house-tops. She'll be sorry for herself before I'm done with her. She'll never steal another woman's husband."

"Don't be a fool," said Philip shakily. "She's stolen nothing from you. You never had any part of me that was worth having. I'm not your husband—I'm only the poor devil you married."

"You're my husband by law and that's good enough for me. You'll have no other wife as long as I live."

"You can gain your point there if you must. There can't be a divorce without your consent, and if I can't offer this woman marriage, I'll offer her nothing. If I can't have her, I can't have her. I love her but that isn't the most important issue. The important thing is that we can't go on as we are. I'll continue to support you—don't worry about that—but I shan't live with you. I can't."

"You'll never leave me," hissed Cora. "I shan't let you. If you think I'm going to be pointed to in the streets as a woman who couldn't hold her husband, you're very much mistaken. I can imagine what Mrs. Greener would say. Oh, no, you shan't humiliate me before the neighbours. No one's going to pity me—and laugh at me —the way I've heard them pitying other women and laughing at them behind their backs. No, you won't leave me. I shan't let you."

"How do you propose to stop me? I have only to pack a bag and walk out."

A cruel, thin smile set hard on Cora's mouth. Her eyes were pin-points. "If you try to leave me, I'll follow wherever you go. I'll turn up where you live and make scenes. I'll come to the office day after day and kick up a fuss. I'll follow you in the streets and tell strangers what you are. Living with me is hell, is it? Just try to leave me and I'll show you what hell really is. I'll make you wish you'd never been born!"

The venom she put into her words was appalling.

"Cora, for God's sake stop and think."

"I have thought. And I've told you what I'll do. I'll keep my word, you ought to know me well enough to realize that. So, it's for you to stop and think before you do something you'll be eternally sorry for."

The more Philip thought the more horrified he became. If he left her, she would do what she threatened, he had no doubt of that. She would have no pity, no compunction. Fear of making herself ridiculous would not stop her, she revelled in even the most degrading scenes. She would make his life a hundred times more hideous than it had ever been. He would lose his job and if he got another, she would see that he lost that, too. And who would take him as a lodger with Cora and her vitriolic tongue at his back like the tail on a kite? She had it in her power to ruin him if he left her, and she would. The campaign of persecution would give her an interest in life; she would live for it, bring to it a host of cunning inspirations, rise every morning bright and eager with a new torture devised for him overnight. Nothing would stop her. He would go to law, get an injunction to prevent her harassing him, but what good would that do? It would take more than an injunction to stop Cora once her mind was made up.

He remembered the case of an acquaintance who was accused by an elderly spinster of having pinched her bottom on a bus. She had gone to his home and told his wife about it, stopped his children in the street and told them their father was a depraved wretch, written anonymous letters to his business associates, kept pace with him on the other pavement when he was walking down the street and shouted accusations at the top of her voice, stood up in the church in which he was a sidesman and cried: "There is a moral leper in our midst!"

Her delusion had developed until instead of pinching her bottom it was something far worse, he was supposed to have attempted on the bus. And people said there must be something in it. Even though no man could imagine himself finding pleasure in pranking with so desiccated a mortal as the spinster, still they said knowingly that there was no smoke without fire.

The demented man had hauled her into court and had her admonished, had brought her to court again and had her fined, brought her a third time and had her bound over to keep the peace with a surety of ten pounds—but he had not been able to stop her. In despair he had tried to take his own life and was shut up in a private lunatic asylum.

If a half-cracked stranger could do that to a man what could not a deserted wife do?

Cora was still talking. "As for this woman, I'll show her. I'll find out where she is, never fear, and when I do, she'll be sorry for herself. She's no better than a common streetwalker. She's a whore, do you hear? A whore. A whore. A whore."

Would she never shut up? Philip's hands were shaking. The fingers of his right-hand curled round something solid and cold and gripped it tightly. He looked down and saw that he was holding the carving knife. The blade was long and pointed. He need only stick it in her and she would shut up. Stick it in her and the tirade would end in a grunt.

But they would hang him. Hang him by the neck until he was dead—and the Lord have mercy on his soul. Dropping the knife, Philip stumbled blindly out of the room. Cora's voice pursued him relentlessly up the dark staircase.

Chapter 8

The train was slowly coming in, the waiting crowd was jostling for position. As it grew nearer it grew bigger and bigger until it almost filled the world. The smoke from the engine smothered everything like fog. On the edge of the platform stood Cora, using her elbows to make the others keep their distance. Philip felt hot under the collar. He hoped no one knew she was with him. She looked such a sight in her faded kimono, with her curl-papers in her hair, with her fattest parts bulging out of her corsets. She was almost as big as the train. The train and Cora dwarfed everything else, made platform and passengers seem tiny.

A hoarse voice like a whisper through a foghorn kept booming in Philip's ear: "Push against her. Push her off the platform. Push her under the train."

The voice of Simmons, who called himself an author and scrounged pints of bitter in 'The Hole in the Wall.' Simmons was drunk. Simmons was always drunk. Someone would hear him if he didn't shut up. But no one looked round. Not even Cora. They were all intent on the train. Cora was so determined to be first that her toes were sticking over the edge of the platform. Easy to nudge her over. Dead easy...

"Push her off the platform. Push her under the train. No one will know it wasn't an accident."

Philip put his hands on the broad back and pushed. It wasn't easy after all. She wouldn't budge. He pushed and pushed, his face reddened, his veins swelled with the effort, but she wouldn't budge. Surely everyone must know what he was trying to do? But no one was looking. Every one—even Cora—was watching the train. It kept coming in. It was so big now that there was only room in the world for the lower half of it and its funnel was lost among the stars.

"Push... Push... Push..."

He did his best. Sweat streamed down his face, but she wouldn't move. She didn't resist. She didn't fight back. She just wouldn't budge. Push as he might, there she was, an enormous jelly, a muddy pink jelly, immovable on the edge of the platform. And the train was coming in. And the hoarse whisper was booming. And in a moment, someone was sure to look round and catch him trying to push the jelly off on to the line. He couldn't stop. He must go on. He lay on the jelly and shoved with his toes, shut his eyes and shoved, bent his knees and shoved, clenched his fists and shoved. And when he had abandoned hope, when it seemed that he would have to go on pushing for ever and ever amen without avail, the jelly slithered over the edge, on the line, under the train.

And the train, at last, came in...

Cora was dead. In the bewildered moment of waking that was Philip's first thought. Cora was dead. There was so much happiness in the thought he could hardly contain it. And then he heard familiar sounds from the next room and the happiness drained out of him Gr-r-raw—whee... Gr-r-raw—whee... No, she wasn't dead. She was lying in bed like a bulging sack, snoring through her open mouth.

Not yet dawn; the grey early light, creeping between the slats of the Venetian blinds, made a dim pattern on the ceiling like the shadow of prison bars. Lying in bed, looking up at the pattern, he knew himself a prisoner as surely as though he had been sentenced at the Old Bailey. A prisoner serving an indeterminate sentence, for whom there 'could be no release' as long as his gaoler lived. People are punished for their mistakes no less than their crimes, but the only mistake that entails lifelong imprisonment is one that is made before a parson while an organ plays 'The Voice that breathed o'er Eden...'

His lot had been hard enough in the past. In future it would be infinitely worse. It had been a mistake to lay his cards on the table the previous night. He had given Cora something to nag about for the rest of her life. Fool to imagine that she might release him! He should have known the simple fact that he wanted a divorce would be enough to make her deny it. The knowledge that his life was intolerable would only add relish to hers.

Before him lay long years of impotent misery which only the death of one or the other of them would end. Cora was only forty-five and there was nothing wrong with her except a disordered liver, the result of too many sweets, too little exercise. She was so lazy that her tissues would never wear out. Unless she fell under a train or stepped in front of a bus, she would go on for another twenty years.

To be married to Cora for twenty more years was unthinkable. Suddenly he knew what he must do. At first the thought was repellent but the more he considered it the more inevitable a solution it seemed. Cora had asked for it, she had only herself to blame if she got it. But he must not be caught. Somehow, he would have to defeat the Law, which demands a life for a life. He remembered what Simmons had said one night, weeks ago, when he was drunk: the perfect murder must be so simple that no one would suspect it to be murder. An arranged accident. "*In the crush you push against* your poor old pal and he falls in front of the train. They don't hang you. No one can prove it wasn't an accident..."

While dawn on slippered feet crept through the silent streets, Philip lay in bed examining schemes for killing his wife. When the alarm clock went off, he started as though he had been asleep.

Washing, shaving, dressing, his brain cells were busy with murder like patient fingers unravelling a tangled length of twine.

Going downstairs, he almost tripped on the broken step near the top. He halted and gave it a long look. Then and there was conceived a plan so simple that from that moment he considered no other. It was ugly, but simple, and—if Simmons was right—simplicity was the keystone of the successful murder. Afterwards he was to wonder how he had failed to see the awful brutality of the plan but from that moment Cora was as good as dead. He no longer thought of her as a living being. She was now only a problem he was on the point of solving.

One excellent feature of his plan was that it required only a minimum of preparation. If he cared to, he could carry it through that day. And time was a consideration. The sooner Cora was eliminated the better. Give her a little longer and she would discover Mary's identity and make trouble for her.

At the office that morning he seemed his usual calm, prosaic self, but all the time he was bubbling inwardly like a boiling pot. Even if he had shown outward signs of excitement, it is doubtful whether the others would have noticed, for it was Saturday and their minds were bent on only one thing; getting away on the stroke of one. Once or twice, going about his routine duties, Philip paused and thought: I'm going to commit a murder. I, Philip Marshall, am about to kill a human being. But the thought carried no conviction. In his mind Cora was already dead and you cannot murder a corpse. All that remained was to dispose of her.

When his employer left Philip went into the inner room and telephoned to Mary. "My dear, I shan't be able to see you this afternoon and probably not tomorrow. I've some urgent business to attend to."

"But, Philip, I want to see you very specially."

"No more than I want to see you."

"There's something I must tell you." Mary sounded distressed.

"It isn't that you don't love me?"

"Oh, no, Philip, never that."

"Then it can keep for a day or two. Lunch with me on Monday."

"Can't I see you before then?"

"I'm afraid not."

Even seeing you on Monday won't be wise, Philip reflected. By that time Cora will be—eliminated—and I shall have to watch my step for fear of rousing suspicion. But see you on Monday I must, even if I hang for it. Before Monday I'll think up some reason for us to meet less frequently for a month or two. I'll have to be careful, careful.

"All right," said Mary dully. "Then I'll see you on Monday at lunch."

"Good bye till then, dear."

"Good bye, Philip."

When the others left the office, Philip opened the Classified Telephone Directory and found the address of a wood-shop in Arnos Grove. He chose Arnos Grove because he had never been there and knew no one who lived there, and because it was the length of London from his own neighbourhood.

At the wood-shop he bought a piece of deal thirty-two inches long, ten inches wide, and an inch thick; those were the measurements of the broken step in his staircase. He was kept waiting a few minutes while the wood was cut, then it was handed to him neatly wrapped in brown paper and tied with string.

Philip held the parcel between his knees on the train from Arnos Grove to Russell Square. At Russell Square he alighted and went to a lavatory. When he came out the parcel was hidden under his coat. He walked to Holborn and caught a Piccadilly

Line train to Hammersmith, choosing a crowded carriage so that it was perfectly natural for him to travel standing (with the wood inside his coat he could not sit). From Hammersmith he walked home, for the District Railway trains were not so busy, and a man is conspicuous standing in a half-empty carriage.

Cora did not expect him home before midnight. When he walked into the house at three, he caught her off guard. There was a scrambling and a rustling as she thrust a lurid magazine and a bag of chocolates out of sight behind a cushion. Philip took the wrapped wood from under his coat and leaned it against the wall.

"What are you doing home in the middle of the afternoon?" demanded Cora peevishly, her sullen face appearing in the doorway of the living-room.

"It's Saturday."

"I could have told you that. I didn't ask what day it is, I asked why you've honoured your home with presence so early."

"It isn't the first Saturday I've come home early."

"It's the first for years. Don't expect any lunch, there's no food in the house."

"I'm not hungry."

Cora leaned forward and peered at the oblong parcel. She glanced at Philip but he did not offer an explanation.

"What's that?" she grunted.

"A piece of wood to replace the broken board in the stairs."

"So, you finally decided to do something about it? That isn't like you. You didn't come home early to try to get round me, did you? If you did, you're in for a disappointment. Nothing will persuade me to give you a divorce, so you can save your breath."

"Cora," said Philip earnestly, "let me go. It needn't be a divorce. Make your own terms. Only—for God's sake, Cora—let me go."

Even as he made the appeal, he realized that it was as futile as a telephone bell ringing in an empty house. There was nothing in Cora to answer it.

She gave him the bitter direct smile of an implacable enemy.

"*I'll never let you go,*" she said, and her tone was all the more chilling because for once it was quiet. "And don't try to leave me. I told you what I'd do and, I warn you, I'll keep my word."

"Very well," said Philip in a tone of finality.

"We'll go on living as man and wife whether you like it or not. 'Whom God has joined let no man put asunder'—that's Scripture, in case you've forgotten. And there'll be some changes made. You'll give me more money. You'll give up this fancy woman of yours, I'll see to that. When I'm finished with her she'll be only too glad to avoid you!"

Philip picked up the wrapped board and went to the kitchen. With a plane and sandpaper, he rounded one side of it until it was identical in shape with the stair-boards. Putting plane and sandpaper away, he gathered up the shavings and threw them in the grate. The kitchen fire had not been lit for days, but the grate was half full of cold ashes. He crumpled some sheets of newspaper and stuffed them in on top of the ashes. He laid the wood-chopper handy on the hearth. In the kitchen cupboard he found a stump of candle in a saucer. With the board under his arm and the candle in one hand he went upstairs.

Through the half-open door of the living-room he glimpsed Cora as he passed. She was sitting on the sofa with her knees spread out, staring into the fire. She did not turn her head. He hoped she would stay like that until he was ready for her.

In his bedroom he placed a chair with its back to the window and set a small table beside it. He took a book from the shelf above his head and laid it open and face down on the table. Beside it, an ashtray. He smoked four cigarettes quickly, making a plausible accumulation of spent matches, ash, and cigarette ends. He lit another cigarette and put it on the ashtray to smoulder.

Going out to the landing he lit the candle, and laid it and the board on the floor. Slipping out the stair-rod he took up the threadbare carpet, made a neat roll of it, and put it to one side of the landing. Then he went downstairs and looked in at the living-room door. There was a tight feeling about his heart, a cold emptiness his stomach.

"I wish you'd taken the trouble to replace the light bulb you borrowed from the stairs," he said, keeping his voice steady by a considerable effort. "It's getting dark and I can't see to do the job. You'll have to come and hold the candle."

"Take the bulb from your room," retorted Cora, without looking round.

"I've had enough of taking bulbs from my room. They never go back. If I take one from anywhere, it'll be from your room."

"You'll leave my bulb alone. It's always the same. The fuss you make when you do a little job!"

But Cora heaved herself to her feet and waddled after him up the stairs. Philip picked up the candle. His hand shook.

"There you go, clumsy!" said Cora. "Dripping grease all over the place. Here, give it to me."

She snatched it out of his hand. "Well, what are you waiting for? Don't stand there staring at me like that. Do you think I want to be here all night? Where are your tools? You'll need a hammer and chisel to prise up the broken board."

"I've got them handy," lied Philip.

"Then get on with it. What are you waiting for?"

"If you stand there," said Philip hoarsely, "I can't see to do the job. Stand here—and hold the candle so—"

He guided her to the middle of the top step and made her stoop so that the light fell on the broken one.

"You're trembling," she said sharply. "What's the matter with you?"

Her back straightened when Philip put his hand on it. There was a terrible moment while she struggled to keep her balance. And then—in one enormous stride it seemed—she went bodily down the stairs.

An appalling thud... A groan...

Philip went down with the clean, smooth board in his hand. He stepped on something that flattened under his foot; the candle. In the faint light from the open door of the living-room he saw Cora lying in a heap at the foot of the stairs. Struggling to rise, her livid face turned toward him, the neck twisted.

"You pushed me!" she panted, hoarse with shock. *"You pushed me!"*

He had not realized it was going to be so beastly. He had not imagined it like this. This was awful. But he could not stop now. He must go on. Even though her eyes were staring in dawning terror up into his, he must go on. He swung the board back over his shoulder. Cora tried to scream but only a harsh croak came from her quivering mouth.

After he hit her, he was not sure that she was dead but he dared not hit her again. In falling downstairs, she might strike her head violently on one step, but not two. He thought he could hear her breathing but there was nothing he could do about it, nothing he dared do.

Hurrying to the kitchen, he chopped the board into kindling, thrust it into the grate, touched a match to the crumpled paper. Sick, trembling, he watched the flames leap up. He set the draught so that the blaze swiftly would burn itself out.

Walking with averted eyes through the hall to the front door, he was sure he could hear Cora breathing harshly, brokenly. It was all up with him if she was. Opening the door, he ran down the path, swung open the gate, took half a dozen paces to the left and opened another gate, ran up another narrow path and pounded on his neighbour's door.

A stout, cheerful-looking man opened the door and looked out at him with mildly startled eyes.

"May I use your phone?" Philip stammered. (In his imagination he had acted this part many times that day but there was now no need to act.) "It's my wife. She's fallen downstairs. I've got to call a doctor."

Chapter 9

Alone in his neighbour's hall, waiting for the call to go through, Philip kept thinking: What if she's still alive? What if she doesn't die? The neighbour and his wife had gone in to do what they could for Cora while Philip telephoned. If Cora was alive and conscious, what was she saying to them at this very moment? Panic tingled in his veins. He had bungled the killing; he knew he had. He was a fool to have tried to do it that way. It might be simple but it was not certain. If Cora was alive—And she *was,* he could feel it. *"My husband did it. He tried to murder me."* Philip could almost hear Cora's high-pitched, furious whisper. He felt like slamming down the telephone and taking to his heels.

The call was answered at last. Yes, the doctor would come at once. Yes, he realized it was urgent. Yes, yes, he would be with Philip in a matter of minutes. Philip was not to try to move his wife until the doctor came, there was no saying what internal injuries she had suffered in the fall.

It was all Philip could do to force himself to walk down one garden path and up the other. What would they say to him when he went in? Or would they say nothing, just stare at him in silence with fearful eyes that said: MURDERER! Perhaps the husband had already gone for the police. Perhaps in a few minutes Philip would be walking down the street with his wrists manacled.

His neighbours were standing just inside the door, a few feet from the motionless bundle at the bottom of the stairs. The man said nothing. He only looked at Philip. It was an odd, disturbed look that might mean anything.

The woman said softly:"You must be brave, Mr. Marshall. Your wife is dead. I can't tell you how sorry I am."

For a moment Philip was overcome with giddiness. The man put an arm about him, a friendly arm. "Brace up, old chap. This must be a terrible shock, but you mustn't give way."

"I'm all right," said Philip thickly. He shook his head and the dizzy feeling passed. "The doctor will be here presently. He said not—not to touch her until he comes."

"You'd better go home, dear," said the neighbour to his wife. "There's nothing you can do. I'll stay with Mr. Marshall for a while."

When the woman had gone her husband shut the door.

"I tried the light switch," he said, "but something must be wrong. The light didn't go on."

"There's no bulb," said Philip dully.

"We'd better find one before the doctor comes. He'll want to examine the—to make an examination."

"I'll fetch the bulb from my room."

"I'd better come with you. You've had a nasty shock. As they went upstairs, Philip said:

"Look out for second step from the top. It's broken. That's how it must have happened. She must have tripped on it and fallen."

They went into Philip's room and switched on the light. Weak at the knees, Philip dropped into the chair that had its back to the window and passed a shaking hand over his forehead.

"Feeling a bit queer?" said his neighbour.

"No, I'm all right."

"I can slip next door and fetch you a drink. Brandy or something."

"No, thanks, I'll be all right."

Philip's elbow was almost touching the book he had left on the table. The cigarette he had lit and laid on the ashtray still smouldered, sending up a thin spiral of smoke.

"I was sitting here reading when it happened. I heard a crash and ran out and—and there she was. She must have tripped on the broken step and fallen all the way down. There was no light on the stairs—light bulbs were my wife's pet economy. She hated to buy them. I've warned her so often, over and over again I've warned her that it's dangerous to save on light."

"Try not to think of it, old man."

Looking up, Philip said: "I don't know your name. Funny, isn't it? I don't even know your name and you've been living next door for about five years."

"More like seven. That's a London suburb for you. You can spend a lifetime in one and never know a soul. My name's Nisbet. I know yours, thanks to my wife." Nisbet laughed complacently. "She's a busybody, I'm afraid, likes to know something about the folk she lives among."

In that case, Philip reflected, she probably knows that Cora and I did not get on together.

Nisbet walked across the room to look at a photograph of a smiling boy hanging beside Philip's bed.

"Your son, isn't it? Fine lad. I know him to nod to. Bit of an athlete, I believe? What's he doing these days? Haven't seen him about lately."

"He doesn't live here now. He—we thought it better for him to be nearer his work."

"I see. This will be a shock for him, poor lad. You'll want him to know without delay, I expect. I can attend to that, if you like. Tell me what to say and I'll send a wire over my phone when I go back."

Philip had forgotten about John. Now he realised that the worst of this sordid business was yet to come. He would have to face his son; that wouldn't be easy. Face him and lie, face him and pretend sorrow; he hated to think of it. He scribbled

John's address and a few words on a scrap of paper and gave it to Nisbet. Almost at once he wanted to take it back, but he couldn't do that. John had a right to know about his mother immediately. Funny to think of Cora as John's mother. Funny? It was impossible. Philip simply couldn't think of her in that light; he wondered if John could.

Someone was knocking at the front door.

"That'll be the doctor," said Nisbet.

"He's been a long time," said Philip. "If she hadn't been dead, she could have died while we waited for him."

"I'll let him in. You sit where you are. You don't look up too much."

With his hand on the doorknob, Nisbet hesitated. "I'll need a light bulb for the hall. Is there another room I can take one from? I don't want to leave you in the dark."

"No, take this one. I don't mind."

In the dark Philip sat and listened to the front door opening and shutting, the murmur of voices. In the dark there was a pounding in his head, as though boilermakers were furiously at work inside it. Soon he could bear it no longer. He rose and went slowly downstairs. Nisbet was standing at the foot of the stairs, his face pale. A tall man in a dark coat—Doctor Veitch—was bending over the huddled thing that had been Cora. "Must have been a hell of a fall," he was saying. Nisbet coughed and the doctor looked round. Seeing Philip, he straightened up.

"This is a bad business, Mr. Marshall," he said, with professional gravity. "A bad business. In falling she must have hit her head on one of the stairs; the mark is perfectly plain. The bump fractured her skull. She must have died instantly."

Thank God for that, thought Philip. Poor Cora! It made her fate less horrible if she had died instantly.

"We'll have to move her," said Dr. Veitch. "Where can we take her, Mr. Marshall? Her bedroom, perhaps?"

It was a long time since Philip had last been in Cora's bedroom. Then it had been in a glorious muddle. It seemed unfair to let strangers see the dirt and disorder with which that poor broken thing had surrounded herself. Philip pushed wider open the door of the living-room.

"In here on the couch, I think."

Philip took her head. She had bled very little. Nisbet took her feet, trying not to look at her face. The doctor went in front of them and removed the cushions from the sofa, throwing them on the floor and thus revealing *Peg's Paper* and the crumpled bag of chocolate creams. Philip had forgotten about them. The doctor picked them up as reverently as though they were sacred relics and placed them on the table. Nisbet grunted as they lowered the body on to the sofa. It was very heavy.

"I'll have to notify the Coroner," said Dr. Veitch, on the point of departure, "and he'll send his Officer to have a word with you. That's customary in cases of accidental death, but you'll find him quite pleasant to deal with. Those chaps are monuments of tact. There'll be an inquest, but that's a mere formality required by law."

An inquest was something Philip had not taken into consideration but he nodded calmly and said, yes, he quite understood. After all, what had he to fear from an inquest? This was a plain case of a woman who had fallen downstairs and fractured her skull. No inquiry could make it more than that.

After the doctor had gone, Philip turned out the living room light and shut the door. Nisbet and he stood in the hall looking at each other uncertainly.

"Come next door for a while," said Nisbet. "The wife will make you something hot to drink."

"It's kind of you but if you don't mind, I think I'll lie down. I'm not feeling very well."

"I should, if I were you." Nisbet shuffled his feet. "Well... I'd better get along. I'll send the telegram at once."

"Thanks."

"And if you feel like dropping in on us later—"

"Thanks very much."

"Not at all. Well... Goodbye for the present."

"Goodbye."

Philip went up the stairs. On the landing he almost fell over the rolled stair-carpet. He carried it to the kitchen, found a bottle of ink, and spilled some on it. When the stain soaked in, he put the carpet in a corner. The blaze he had lit in the grate had long since burned itself out. He raked the ashes until those from the wood and paper were thoroughly mixed with the dead ashes of the old fire. He went up to his room, treading softly as he passed the door behind which lay the thing that had been his wife.

He pressed the light switch in his room but nothing happened. The bulb was down in the hall. Well, there was always the one in Cora's room, she would not need it any longer. But he could not enter her room to fetch it, although she was downstairs, not there. The frowsty, unmade bed, the clothing strewn everywhere, the spilt powder on the dressing-table, the tangled hairs on her comb; these things and more would recall to him the presence of the dead woman and that was not to be faced.

He went and got the bulb from the hall and plugged it into his socket. He switched on the light and almost at once switched it off again. He sat on his bed, lit a cigarette, tried not to think.

If I had known what it would be like I'd never have done it. Why didn't I realize how awful it would be to kill her like that? All I thought was how simple, how easy. The stark brutality didn't strike me. If it had, would I have let her live? Surely, I couldn't have gone through with it if I had known what that moment of striking would be? But I couldn't have known. Nothing I could have imagined would have been one tenth so horrible as the grim reality. To know how terrible killing is you've got to kill.

Authors glibly describe horrors, but they don't really see the pictures they've drawn with words, or they'd realize how inadequate words are. Old ladies revel in printed pages dripping blood, but they don't stop to think about what they're reading, their eyes race on ravenously, avid for more thrills. They read about a man's brains being spattered on a wall by the impact of a bullet, but the grisly horror of it doesn't sink in, they don't see the picture, they only get the thrill.

To know what murder is you've got to commit it. And when you've committed it, if there is a hell, you know what that is too.

Philip could not sit there any longer. Sitting in the dark, going over the killing in his mind, was driving him mad. Tiptoeing downstairs, he snatched his coat and hat from the hallstand and went out. He stood on the pavement for a moment wondering where to go. There was nowhere he wanted to go, he only wanted to get away; but how can you get away from something you take with you? For an hour or so he wandered about the streets of the neighbourhood. He passed one or two acquaintances, only realizing after he had passed that he had not returned their nods. It didn't matter. Tomorrow they would hear about Cora and say: 'So that why he didn't seem to see me last night. Poor fellow, he must be feeling it more than you'd have thought.'

Finding himself outside a cheap restaurant he made the discovery that he was hungry. He went in and sat at a table. His eyes wandered up and down the menu as his feet had wandered the streets. What did one eat? All the words for food looked unfamiliar. A steak? A tender steak that you slice with a knife and red juice runs out? No, not a steak. Not anything with blood. He ordered eggs. Ate one egg. Pushed his plate aside. Sat for a time staring at the wall. He rose suddenly and walked out.

The Italian proprietor, a once-white apron round his bulging middle, came running after him.

"Please you forget to pay. Two fry eggs, is eight pence."

Philip handed him a shilling and walked on.

Where to now? He did not know. He could not go back to the silent house, the empty house that was so full of Cora. Soon the Nisbets would come and offer him hot drinks and ask him to go in and sit with them. Nice people, kind people. It would have been pleasant to be friends with them during the seven years they had lived next door, if only Cora had been able to get on better with people. Funny that it was through her death he had come to know them. They were the sort of pleasant, ordinary people, Philip had always wanted for friends, but tonight his only wish was to avoid them. He couldn't face them and play the hypocrite, pretend to be heartbroken over Cora's death. They would want him to spend the night with them— 'No, *it's no trouble at all. It won't take a minute to put sheets on the bed in the spare room'*—and he wanted to be alone. But how could he be alone when wherever he went Cora went with him?

He caught a train to town and went to a hotel. The clerk at the reception desk offered a pen and asked about his luggage.

"I haven't any. I'll only be stopping one night. I'll pay in advance if you like."

From his room Philip telephoned for a bottle of whisky. It came with a syphon of soda. He diluted his first drink but after that he drank the whisky neat. He sat on his bed staring at the wall and every now and then he remembered the glass in his hand and took a swig at it. It was the first bedroom Cora and he had shared for a long time. For the most part he sat in silence but once he said:

"You asked for it. Damn you, you asked for it. You thought you had me where you wanted me but now you know your mistake."

The bottle did not last long. He ordered another. In the small hours of the morning, he fell asleep across the width of the bed, fully clothed, leaving the light on. There was half an inch of whisky left in the second bottle.

Chapter 10

On his way home the following morning Philip felt too groggy to think about his crime. A thick head has little patience with a nagging conscience. Nearing his house, he saw John standing on the doorstep, using the knocker with an air of frustration. The mere presence of his son had always meant happiness to Philip but now he was reluctant to face him. Torn between a desire to hurry to the boy, and an equally strong desire to turn on his heel and hasten away from him, Philip walked on slowly, arriving at the gate at the moment when John, giving up hope, had abandoned the knocker and was about to go.

John was wearing a black tie. He must have gone out and bought it when he received the wire. It looked as out of place on him as a crepe bow on a sunflower.

"Well, John," said Philip lamely.

This was the moment he had been dreading the moment when he must meet his son's eyes. But it was John who flinched when they shook hands. John had a guilty look, as though his conscience were eating him alive. He glanced resentfully at his father's tie—a blue one with polka dots—and his father's unshaven chin.

He was pale and his shamefaced air made him look more youthful than ever. Philip knew what was in John's mind; he was fretting because he was not really heartbroken over the death of his mother and he felt he ought to be. The tie, conventional badge of sorrow, was not enough; he ought to be in mourning inside as well as out; and because his inward mourning was spurious his conscience was making him squirm.

"I came last night as soon as I got your wire but although I rang and rang, I didn't get an answer."

"I didn't feel I could spend the night in the house," replied Philip, fumbling for his keys.

"My God, no," said John quickly. "No, you couldn't do that."

Philip opened the door and they went in. The stagnant air struck chill and musty. The house was as unfriendly as though it had been left to itself for long years instead of a single night. It had acquired the personality of a funeral mute. From force of habit, Philip hung his hat and coat on their peg. After a momentary hesitation, John hung up his hat. Philip felt his big son shrink a little as the atmosphere of the place wrapped itself round them.

"The people next door were very kind," said John, with a shiver. "They heard me ringing last night and made me go in for a cup of coffee."

"Nice of them," said Philip.

They avoided each other's eyes. John was staring at a rust-coloured smear on the floor between their feet. He looked sick.

"That was where she—" he said, as though the words were being forced out of him.

"Yes. The doctor said she didn't suffer. Death was instantaneous."

"I'm glad of that," said John, shivering again.

They stood, as though waiting for something, at the door of the room in which Cora lay. Philip moistened his lips.

"Do—do you want to see her?"

He hardly knew why he made the suggestion, except that it was customary on such occasions. The words had slipped out almost against his will. They had asked Philip that question when his own mother died, thirty years before, and although Philip had loved his mother, he had not wanted to see her lying dead. John looked frightened. Wordlessly, he shook his head. That was a relief. If John had said 'Yes' Philip would have had to find an excuse to put him off. He could not have let him go into the living-room and look down at what was lying on the sofa.

"Well..." Odd, this feeling that John was a stranger in the house. It was present in John as well as in Philip. "Well... We'd better go up to my room—your old one."

Entering his old room, John felt like a convict returning to a prison cell after a period of freedom. It was almost exactly as he had left it on the afternoon, a year ago, when he had slung some clothes into a bag and stormed out, vowing never to return. For a moment he had an illusion that he had never been away, that his freedom was only a dream. Was it ten years ago—or only yesterday—that he lay across that iron bed, sobbing after being punished unmercifully by his mother for some trifling fault? The awful mauve roses on the wall-paper, as big as saucers and spaced at irritatingly regular intervals. How many times had he counted them when sent up to bed in the middle of a sunny afternoon? The bookcase above the bed was new. Cora had never allowed him to keep books in the room for fear reading might enable him pleasantly to while away a period of punishment. It was odd, he thought, that for the past year his mother had been dead to him although she was alive, and now he had only to step over the threshold of his old room and she became frighteningly alive, although she was dead.

Not all the memories the room recalled were unhappy ones. There were some pleasant relics of his boyhood; boxing gloves on a nail above the fireplace; a home-made model yacht; a row of silver cups he had won for running and swimming; photographs—in which he figured— of school football and cricket teams.

"You haven't changed the room much."

"No," said Philip.

"I wish you had. It reminds me of things I'd rather forget. It's like—like coming face to face with the ghost of my boyhood."

"That's why I haven't made many changes. I wanted to feel that I still had something of you."

"You've always been fond of me, haven't you?" said John, in the embarrassed tone an Englishman uses to speak of sentiment. "I don't know why. I'm not worth it."

"If I said, 'No, you're not,' you'd be bloody annoyed," said Philip, with a smile, "so let's leave it that I'm fond of you. There doesn't have to be a reason. I must shave. Will you stay here or come and talk to me in the bathroom?"

"I'll come and talk to you," said John quickly. He had no wish to be left alone with his thoughts.

Perched cross-legged on the edge of the bath, watching his father shaving, John could not help remembering the bare-kneed boy who had done that so often. The boy had talked incessantly, for he loved to tell his father in minute detail about everything that happened to him and he had to make the most of his opportunities, for there was always the danger that at any minute his mother might walk in on them and spoil everything. John recalled long walks with Philip; visits to the Zoo; afternoons on the river. Spates of talk, warm silence. What a good companion his father had been! And how his mother had hated to see them together! She had done her best to limit their outings and her sour expression when they returned from one of them had always taken the edge off their happiness.

His mother, his mother; always his thoughts came back to her.

"If I'd known she had so short a time to live I shouldn't have gone away."

"Yes, you could have stuck it out a little longer," Philip agreed, "if you'd known. But you didn't know. She seemed good for another twenty years. And you had your own life to lead. So don't reproach yourself for leaving a home in which you were miserable. Oh, I know how you feel. While she was alive you could have given a hundred excellent reasons for leaving her but now she's dead you think it's indecent to remember them. That's the unfair thing about death, he gives his victims the last word."

Philip was wishing he had as little reason as John for feeling guilty. Had the fall that killed Cora really been an accident, he would be the happiest man in the world at this minute. Why pretend? Cora was a bad wife, a worse mother. It was natural for them to be glad to be free, so why feel guilty about feeling glad?

"What will you do now?" asked John. "You won't want to live here alone?"

"I'll find a room in the neighbourhood."

In Philip's mind was a half-hope that John would suggest sharing a small flat with him, but John didn't. Philip tried not to feel hurt. It was natural, after all, for the boy to have found other interests in the year they had been apart. The reflection made him remember that he himself had found an absorbing interest; Mary. He realized with a shock of surprise that since noon the previous day he had not thought of Mary.

They went to the bedroom and Philip put on a clean shirt and a black tie.

There was a knock at the front door, a commanding double rap, charged with authority. Philip went down to answer it. Through a frosted-glass panel he saw the outline of a police helmet and his muscles tightened, his mouth became dry. Keep cool, he told himself. There's nothing to worry about. It was an accident. Squaring his shoulders, he opened the door. He felt easier when he saw the face of the policeman who was standing outside. It was round and pink, with sleepy blue eyes; the face of a middle-aged baby, not that of a man who would go out of his way to make a murder out of an accident.

"You Mr. Marshall, sir?"

"Yes. What can I do for you?"

"I am the Coroner's Officer and it is my duty to inquire into the death of your wife."

"Come in," said Philip, opening the door wider.

As he crossed the threshold the Coroner's Officer took off his helmet and hung it over his arm by the strap. He was bald and the round pinkness of his head made him look more than ever like a baby, a circumstance Philip found peculiarly comforting. He began by asking routine questions; how old was the deceased, what was her full name, what was her maiden name, how long had they lived in this house; and jotted down the answers in a black-bound notebook.

"Who was her regular medical attendant, sir?"

"Does that matter? She died from a fall. The state of her health had nothing to do with it."

"It's one of the questions I must ask, sir. In accident cases there is always the possibility of suicide. If I failed to inquire into the medical history of the deceased the Coroner might have something sharp to say to me at the inquest."

Philip realized then how important it was going to be to consider everything he said and did. If routine compelled a Coroner's Officer to look for suicide in even the unlikely case of a death from falling downstairs, how much more thoroughly must he be required to investigate the possibility of murder? It was an unpleasant thought, but Philip did not let it shake his nerve. Let this man look for evidence of murder; there was none for him to find.

"Doctor Veitch has been our medical man as long as we've lived in this house," he replied calmly. I'm glad to say we haven't required his services very often."

"It was Doctor Veitch you called in last night?"

"Yes." Philip was glad to be able to answer in the affirmative. It was disturbing to note how significant even the most trivial-seeming question could be.

The sergeant wrote in his notebook. His eyes shifted to the brown stain on the floor and his lips tightened.

"That was where you wife lay after the fall?"

"Yes."

"Where were you at the time, sir?"

"In my room, reading."

"Which room is that?"

"The first on the left at the head of the stairs."

"What time would it be when you heard the fall?"

"I can't say positively. Between half-past four and five, I imagine. It was beginning to get dark. My neighbours might know more exactly. I ran next door to phone for a doctor as soon as I realized that my wife was seriously hurt."

"How do you suppose she came to fall, sir?"

"There was no light on the stairs and there's a broken board near the top. In the dark she must have tripped over it. After she fell, I found a candle on the floor in the hall. It was a habit of hers to use a candle in a saucer to light her way up and down. I've warned her against it repeatedly."

"You heard the fall and ran down?"

"Yes."

"Was your wife conscious when you reached her?"

Philip saw Cora's twisted body struggling to rise, a picture he was never to forget. He saw her shocked face staring up at him, heard her croaking: *'You pushed me! You pushed me!'* Yes, Cora was conscious when he reached her—that was what had made it so hard to kill— but she would not have been if her death truly had been an accident. She was supposed to have hit her head in falling and, according to the doctor, the blow had killed her instantly. If it had been an accident, she would have been dead when he ran down to her.

"No," he said. "No, she wasn't conscious. I thought I could hear her breathing but that may have been imagination. From the way she lay I knew she was badly hurt, so I thought I'd better summon a doctor at once."

"No carpet on the stairs," commented the Coroner's Officer, making a pencilled note of the fact.

"We took it up yesterday afternoon."

"Oh, sir? Why?"

"I spilt ink on it. Having some letters to write, I was going up to my room with the bottle in my hand and it slipped through my fingers and made an unholy mess. We took the carpet up, intending to send it to the cleaners."

Footsteps crossed the landing above and John appeared at the head of the stairs. When he saw the policeman, he looked startled. Philip was annoyed. Damn it, why need the sight of a police uniform make the boy look as though he had done a murder, when he didn't even know that murder had been done.

"This is the Coroner's Officer, John," he said. "He is making some routine inquiries." To the sergeant he added: "This is my son."

John came slowly down the stairs.

"You were not at home when this happened?" asked the Coroner's Officer.

"No," said John. "I—" He looked at his father.

"My son doesn't live here," explained Philip.

"Then I'd better have his address."

The Coroner's Officer wrote John's address in book. He hung his helmet on the post at the foot of the stairs and went up to look at the broken step. Bending down, he peered at it closely. Taking a penknife out of his pocket he scraped at something with the point. "Candle-grease," he muttered.

"I told you she was carrying a candle."

"Quite sir. A candle in a saucer, you said. You'd expect the grease to drip into the saucer, unless she tilted the candle to look at something. Odd that grease should drip on the broken step. It almost looks though she paused to examine the step before she tripped over it."

"She'd hardly do that," said Philip.

The Coroner's Officer gave him a long look. "That's what I was thinking, sir," he said heavily.

He stood looking at Philip with the flake of candle-grease in one hand and the knife in the other. His face had hardened disconcertingly. It wore the strained expression that often accompanies deep thought on the part of those unaccustomed to it. Philip had no need to be a mind-reader to follow what was going on in the sergeant's round head. The man's thoughts were elephants moving ponderously through a jungle, each holding with its trunk the tail of the one in front; and the hindmost had 'Murder' written across its broad rump. It was absurd. It was preposterous. You can't make murder out of a blob of candle-grease, even if you find it where it shouldn't be; but that was precisely what the sergeant's slow mind was doing.

"You and the deceased were alone in the house at the time of the...happening?"

"That is so."

"You have no servant? The deceased did her own housework?"

"A charwoman came in occasionally."

"I'd better have the charwoman's name and address, sir."

"Her name is Meggs. I believe she lives near Devonshire Road. I don't know where exactly."

"I dare say I shall be able to find her, sir."

"Is all this necessary?" demanded John suddenly. "My mother died from a fall."

"There are certain investigations which must be made, sir, in all cases of sudden death," replied the Coroner's Officer stolidly. To Philip, he said:

"It will be necessary for the Divisional Surgeon to examine the body. A post mortem may be held. In that case, the remains will be taken to the mortuary sometime this afternoon. Do you expect to be in all day, sir?"

"No," said Philip, "I don't. I'm going out for lunch shortly and then I shall be looking for temporary lodgings." He took a key-ring from his pocket detached a key. "If I'm not in when you bring the Divisional Surgeon, you can admit yourselves with this. Let me have it back when you've finished with it."

Pocketing the key, the Coroner's Officer shut his notebook and snapped a stout elastic band round it. "That's all for the present, Mr. Marshall. If you find suitable lodgings, please leave the address a local police station."

After he had gone John turned startled eyes on his father.

"From his manner you'd think there was something fishy about Mother's death."

Philip's heart skipped a beat. He forced a laugh. "The manner goes with the uniform."

"Why should a post mortem be necessary? What does he expect to find?"

"I don't know. It doesn't much matter. There isn't anything to find."

"Sunday's a bad day to look for a room. If you don't find one, you'd better come back with me. Mrs. Lemon might be able to put you up for a few days."

"How would you explain me? You're supposed be an orphan."

John reddened. Before he could say anything, Philip, smiled and added: "I'll find a room. Coming from the station this morning, I passed a shop window with a lot of cards in it advertising rooms to let. I took the addresses. There's sure to be a passable one among them. Meanwhile, I'm hungry. Let's see what we can get in the way of lunch at 'The Hole in the Wall.'"

Philip packed a bag and they left the house. As they walked down the street John turned his head and looked back.

"It doesn't seem right," he mumbled, "leaving her alone."

Philip did not answer. He knew that Cora was not alone, that never again would she be alone; that always, to the end of his life, she would go with him wherever he went.

Chapter 11

That evening the Coroner's Officer called at Philip's temporary lodgings and gave him a summons to attend the inquest at ten the following morning. In handing over the paper, the cherubic officer's manner was formal and brusquely official; it left no room for doubt that his suspicions had hardened in the handful of hours since their previous meeting. A suspicious baby, the simile was absurd, but that was how the man appeared to Philip.

When the officer left, Philip telephoned his employer at home, told him of Cora's death and requested permission to absent himself from the office for two days. Henry Sturgis was almost overwhelmingly sympathetic (he never suspected the true state of affairs between Philip and his wife). "Take as much time off as you need. There are no end of things you'll have to do. Don't think of coming back until after the funeral, at least. Not then, if you think a few days' rest will do you good. If there's anything I can do—"

"Thanks very much," said Philip, "but there isn't anything."

Even then, Mr. Sturgis did not ring off. "You have my heartfelt sympathy, my dear chap. I know what it is to lose a good wife. When the first Mrs. Sturgis died, I thought the world had come to an end." (You must tell me all about it, said Philip, in silence; but not today, please...) Henry Sturgis wanted to tell him all about it then and there. It was a long story, full of drip and droop; he had told it often and he never tired of the telling. To cut it short, Philip said quickly:

"I knew you'd understand, sir. Thank you very much," and hung up, leaving his employer's story in mid-air.

In the morning Philip telephoned Mary and told her he

must put off their luncheon engagement and might not be able to meet her for a day or two. Mary's voice sounded peculiarly thin and flat.

"Is there something wrong?" he asked, but she did not answer. "Mary," he said. "Mary, dear, what is it?"

She did not speak, but he thought he heard a sob coming over the wire. In a panic, he said:

"Look here, I'll meet you outside your office this evening."

Still, she did not answer.

Impatiently, he repeated it, and finally she said:

"Alright," in a very small voice.

Frowning, he hung up the receiver. Now what the devil, he wondered, could all that have been about?

He turned up early at the Brentford Fire Station where the inquest was to be held. When the set hour approached only a scattering of people had appeared. Philip eyed each one of them warily. There was none who looked like a reporter, but then he had only the vaguest idea what a reporter looked like; a prying eye, perhaps, and a notebook in the hand. Well, there was no one here like that, these were only idle curiosity seekers. Most of them looked as if they were on the dole and had come in to get out of the rain which had been falling with gentle obstinacy since dawn and seemed likely to go on until dark. There was a small jury, comprised of local tradesmen. The Coroner's Officer was there, standing stiffly erect against a wall. He granted Philip one severe look, then turned his eyes to the window.

At ten minutes to ten Nisbet came in. He looked about him and, seeing Philip, walked over and sat beside him. Beyond an exchange of greetings, neither of them spoke. John appeared a moment later.

"Good morning, Dad."

"'Morning, John."

"Hello, Mr. Nisbet."

"Good morning, young fellow."

The boy shuffled his feet, twitched at his tie, sat down and glanced about him, squirming in his chair. "Barn of a place, isn't it?" he whispered huskily. "Hanged if I can see what they want with an inquest, anyway."

Philip replied, rather wearily: "They always do have one in cases of accidental death." He had spoken and heard that sentence so often lately, it was becoming a formula. Once or twice Nisbet coughed and moistened his lips as though about to speak, but it was obvious he did not know what to say. He was weighing sympathetic utterances in his mind and rejecting them, one by one, as trite and insincere. Perhaps his wife been talking to him about the true relationship of Philip and Cora. She could hardly have lived next door to them for seven years without knowing that they hated the sight of each other.

The Coroner was late. He came in at last with a plump man in a raincoat who carried a black bowler hat, cast a sluggish eye round the place and seemed to yawn, not with his mouth but with his whole body. The Coroner placed a brief-case on a table, drew a chair closer to it, and sat down. The plump man in the raincoat leaned over the back of the chair and spoke for a long time into the Coroner's ear, his lips scarcely moving. Through rimless eyeglasses, the Coroner threw a sharp glance at Philip.

The proceedings started with Philip being called to give evidence. He was asked two questions:

"You have seen the body? You identify it as that of Cora Marshall, your wife?"

He answered both of them in the affirmative. To his amazement, the Coroner then said:

"Thank you, that will be all for the present."

For a moment, Philip remained seated, unable to comprehend

that no more was wanted of him. The Coroner gave him another sharp glance and repeated:

"That will be all."

In a mental fog, Philip rose and walked to the body of the court.

Dr. Veitch was next.

"You say you left home as soon as you were summoned but the woman was dead when you reached the house? In your opinion, how long had she been dead?"

"Ten minutes, perhaps. A quarter of an hour at most."

"And the cause of death?"

"A severe fracture of the skull caused by striking her head on a stair-board in the course of the fall."

"Thank you, Doctor. That will be all."

Adjusting his glasses, clearing his throat, turning with blank face to the jury, the Coroner said, in a clear, precise tone:

"For reasons I shall not explain at this time, I am adjourning this inquest indefinitely. You will be notified when required to attend again. Since a thorough medical examination of the deceased has already been made, permission is granted for burial as soon as the relatives see fit. Good morning, gentlemen."

He rose and walked out in sober dignity.

With a startled question written all over him, Nisbet turned to Philip.

At the back of his mind, Philip had expected, dreaded, something like this. Now that it had happened, his mind was empty. He dared not look at John, who was gaping at him.

"What the devil does this mean?" gasped John hoarsely.

"How the hell should I know?" retorted Philip in futile anger.

Abruptly, he stood up and walked to the door, half expecting that the Coroner's Officer or some other policeman would bar the way. But no one prevented him leaving the building.

Outside it was still raining with soft persistence, as though it always would. Philip turned up his coat collar, pulled down his hat brim. Without looking back, he knew that John walked at his heels, which meant he was in for some awkward questions, and he felt that speech at this moment would choke him. Oh, for a passing bus on which to spring, on which escape…

"Dad—" John was having trouble with his voice. "I suppose there couldn't have been anything… anything peculiar… about Mother's death?"

Philip turned on him. "You mean, did I kill her?"

"Good heavens, no." John's eyes were round with innocence and horror. "I hadn't thought anything like that. I only meant—well, could it have been suicide?"

"A woman wouldn't commit suicide by throwing herself downstairs."

"No, of course not," said John, sounding immensely relieved. "Then, that's all right. The adjourned inquiry had me worried for a moment. But there's really nothing to worry about, is there?"

"Not a thing in the world," said Philip. You babe, he thought, you blessed, innocent babe.

"Well, I'd better go on to the office. We're pretty busy."

"I suppose you'd better. See you soon?"

"Well…" Uncertainty made the boy's voice waver. "I don't know. I think Gladys expects me to spend the evening with her."

"Gladys?"

"You know—my landlady's daughter. Women are funny. Give them the least encouragement and they start holding on to you."

Philip knew that. My God, didn't he?

"Well, there's always the funeral," he said dryly. "I'll see you there."

"Yes, I'll see you at the funeral." John looked almost frightened at the thought.

"Don't come if you'd rather not. A funeral is an unpleasant experience, to say the least of it."

"Oh, I'll come. One couldn't very well stop away." To John the suggestion was profoundly shocking. "When will it be?"

"Tomorrow morning, I suppose. I'll make the arrangements today and let you know."

"Well... Here's my bus."

It was Philip's bus, too, but he made no move to board it. He let the boy go alone and waited in the rain for the next.

*

Rain all day. A steady, monotonous drizzle that soaked through everything to the skin. His clothes sodden, his shoes squelching, Philip tramped the streets on various errands. To the undertakers, to arrange for the funeral. To the cemetery, to make more arrangements. To a florist, to order a wreath. What to write on the card was a problem, and in the end he left it blank.

In the evening the rain kept him company while he waited for Mary a short distance down the street from her office. She came at last, walking with painful slowness as if reluctant to meet him. He was shocked by her face. Distraught, grey, haggard. It told at once the agony she had suffered all day. Mary stared at him as though afraid. Philip was at a loss for words. Under a lamppost they stood in the rain, looking at each other helplessly.

"Philip," she said, "you must tell me. I've got to know. Don't lie. Philip, I want the truth."

"I'll tell you the truth, I promise that. What is it want to know?"

For what seemed a long time she fumbled with the catch of her bag. It opened, spilling compact, purse, and keys on the wet pavement. Philip made a move to retrieve them but Mary shook her head.

"They can wait. This is it. This is what I've got to know about."

She handed him a newspaper clipping.

It was about the death, on Saturday, through injury sustained in falling downstairs, of a Chiswick woman, Mrs. Philip Marshall. That was all there was to it, but for Mary it had been more than enough. Since reading it she had been through an emotional hell.

"This Mrs. Philip Marshall; she was your wife?"

"Yes," said Philip. "She was my wife."

"Philip, for God's sake tell me the truth. Was her death an accident?"

"No," he said. "It was not an accident."

"It's what I feared, then. You killed her."

"Yes," he said. "I killed her."

To lie did not occur to him. At the moment he could not have lied, even if he had wanted to do so. There was fear in Mary's eyes but it faded into bewilderment as she looked at him. He looks no different, she thought. In spite of what he has done, he looks no different. He is still Philip. A little pale, a little overwrought, that is all. How could that be? How can one murder without undergoing drastic change, without altering the story written on one's face? This man who had murdered, who stood silently looking at her in the rain, was still Philip. The Philip she had known. The self-same Philip. She did not know what she had expected, but she had not expected that.

"It was my fault," she said, only just aloud.

"Mary, you don't know what you're saying."

"It was my fault. I am to blame."

With that, she was gone. Philip started to follow her, then

turned back and scooped up her scattered belongings from the glistening pavement. Thrusting them into a pocket, he ran after her as quickly as he could but, turning a corner, became entangled in a scurry of drenched beings who were hastening to the Underground, to buses, to the shelter of doorways. It was no good. He would never find her in this. Still seeking her in vain, he almost walked into the stout man in raincoat and bowler hat who had talked in earnest whispers to the Coroner at the inquest.

On his way home, in a late edition of an evening newspaper, he found a few lines on an inside page, headed: *Surprise Inquest Adjournment.* He read the lines without emotion.

*

They buried Cora the next day. The only mourners—if mourners one could call them—were Philip and John, unless one included Mrs. Meggs, the charwoman, who brought a moistly clenched fistful of white roses to lay on the grave. She kept darting malicious glances at Philip and muttering under her breath, even during the brief service. The Coroner's Officer and the stout man in raincoat and bowler hat were there as well, looking solemn and saying nothing. The burial service ended with a light patter of soil on the coffin from the thin white hand of the clergyman. As the little group filed from the graveside, two men with sleeves rolled up started shovelling earth in earnest.

Walking away from the cemetery with John, Philip heard a hoarse whisper: *"You bloody murderer!"*

He not look round, but he knew from whom it had come; Mrs. Meggs. Out of the corner of his eye, he stole a glance at John's face and was reassured. The boy had not heard it.

From the cemetery, Philip went straight to the office. Every time he encountered his employer that afternoon Henry Sturgis eyed him oddly. At last Sturgis called Philip into the inner room.

"Look here, Marshall. It's a dashed awkward thing to ask a man—but there wasn't anything fishy about death of your wife, was there?"

"Nothing whatever," replied Philip steadily.

For a while Henry Sturgis studied Philip's face and then he nodded his head as if satisfied.

"Glad to hear it. Thought I knew you well enough to be sure you wouldn't be up to anything shady. Only asked because a bloke in a raincoat has been here pestering me with questions about you. There wasn't much I could tell him but his manner made me wonder."

"My wife died from an accidental fall," said Philip. "No amount of questioning will make more out of it than that."

During the afternoon, Philip left the office for a few minutes and telephoned Mary. Whatever happened, he had to see her soon. It was a need that would not be denied. To his surprise, she agreed without hesitation to meet him that evening.

They met in a teashop. Mary was no longer afraid of him, only afraid for him—miserable with fear for him, and consumed with pity for Cora, this dead wife of Philip's whom she had never known. She tried, haltingly, to explain how she felt.

"I can't think of Cora like that," said Philip. "For the sake of my sanity I've got to hate her. It isn't easy. I could hate her while she was alive but, somehow, now she's dead I can't. But I must. If I start feeling sorry for her, I'm done."

"It's all my fault. I am to blame."

"What do you mean by that?"

"I can't tell you now. The words won't come. As soon as I can, I'll tell you."

"You think I killed her in order to marry you," said Philip. "You mustn't think that, it isn't true. I did it because we were poisoning each other with hatred and she wouldn't let me go. Don't blame yourself. I was prepared to give you up—if only she'd let me go."

Mary told him that a man had come to her office and her lodgings, asking questions.

"I didn't tell him anything but I had an awful feeling that he knew everything. He was slow and quiet but he scared me. Oh, Philip—they won't—won't do anything to you, will they?"

"No," said Philip, "they won't do anything to me."

Under his breath he added: "I hope…"

On their way to the Underground, Philip had an idea that someone was following but he did not look round. He was past caring.

Chapter 12

In the middle of the following morning Philip looked up from his desk and saw someone standing at the office counter, eyeing him as placidly as a ruminative bovine. It was the heavy man in soiled raincoat and dusty hat who had spoken softly and long into the ear of the Coroner at the adjourned inquest. He was chewing gum with slow rhythmic movements of the jaw and looked as though he might have been standing there, just gazing at Philip, for hours. Philip rose and walked to the counter.

"Detective Sergeant Huxley of the Criminal Investigation Department," said the man, in the confidential whisper of a bookie's runner. He showed his warrant-card, cupped in a large hand so that no one but Philip caught so much as a glimpse of it.

"What can I do for you?" Philip spoke with a lightness he was far from feeling.

"My Inspector wants a word with you."

"I'll get my hat."

"Oh, not now. It'll keep. After work will do. My Inspector would like you to meet him at your house at eight this evening."

"At my house? I've moved, you know."

"Yes, we know." Sergeant Huxley's slow drawl suggested that he knew everything there was to know and was bored by it all. "But you haven't given up the tenancy."

"No, that's so. Very well, I'll be there at eight."

That evening, an hour before the time of the appointment, Philip let himself into the house in which he had lived for over twenty years. Already the hollowness, the chill, of empty houses had settled on it. His footsteps echoed as he walked from room to room. There was nothing he wanted here. Every piece of drab furniture was an enemy. Tomorrow, he thought, I'll call in a dealer and get rid of the lot. That is, he amended, if tomorrow I'm still at liberty...

The kitchen stank abominably. He opened a cupboard, took out some bearded scraps of food, and threw them in the dustbin. The atmosphere in Cora's room was worse. Odour of human hair, of heavily scented powder, of soiled clothing, of stale sweat. Unwashed stockings hanging on the bed rail. Corsets on the back of a chair. Undergarments in a heap in a corner. A hairnet on the mantelpiece. A brush matted with hairs on the dresser. He opened the wardrobe and looked wryly at the jumble of wearing apparel within. Tomorrow, he thought, I'll burn all this. For the present, he made a pile of Cora's possessions in the middle of the floor, emptying drawers on to it; snatching dresses from hangers to add to the pile.

In a musty corner he came upon a locked tin box. Placing it on the floor, he burst it open with his heel. There was nothing in it but a wad of letters and papers tied together with chocolate-box ribbon. He put them in his pocket for future reference. In his own room he found evidence that his belongings had been thoroughly searched and remembered that the spare key he lent to the Coroner's Officer had not been returned. Well, let them search, they could have found nothing that mattered. There was nothing for them to find.

The hour of eight sneaked up on him like a thug. A shrill ring that echoed through the house was his first warning that time had slipped away. Going down to answer the ring, he almost tripped on the broken step. Halting, he looked at it with an odd half-smile. Funny if he'd fallen and broken his neck. Rough justice, that would have been.

Unlike his subordinate, who was standing in shadows behind him, Inspector Haddow was lean and had eyes sharp as needles. Philip let the police officers into the living-room, apologizing for its untidiness and lack of comfort. The Inspector said that it was quite all right. He added that the purpose of his visit was to make routine inquiries into the death of Philip's wife.

"Routine inquiries, Inspector?" echoed Philip. "Surely not routine? I should have thought Scotland Yard much too busy to take so much trouble over an accidental death."

"Perhaps you're right," agreed Inspector Haddow, looking him in the eye. "Routine is hardly the word. As a matter of fact, we're here because the Coroner's Officer decided that the death was not quite what it seemed."

"What else could it be?"

"Well, for one thing, it could be murder."

"You're joking." Philip tried to sound as if he really thought so.

"Hardly."

"But my wife and I were alone in the house. That would mean I killed her."

"Yes, that's what it would mean."

"Well," said Philip lamely. "I didn't."

"I hope not," said Inspector Haddow heavily. "I hope not. There are some questions I wish to put to you. I must inform you that you're not compelled to answer them."

"Oh, I'll tell you anything I can. I've nothing to hide."

"Good. We'll start at the beginning."

They did. To be precise, they started at the beginning no less than five times. Philip told his story and retold it until he was heartily sick of it. In the background, Sergeant Huxley sat stolidly and wrote down every word that was uttered.

"You say you were reading in your bedroom when you heard the fall?"

"I've said so half a dozen times. That, at least, should be clear enough."

"Quite. Now, to return to a point we discussed earlier—"

Over and over again, each point was covered until Philip's story, slight to begin with, was positively threadbare. At last, the Inspector rose. But this was not the end, only a fresh beginning.

"Now, about the stair carpet," he said. "You say you spilt ink on it and it was taken up to be sent to the cleaners? You don't mind if I have a look at it?"

"Not in the least."

Philip took them to the kitchen. They unrolled the carpet and spread it on the floor. For a while they all looked at it in silence. So worn that, in places, the linoleum could be seen through it. So stained that the original colour and design were not apparent. In comparison with other marks, the ink-stain was an embellishment rather than a blemish.

"This," said Inspector Haddow, as though there must be a mistake, "this is the carpet you were sending to be cleaned?"

"It is," said Philip stoutly. Looking at the carpet, he realized how preposterous that part of his story was, but he must stick to it—or confess the truth.

"From what you've told me I should not have thought your wife an extravagant woman."

"She wasn't."

"And yet, she was going to spend money on *this*"—he spurned the carpet with a toe. "Come now, Mr. Marshall, that isn't a likely tale. Look at it. The thing's worn out. It's threadbare. It's fit for nothing but the dustbin."

"I agree," said Philip, "but I'm looking at it now with your eyes. To my wife and me this was a familiar possession for twenty years. We'd be the last to see how far-gone it is."

"I'll warrant it wasn't cleaned in all those twenty years."

"Probably not."

"You waited, in fact, until there was no point in cleaning it before you decided to have it cleaned. Pity you did. If it hadn't been taken up, your wife wouldn't have fallen."

"That is by no means certain. Even when the carpet was down the broken step was treacherous."

"I suppose the step had been broken for a long time?"

"Yes, quite a long time."

"But your wife had not fallen before."

"She had tripped on it on previous occasions. We both had. She hadn't broken her neck, if that's what you mean."

They returned to the living-room. There was an air of permanence about this inquisition, as if it had just got into its stride and would go on for ever.

"A convenient accident for you, wasn't it?" said Inspector Haddow.

"What do you mean?"

"Well, for one thing, your employer tells us he offered you a partnership if you could raise a thousand pounds. Your wife's money will come in handy for that, won't it?"

"My wife's money? What money? What are you talking about?" Philip was utterly dumbfounded.

"Come, Mr. Marshall, you don't ask me to believe—"

"I don't ask you to believe anything. You can believe what you like—but my wife hadn't any money. What makes you think she had?"

"I'm told that in investments and savings she had over twelve hundred pounds. A tidy sum. Sufficient to pay death duties and secure that partnership."

Had he been turned inside out; Philip could not have been more at a loss. There wasn't anything to say, or anything to think, or any way to grasp it. It was like being an earth-dweller for half a life and suddenly finding yourself floating down a canal on Mars and discovering you had lived there always. Wonderingly, as though it might be a figment of his imagination instead of a reality he had lived through, he recalled the stifling parsimony of his wife. Investments? Savings? Twelve hundred pounds? No, no! His mind boggled at it. It simply did not fit, could not be. He shook his head like a swimmer coming up after a plunge.

"This is absurd. It can't be true."

"You didn't know it?"

"I hadn't the slightest idea she'd saved a penny. I still can't accept it. The idea's too fantastic. In any case, if she had any money, she certainly wouldn't leave it to me."

"And yet, I have definite information that her will is in your favour."

"I don't believe it."

After all, there are limits to human credulity. Cora leave him money? Not a penny if she could help it. Rather than let it fall into his hands she'd have lit a fire with it.

"How long ago is this will supposed to have been made?"

"More than twenty years, I'm told."

"That's funny," said Philip.

Now he remembered. On their honeymoon (had they really gone on a honeymoon? —that, too, seemed unreal) they had made joint wills in favour of each other. A mere gesture, for at the time neither of them had anything to leave. That must be the will to which the Inspector referred. It was a good joke on Cora, for there was no doubt—not one doubt in the world—that she had meant to destroy it and make another long ago. Typical of her to put off and put off until at last it was too late. Yes, the joke was on Cora. There could be no revision of wills where she had gone. At this moment her wraith must be wrung with the fury of frustration. And yet, when you came to think of it, the funniest thing of all was the fact that leaving Philip her money was probably the worst trick she could have played him. Philip did not need the Inspector's accusing eyes to tell him that it made the case against him black indeed.

"It's the first I've heard of all this. You won't believe that, but it's true. She was always grumbling about lack of money. The things we couldn't afford. Sufficient hot water...decent food..."

The Inspector did not tell Philip he was a liar. But his eyes did.

"Leaving aside, for the moment, the question of the money, let's come to the divorce you wanted and to which she refused to agree."

"Oh," said Philip dully, "so you know about that."

"We know a great deal more than you think. I advise you to be frank."

"But how *can* you know?"

"We won't go into that. But we do know. The night before your wife...died, she flatly refused to divorce you. There was a violent quarrel. Next day she fell downstairs and was killed. I may have a suspicious mind, Mr. Marshall"—the Inspector's voice was knife-edged with irony— "but the facts look significant to me. They'd look significant to a jury."

He said it menacingly, in the hope of startling Philip into unguarded speech but Philip was not even listening. Philip was wondering who could have told about his fruitless request for a divorce. And, quite suddenly, he knew. It was simple, when he remembered how slight was Cora's self-respect. Cora had been in the habit of pouring the intimate details of her private life into the willing ear of her charwoman. On the morning after the argument, she must have told Mrs. Meggs about it. After the murder, Mrs. Meggs must have told the police. It added up; but you had to do your reckoning with the mind of a Cora. It was disconcerting and in a sense amusing to reflect that Mrs. Meggs must know as much about him as though she had been his wife. His habits. His weaknesses. His deficiencies as a lover.

His failure as a money-maker. All the destroying frailties a man strives to hide from the world outside his home. Yes, Mrs. Meggs had come as close to his skin as a bedbug.

"That divorce was vital to you, wasn't it?" The Inspector continued mercilessly. "You must have been desperate when she refused it. Somehow, you had to get rid of your wife so that you could marry the other woman and give your child a name."

"The other woman?" Philip gaped. "My child? Good God, man, what are you saying?"

"I should be a poor investigator if I hadn't found out about your friendship with Miss Grey—and that your friend Miss Grey is pregnant."

The world was empty of all that mattered. Empty and filled with bitterness. There was nothing to which Philip could cling, in which he could trust and believe. Without question, he accepted what the Inspector had said. Now that he thought about it, the proof was so obvious it was incredible he had not known it before. Voices in his ear: *"So you're the man. Married, too, by the look of you"*...*"It's none of my business—but you'll do right by that girl, won't you?"*...*"There's something I must tell you. It may make you hate me."* A woman crying on a bench in an empty square. She said she was crying because she was lonely. What else could she say? You don't tell a stranger the truth, if the truth is a fatherless child. But Philip had not been a stranger, not for longer than the first half-hour of their acquaintance. She could have told him. Oh, yes, she had tried—he'd grant her that—but why hadn't she persisted, forced him to listen? Lonely, was she? No bloody wonder.

Philip could have told the police officers that Mary's child would not be his; that until that moment he had known nothing about it. But he did not tell them. For some mist-shrouded reason he preferred to be considered a murderer rather than a blind fool duped by a girl.

There was a drumming in his ears; the overture to disaster. Now stretched before him the dragging weeks of a trial that could have but one conclusion. A long-drawn-out judicial orgy with a dangling rope at the end of it. "And may the Lord have mercy on your soul . . ." And then, Philip remembered something and it gave him hope. These policemen had not cautioned him. In accordance with regulations, they must do that as soon as they made up their minds to arrest. There could be but two reasons for the omission; either they were ignoring the rules in order to trap him; or, in spite of all the evidence, they were still not quite sure.

"You don't seem to have much to say," remarked Inspector Haddow dryly.

Philip corseted his wobbling mind. "What is there to say? You think I killed my wife. Well, I didn't. I admit I was unhappy with her. Perhaps I even wished her dead. But her death was accidental. I had nothing whatever to do with it."

He waited for the formal caution, but it did not come. Inspector Haddow rose. In the background Sergeant Huxley moved to the door.

"Well," said the Inspector, "that's about all for the present."

He turned to his subordinate and a significant glance passed between them. Sergeant Huxley went down the passage, opened the front door, walked out to the garden. Philip made a move to follow but Inspector Haddow blocked the way. In an easy, conversational tone, he said:

"You haven't a hope of getting away with this, you know."

"You're bluffing, Inspector," said Philip calmly. "Bluffing and you know it. That's why you got rid of your assistant. It's against regulations to play tricks like this on a suspect, isn't it? You wouldn't want a witness present."

"You killed her, all right," said Haddow, watching Philip closely. "I haven't a doubt of it."

"Then why don't you arrest me?"

"In a murder case we look for a motive. Sometimes it's money, sometimes a woman. You have two beauties. The money you needed for the partnership and the woman you had to marry. Those two things alone would condemn you in the eyes of a jury."

"Then why don't you arrest me?"

"The spot of candle-grease on the broken step; wouldn't she have stooped to examine it before tripping over it, you know. And your story about taking up the carpet to send it to the cleaner—that's thin, pitifully thin."

"Then why don't you arrest me? Shall I tell you? Because you know you couldn't get a conviction, that's why. No matter how convenient my wife's death was for me, it could still be an accident and no jury could condemn me in the face of that possibility."

"I'll grant you've been clever. If you'd done it any other way, you'd be in jail now. But people do fall downstairs—and it's hard to prove she was helped by a push. If you'd tried to pretend you weren't home at the time—if you'd done a single damned thing but exactly what you did, we'd have you. Oh, you're smart lad, all right—but even the smartest slip up in the end. Don't kid yourself that you'll be the exception, I have almost enough on you now to convince a jury. A little more, a very little more, is all I need. And I'll get it. Make no mistake about that. I'll get it."

"And now," said Philip pleasantly, "I suggest you join your assistant and tell him your bluff fell flat. In a bout with the law, Inspector, there is no better armour than knowledge of one's innocence."

"Innocence!" snorted Inspector Haddow. "Don't make me laugh."

But he went.

Chapter 13

You could have told me, he said, lying in the dark alone. For the hundredth time he said it, and there was pain in his heart. You could have told me. She did not answer, for she was not there. He was alone in a house full of people whom he did not know. A house full of lodgers, one to every silent room in the place, and there is no way to be more alone than that. You could have told me, he said, and tried to answer for her but could not, his pain being too great. The clock said three. An hour later he glanced at it and it said a minute after three. He picked it up and put it to his ear. Yes, it was ticking. No, the hands had not stuck. You could have told me, he said, continuing the one-sided argument.

Another slug-slow, sick-drear hour dragged past and it was two minutes after three and he got up and put on his dressing-gown.

There must be things to do to keep his mind from running frantically in circles, as in a maze. Things to think about, apart from the one thing that was all he could realize. Lighting a cigarette was a beginning, a matter-of-fact, everyday thing to do. Watching the red-glowing tip one could be hypnotized into a state of nothingness, of not-being, of suspended existence. But as he flipped the match out of the open window, to be extinguished in the still, deep pool of night, he said, reproachfully and not aloud: You could have told me.

Did you think I should be scornful? Of what? Of your child? How can one scorn a baby? The very idea is absurd. Did you think I should despise you? If one believes in God—or in man—it is impossible to despise a woman for the swelling of life within her. That is God. That is man. Did you think I would stiffen my face because your child has no father? But he has. I am his father. My son is his father. The whole world is his father. His ancestors lie in every cemetery. His roots are in life, in death, in the ages, and they reach into the future. Realizing that, how little matters the brief existing planter of the seed.

You could have told me. I should have understood. You made a fool of me. That is what I cannot forgive. For that, I hate you. That is small of me, but then, I am small. I am a man. A man—so small a thing as man—must not lose face. He can accept humiliations, disasters, and absorb injuries, but he must not lose face. That is what you have done to me. You have made me lose face. How can I forgive?

There must be things to do to keep his mind from going cold with bitterness. Another cigarette was a thing of small moment but lighting it helped. Smoke curled round his head, blew away from him. In the splash of light from the match he noticed a bulge in the breast of his coat which clothed the back of a chair. There was a packet of papers in the pocket. Letters and papers tied together with chocolate-box ribbon.

He turned on the light, blinking as it burst over him. A small, perplexed man with a bald spot, blinking in the light, clad in faded pyjamas that had shrunk in the wash. He took out the packet of papers and sat on the bed to examine them.

The mortal remains of Cora Marshall, if one excepted the flesh and bone that lay, waiting for disintegration, in the cemetery. The joint will, yellowing with age, which they had made twenty-odd years before, and which now made him her heir. A little bundle of share certificates. A savings-account book, filled with revealing entries (there was no entry, 'the blood and soul of Philip Marshall,' but there might well have been). A few letters which he recognized with growing disbelief; letters he had written her long, long ago, when they were first engaged.

He had tried then, how desperately he had tried to invest Cora with glamour and loveliness, for he had needed these things in his life. He had written out his heart to her with the unencouraged hope that if he called her kind, she would be kind, and if he dubbed her beautiful, beauty would garb her like a cloak.

The letters were poetry, inarticulate and groping. Apart from their son, they were the one beautiful thing that had grown out of them. And Cora had kept them. Philip wondered why. He could never truly have known his wife, for the Cora who preserved his youthful outpourings was not the Cora who had shared his bed and board. He began to wonder if the fault had been his, if some well of goodness in Cora had dried in the sands of his post-marital disillusionment. Had he, like Frankenstein, himself created the monster that destroyed him? Had another Cora been imprisoned alive in the monster? If he had struggled and persevered, could he have freed some inner being fine and good? Woman, thy name is Mystery. Cora, fat, nagging, mean, suspicious, stupid… Cora, preserving his love-letters when their love was at an end, if something can end that never truly had beginning.

One by one, he put matches to the letters, watching them burn, and sent the ashes floating out into the night.

Turning out the light, he stretched himself on the bed. And now, the image of Mary was blurred by that of Cora. You could have told me. Told me about your baby; told me of the beauty imprisoned in you. If I had seen that inner you, the one that kept my letters, struggling for freedom from the monster... If I had known the truth (if this is truth, if what I took for truth was falsehood) …

Cora. Mary.

Mary. Cora.

Struggling to disentangle them, struggling to force back the head of truth and look into her face. Weary of the struggle, tired so tired...confused, so terribly confused...surrendering at last to the blessed oblivion of sleep.

*

They met the next day, Philip and Mary, in a corner of a restaurant crowded with city workers, to whom time was a menace and a threat, for whom the hands of the clock were exclamation marks. Typists. Clerks. Office-boys. The hungry haste of a farmyard at feeding time. There was no need for Philip to say anything, a glance at his face told Mary that he knew.

"They've told you. What must you think of me?"

"I thought of you all night. In the night, I used up all my words. There isn't anything to say."

"I tried to tell you."

"I know that now."

"I could have forced you to listen but...I was afraid."

"You tried, hard enough. Don't think I'm blind to that. I made it impossible for you to tell me. That isn't your fault."

"I want you to know how it happened. I want to tell you."

"Oh, that. That isn't important. What does it matter how it happened? You needn't tell me."

"I want to tell you. You must know how it was."

A waitress paused, as if in flight, beside them. Order-pad in hand, pencil poised. Her eyebrows asked a question, made a time limit for answering. They ordered food they knew they would not eat. The waitress went on like a bird that no sooner alights on a twig than it is away again.

"It was in the second period of my life in London. All I told you that night was true. Not the whole truth, but all true.

First, I was dying with loneliness, and then I got to know these people. The people to whom life was a gossip column. It was fun, in a lot of ways. Not the sort of fun we've known, but fun. Boys and girls, my own age who laughed at the serious things of life in a way that made you join in. This boy…I was crazy about him…he was good-looking, clever, not the sort I'd ever dared hope would take to a plain girl like me. Even a plain girl has her dreams, you know. Oh, he shocked me, right down to the roots…but to be a prude was to lose him and I couldn't let that happen. To me he was marvellous. I'd have given my eyes to hold on to him. I didn't see that in the end I was bound to lose him, no matter what I did. He said no one was a prude anymore; life didn't give you time. I don't think he tricked me, that wasn't how it was. I tricked myself. The first time I met you…that night...I had telephoned him. I won't tell you what he said, what he suggested, when I told him about—about—"

"Look," said Philip earnestly, taking her hand in his. "Forget about him. He doesn't matter. He never did. The fact that he was unworthy of your love and trust doesn't make either of them less beautiful."

The waitress thrust some dishes between them and distributed cutlery with brisk efficiency. Over the unwanted food, they looked at each other miserably.

"We've made a nice mess of things, haven't we?" asked Philip.

"A little while ago I wanted to kill myself," said Mary huskily, "and you prevented me. Philip, that may be the answer for us now. I wouldn't be afraid to die with you."

"It may be the answer for me, my dear. Never for you. What affinity with death can you have, with life stirring within you? Are you afraid of this child?"

"I'm afraid for its future. That's why I didn't trust you—at first. I thought—it was rotten of me, but it was for my child, not for myself—I thought, here is a man no longer young, unmarried, and who probably will never marry. What harm can it do, I thought, if I get him to marry me and give my child a name. That was all I wanted, Philip. You could have kicked me out ten minutes after. Married, I could have gone back to my aunt, a deserted wife with a child on the way. She'd have understood and forgiven that. She never could understand or forgive the other. But when I knew you better, I found I couldn't do it to you. That was when I thought of death."

"You're going to live, Mary. Through you, perhaps I'll earn the right to life. Out of all this, some good must come. We'll give your child a name, a home, a chance in the world. That's our reason for being; our sole salvation; our only small excuse for all we are."

"You can't marry me, Philip. The police already suspect you. If you marry me, they'll know."

"They know now."

Mary shuddered. "I'll go to them and tell them it isn't so; that you are not the father."

"Humiliate yourself for me? I shan't let you. Besides, what good would it do? They'd believe what they want to believe, not what you told them. Even if they did believe you, they have plenty of other reasons for suspecting me. I'm offering you a poor thing, Mary, when I offer you myself. Will you take me?"

"I love you, Philip," was her answer.

Chapter 14

In the back garden a smouldering fire consumed the mountain of rubbish that had piled up on two people in the course of twenty-odd years. At the front an old woman and a young girl moved slowly off, pushing a handcart piled high with Cora's garments. At the kerb stood a furtive van and, like the alternating figures of a husband-and-wife weather-gauge, the dealer's men popped out of the van, into the house, out of the house into the van, stripping the place of furniture, more as a favour to Philip (the dealer said), than anything. One of the men was stringy, with a cast in his eye and a drip at the end of his nose. The other was podgy, with eyes that lovingly envisioned beer and a mouth drooling at the thought.

In an upper room, Philip packed in a case half-filled with straw, the cups John had won for running, rowing, and swimming. He wrapped each cup in tissue paper, and bedded it down with care. This was a task he would trust to no one else. The things of value that were John's, Philip was sending to his son. Some of the rest—old exercise books, forgotten toys—he was keeping for himself. He stood for a while holding a frame of butterflies and wondering into which category it belonged. In the end he added it to the trophies in the packing-case. Let John decide for himself whether it was worth keeping. In a clutter of small articles at the bottom of a cupboard, he found a little bottle of cyanide of potassium crystals. A pinch of the stuff would kill a man but John had used it for killing butterflies. Philip laid the bottle with a heap of refuse earmarked for burning; but, before he fed the fire again, he rescued it—he didn't know why—and put it in his pocket.

While he worked, he wondered how to tell John about his

forthcoming marriage. At last, there was no more to do but lock the house and take the keys to the agent; and he had not yet made up his mind about how to tell John. Walking away from the house, gladly, without once looking back, Philip thought: What am I to say to him? How is he to understand so sudden a re-marriage to a girl less than half my age? With his trite mind and orthodox views John was bound to consider such haste indecent. The adjourned inquest had shaken him. In spite of his innocence, he was sure to put two and two together and arrive at a sinister total. Philip decided not to tell him; not yet. He knew this decision meant only a postponement, at best, of a reckoning with John, but he felt that a postponement, however brief, was to be desired.

Two weeks later, Philip obtained a day's leave-of-absence from the office on the pretext that he was feeling unwell—his employer was another from whom the marriage had best be kept secret—and Mary and he were joined in matrimony by a registrar. Mary's landlady, more grotesquely ugly than ever in pink frills, insisted on being present. At the last moment, the registrar's clerk went out to the street to find another witness and brought back a familiar stout figure in a raincoat and bowler hat. After the brief ceremony, Sergeant Huxley of the Criminal Investigation Department told bride and bridegroom he hoped they would be very, very happy. There was an inscrutable expression on his sleepy face as he said it.

"Of course, they'll be happy," said Mary's landlady heartily. "Weren't they made for each other? Anyone with half an eye can see that, I should hope. Come on, dears," she added. "I've ordered the wedding breakfast at 'The Star and Garter'. Champagne and oysters and roast duck and strawberries—and it's my treat. No, you mustn't thank me. It's a pleasure, I'm sure.

"Well," she said, half an hour later—the three of them were

seated at a table with an immense floral decoration also of her choosing, in the shape of two hearts pierced by an arrow— "This ain't my idea of a wedding. You sit there as though you'd been married ten years instead of an hour. Here, you"—this to the waiter— "let's have another bottle of champagne. And let's have it in bigger glasses, this time."

To please her, Philip and Mary tried to be bright. But when the meal at last came to an end they were both relieved. Pretending that this was a normal wedding was a strain too great to be sustained.

"Philip," said Mary, when they were alone, "you're not sorry?"

"No, my dear, I'm not sorry. I only feel that all this is, in some way, an anti-climax. There has been so much between us from the first that didn't rely on a licence or on some words mumbled by a registrar."

"I know. There was something unreal about the wedding ceremony, as though it had nothing whatever to do with us. Philip, you won't be cross if I admit to you that I've never truly conceived us in the role of husband and wife. I can't now. We were such tremendous friends, there didn't seem room for anything else in our relationship."

"Nothing is changed, Mary. We'll still be the same to each other. Marrying was just something we had to do."

"Yes, it was something we had to do."

"We'll take time to adjust ourselves. In a way, you are to me more a much-loved daughter than a wife. Let's keep it like that for the present. Until the child is born, at least. Then we can take stock of our lives and decide what we want to do with them."

"I'm not—not trying to hedge, Philip," said Mary uncertainly.

"I know you're not. And neither am I. But we know what we have now and we don't know for what we might exchange it. Time will tell us what we are meant to be to each other."

Philip tried not to think of the most important reason for his reluctance to live with Mary as husband and wife. In some strange way he felt himself not truly alive but only existing, as it were, on ticket of leave. So much hung over his head, so much uncertainty, so little hope for peace. In all the circumstances, he considered he had no right to broaden the relationship between himself and Mary. If Nemesis overtook him—and in every nerve and fibre he knew it would—he wanted her to have as few adjustments to make as possible.

There was no honeymoon. They went straight to the flat they had taken and furnished simply a few days before. It was small; two bedrooms, a living-room, a kitchen, a bathroom, a tiny hall; but within its four walls Philip was to spend the happiest months of his life. They were not by any means carefree months; his sleep at night was troubled and broken, and over him at all times hung the threat of arrest; but there were precious minutes and hours and days that made up to him for the drab bleakness of the life which hitherto he had led.

His fears were partly relieved by the reopening of the inquest on Cora which fizzled out, like a damp fire cracker lit with great ceremony, in a verdict of accidental death. That did not mean, he knew, that he was now free from danger. It only meant that no further evidence against him had been forthcoming and what evidence existed was not enough. The case still lived in the files of New Scotland Yard, waiting for a little more (so very little) to give it strength and body.

Philip's employer had said no more about the partnership he had offered and Philip did not bring up the subject. Philip had taken Cora's will to a lawyer, who offered it for probate, and the money would soon be available; but Philip had no intention of using it for his own advancement. The thought of benefiting financially by Cora's death was repellent. He did not know what he was going to do with the money. That was one more question he was leaving in the capable hands of Time.

Mary was a good cook, an excellent housekeeper. She kept the flat bright and cheerful. Homecoming was a nightly pleasure to which to look forward through the working day. Evenings were a joy. They spent them walking in the parks or by the river or at their own hearth, with a book. Sometimes they talked a lot, sometimes they were silent; it didn't matter which. Their companionship was like an old coat that has fitted itself snugly to the contours of the wearer. When they were apart life was suspended for both of them; when they came together again they were one harmonious whole.

One evening, when they were washing up after supper (a task Philip enjoyed and insisted on sharing), Mary said:

"While I was shopping today, I met a girl I used to know. One of my father's pupils. You remember, I told you about the parties Dad and I gave—lemonade and cake and games and songs pounded out on the piano. She came to most of them. She was great fun. She's married now and living in Edgware."

"Did you arrange to meet her again? You need fun in your life, my dear."

"That's something I want to talk to you about. She noticed at once—that I'm going to have a baby. I told her I'd been married for ages. She wanted, there and then, to fix a date for us to go over to dinner with her and her husband."

Over the rim of the large plate he was drying, Philip smiled at Mary. "And so?"

"Well, I didn't know whether you'd want to go."

"Why not, if they're nice people?"

"Well, Violet hasn't altered much since the age of fifteen. Oh, she's a nice kid, but—well, not very brainy. From what she said, I don't think her husband is, either. You might be bored."

"I'm not exactly the intellectual type either, my dear. The point is whether you'd care to go."

"I would, rather," said Mary, wrinkling her brow. "For one thing, Violet will be writing home and telling everyone I'm married and going to have a baby. If she's seen you—I mean, well, the more she has to write about the more normal and straightforward everything will seem."

"Then let's go one evening soon."

"You're sure you won't be bored?"

"If I am, so much the better," laughed Philip. "A bored husband—what could be more normal than that?"

But when the appointed evening came, Philip was not bored. Mary's friends, the Ramsdens, were very young; very much in love; very proud of their new little house and their new little car. They were silly, in a way, but it was in an appealing way; the silliness of puppies at play. They liked Philip and wanted him to like them and they went through their tricks to amuse him. At first, Mary kept glancing anxiously at Philip, but when she saw how wholeheartedly he was enjoying himself she relaxed and let the party spirit take hold of her as well.

For the first time since a certain fateful Saturday afternoon, Philip spent an entire evening without once thinking of Cora or of hanging by the neck until he was dead.

More intellectual company could not have done that for him.

Chapter 15

"For you, Mr. Marshall," said the office-boy, turning from the telephone. It was a morning about two months after the wedding. Philip crossed the room and took the receiver from the boy. "Marshall speaking," he said.

"Hello, Dad. It's me—John."

Hearing his son's voice was such a surprise that for a few moments Philip was at a loss what to say. In silence he stood gripping the receiver, groping for words in an empty mind. At the other end of the wire, John said impatiently:

"Hello. Hello. Are you there?"

"Hello, John. Sorry. I was thinking."

"I rang up your lodgings last night. They said you'd left."

"Yes. I moved some time ago."

"You might have let me know."

"I didn't think you'd be interested."

Another lengthy silence and then John said, humbly:

"I suppose I deserve that."

"I didn't mean to snub you. Nice of you to give me a ring."

"I want to see you, Dad. There's a lot on my mind. When can we have a talk? This evening?"

"This evening? You're in a hurry all of a sudden."

For the life of him, Philip could not hold back the reproach, nor keep the hurt bitterness out of his voice.

"I know. I've left you alone until it suits me to do otherwise, that's what you're thinking, isn't it? Maybe you don't want anything to do with me. I can't blame you if that's the way you feel."

"Don't be a fool, John," retorted Philip sharply. He wanted to say a lot more than that—*I'm your father, boy. Get it through your thick skull that I love you. Nothing you could do would alter that. I'm aching to see you; have been for weeks*—but the office was full of ears. "I'll meet you this evening. It had better be about eight, for I must go home first. Where shall it be?"

"In the lounge of the Osterley Hotel, Dad, if that is convenient for you. It's near my digs."

"Right. The Osterley at eight."

"Goodbye till then, Dad."

"Goodbye."

Over the evening meal, Philip told Mary about the appointment. Her eyes lit up. No need to tell him she was glad; it was written all over her.

"I'll have to tell him we're married." Philip was worried about that. "It won't be easy. How is he to understand why I didn't tell him before?"

"Be patient with him. You're excited, aren't you? Tickled to death about seeing him again?"

Philip took one of her hands in both of his.

"Mary I'm so excited I could burst. If only you and he can be friends—what fun we could have together, the three of us."

"Don't count on that, Philip."

She looked at him very earnestly. There was a wealth of love in her gaze and something more; something that made him, unaccountably, close to tears.

"If this means that he wants you again on the old footing, you mustn't let me stand in the way. Please, Philip, dear, you've got to understand that. If he holds out his hand to you, take it. You've been good to me—so very good—but don't spoil things for yourself by insisting that he accept me. There's my aunt in Lytham. I can go to her...now."

"Try to leave me," said Philip gruffly, "and I'll drag you back by the hair. I need you. Nothing can change that."

That evening, watching his son come across the lounge to

him, Philip felt the old thrill of pride and pleasure. The boy was beautiful. There was no other word for it. Tall. Broad. Straight. Clean-limbed as an athlete. Graceful as a dancer. Clear-skinned as a child. For the thousandth time he marvelled that from his loins, from Cora's womb, this being had sprung. There was only one fault to be found with him, his soft, full-lipped mouth betrayed weakness, lack of decision.

As a small boy, John had always smiled readily, his face shining with happiness, at sight of his father. That ready smile bloomed again as he neared Philip.

"Dad," he said, "this is great."

"I'm glad to see you, boy. You're thinner. What have you been doing to yourself?"

John took a deep breath and it seemed that words were going to pour out of him in a torrent but a cloud passed over his eyes. He hesitated, his tongue came out and moistened his lips. Playing for time, he said: "You're not precisely fat yourself. You look harder, though—tougher. Don't tell me you've taken up golf."

"No." Philip smiled. "No, I haven't taken up golf. It must be something else. I'd better give you my new address. It's in Bedford Park."

An odd expression came over John's face. "I—I heard you were living in that neighbourhood. A friend of mine said—said he'd seen you."

"Oh?" Philip was wary. There was something the wind. "What else did he say?"

"Oh, he talked a lot of rot. I ticked him off for it."

"What sort of rot?"

John blushed. He squirmed. "The damned fool said you were living with a woman," he blurted out.

"That's perfectly true. I *am* living with a woman—only I happen to be married to her."

"God Almighty," said John, staring. After a pause he added: "You might have told me."

"Yes, I should have told you. Only, well, we've been almost strangers for quite a time. I didn't know how go about it."

"I told this ass he was crazy," said John, as though he still didn't believe what his father had said. As though in some way his disbelief could annul Philip's marriage.

"You, living with a woman. That was a likely tale. How was I to know? I suppose you're not joking?"

"No, it isn't a joke."

"A bit—a bit sudden, wasn't it?"

"Perhaps I ought to have bowed to convention," said Philip irritably, "and been a respectable and lonely widower for a year. But I'm afraid I didn't see the point."

"No. No. You'd a right to suit yourself. After all you weren't too—too happy with Mother."

"No, I wasn't too happy with your mother."

A masterpiece of understatement, that.

"I—It's none of my business but—I suppose you knew her before...before—"

"Yes, I knew her before."

"You'll think me stupid but I still can't grasp it. Not knowing anything about her makes it all a little unreal. I don't know what to say."

"You're struggling with the picture of your dry-as-dust little father in a romantic role? Forget it. My wife is young. As young as you are. But when she married me, she wasn't looking for the Great Lover type. We began as good friends—the sort of friends you and I were once— and that's how we've got on."

"You're happy?"

"I never knew before what happiness is."

"Then that's all right." John took a deep breath. "Gosh,

though, you've taken the wind out of my sails. I'm afraid my news is going to fall a little flat. You see, I'm going to be married, too."

"That's splendid," said Philip, trying to sound as though he really meant it. "Who is the girl?" He was afraid he already knew.

As though he'd rather not have told, John answered reluctantly: "It's Gladys Lemon. You know, the daughter of the people I live with."

"I see." That utterance was neither inspiring nor helpful but it was the best Philip could manage. "What are your plans? I suppose you'll wait a bit? You're rather young, you know."

John looked unhappy. "We thought we'd marry in about a month's time. Gladys's mother doesn't believe in long engagements."

"I thought you'd want to make something of yourself before thinking of marriage? You've always dreaded being chained to a desk for life."

"I'll get over that. I'd probably never amount to anything, anyway. Oh, what's the good of chewing the fat about it? It's all settled."

"Like that, is it?" Philip watched his son narrowly.

John looked the other way.

"This is going to mean more awkward explanations. Aren't you supposed to be an orphan? It isn't going to be easy, bringing me in at this late date. Or am I to be left out?"

"That's why I rang you this morning. I've told Gladys about you. I want you to meet her. She's coming here presently."

"That wouldn't be Gladys over there, by the door, would it?" Philip nodded toward a hard-looking young woman, with hair of counterfeit gold, who had just come in.

"Where?" John craned his neck. He rose. "Yes, that's Gladys. I'll bring her over."

He threaded his way between tables to the other side of the

lounge. The quick glance he darted at Philip before he went told its own story. A youngster proud of the girl of his choice would not have been quite so anxious, quite so doubtful, about his father's first impression. Watching the girl greeting his son, Philip's heart sank. They came toward him and, just looking at her, Philip knew all about her as intimately as though he had seen her grow from childhood. The way she walked, with a see-what-I've-got swing of the hips; her little dark eyes, on guard, furtive, speculating; her brazen make-up, devoid of taste and artistry, designed to be provocative and succeeding only in being vulgar: all these things and many more gave her away. When she spoke, her voice went through Philip like a sword.

This was another Cora. With the added danger, to the man who married her, of a nature in which sex predominated and an attitude toward it that was frankly animal. Good God, how could the boy be such a fool? He had only to look at her.

"I'm ever so pleased to meet you, Mr. Marshall." Her carmine lips smiled but her eyes weighed him up. "When John told me, you could have knocked me down with a feather. Ain't he the sly one, keeping you dark so long? I'll have to watch him, after we're married." She put emphasis on the last word, intending Philip to get it straight from the start. "What Ma will say I reely don't know."

"You haven't told her yet?"

"Oh, no. John thought we'd better wait a bit before telling her about you."

She was lying. Philip was quite sure of that.

He invited her to have a drink. At first, she was coy, pretending to be shocked at the very idea. Then she said, "Well, just a small port." She tried to sip it as though this were her first but it was not a skilful pretence. There are people who don't need to acquire a taste for alcohol, who have it in their blood, who would take to it as babies if it were offered in a feeding bottle. This was one of them.

For the first time in his life, Philip consciously played the hypocrite. He laid himself out to charm the girl—and succeeded.

"Your father's a duck," Gladys told John, who writhed. Confident she had won Philip—she told herself complacently that she knew how to handle men—she let herself be persuaded to have another port. And another. While John grew hot under the collar, she talked a lot in a shrill voice. She talked too much. A great deal too much. Every word laid bare her soul, as small and shrivelled as a dried pea.

Long before she was ready to go, John took her home. He said he would be back. Philip ordered a large brandy and waited. When John returned, he looked anxiously at his father.

"She's not like that really. The port must have gone to her head. She isn't used to it."

Philip said nothing. John tied his fingers in knots.

"You'd have to see her home to understand her. She hasn't had—much of a chance."

"Do you love her?" Asked Philip.

John grew red. "I've asked her to marry me, haven't I?"

"That doesn't answer my question."

"Of course, I love her. Certainly, I love her. What makes you think I don't?"

"I know you don't. If you did, I shouldn't ask the question. I'd see the answer in your face. John, what's behind all this? The girl isn't in any trouble?"

"Good God, no!" John looked open-mouthed at his father.

"Then why are you marrying her? Tell me the truth."

"I don't know what you're getting at. Any one would think there was something wrong with her, the way you talk. Oh, maybe I'm not so terribly in love with her, but how many men are, when they marry? There are other reasons for marriage than just being in love."

"I didn't think you knew that. Perhaps you can tell me some of them?"

"Well, a man needs a home. An interest in life."

"You're rather young to be smitten with an urgent desire for home-making. And if you need an interest in life, isn't ambition big enough?"

"It's no use talking, Father. We're engaged and I'm going to marry her. It's my affair."

"I can't deny that. I'm only trying to find out the whole of it."

"Well, for one thing, she loves me. That's something to start with, isn't it?"

"It is, if it's true. What makes you think so?"

"I know so. Why, even her mother noticed it—and you wouldn't call her particularly observant."

"Oh. What did her mother say?"

"Only that Gladys is crazy about me."

"When did she say this?"

"Dad, I'm not a kid any longer. Must I submit to a cross-examination?"

"You needn't, I suppose. It's only that I know you're making a terrible mistake and want to save you from it if I can."

"You're wrong, Dad. Maybe you can't understand what I'm doing but—well, I do. That's the important thing. There are some things that matter to a chap—his honour, for instance."

"What's your honour got to do with this?"

"It isn't what you think. I haven't—haven't—touched her, if you must know. It's only—only— well, a chap can't let a girl down. It's my fault she's in love with me. Her mother pointed that out. I was lonely. I took her out a good deal. There's nothing much in that, I suppose, but Gladys took it seriously."

"Or so her mother told you."

"Well, yes. She said the poor kid couldn't eat or sleep for thinking of me. I was the whole world to her. Her mother was scared what Gladys might do if she learned that I was only—amusing myself."

"You took her to the pictures, I suppose. Bought her chocolates. Probably you held her hand. There's nothing in that to give her a lien on you."

"Well, but don't you see, Gladys took it seriously? Her mother and I had a long talk. She pointed out that I might be ruining a girl's life. Put like that, what could I do?"

"You could have told the woman not to be so damned silly—or so blatantly scheming. You could have changed your lodgings."

John looked shocked. "That wouldn't have been the honourable thing to do."

"Honourable fiddlesticks. It would have been the sensible thing. Couldn't you see the trap you were being coaxed into?"

"It wasn't a trap. And, if it was, what can I do?" He was like a bewildered small boy. "I've worried myself sick at night. I know it's a serious step. But I've promised to marry her. I can't back out."

"Don't be a fool. This involves your whole life. You can't afford heroic poses."

"That's unfair. When I was a kid, you tried to teach me always to do the decent thing. Now you want me to be a cad."

"I want you to use your head before you make a mistake that will ruin both your lives."

"It won't be as bad as that. Gladys and I will rub along together somehow."

"She'll make your life a misery. I know the type. She'll grow fat and shiftless and lazy before your eyes. She'll squander your money and trick you with other men. She'll nag—night and day she'll nag—she'll drive you insane. By marrying her you'll give up your chance to amount to something—and she'll make you eat dirt for being a failure. It's a life sentence you're passing on yourself, John. You'll be chained to her as long as you live."

But John could not think as far ahead as that. At twenty-three the awful infinity of the years is never apparent.

"You're piling it on a bit thick, Dad."

"Not half thickly enough." Philip tried another tack. "John, if this hadn't happened, if you hadn't promised to marry the girl, what were your plans?"

"It's hardly worth discussing now but I was planning to go abroad. Australia—South America—South Africa —I hadn't decided exactly; some place where there's room to breathe and a chance for a healthy chap who's willing to work to make good and be somebody. But that's all over. Gladys wouldn't like the life. We've thrashed it out. It wouldn't be fair to her to—"

"For the moment, let's consider what's fair to you. John, I have some money—quite a lot—which your mother had saved. In the back of my mind, I've had it earmarked for something—I didn't know quite what— and now I know what it is. There's enough to take you anywhere you want to go and give you a decent start."

There was a bitterly regretful look on John's face as he said no, but he said it.

"Thanks a lot, Dad. But I'm tied to Gladys."

"Tied!" repeated Philip angrily. "Yes, that's what you'll be. Tied. Tied hand and foot! Do you think I don't know? Haven't I been through it? Haven't you seen the kind of life I led with your mother?"

"That was different, Dad."

"In what way was it different? Your mother was a girl, pretty much like Gladys—at first. I didn't fall in love, any more than you have. We worked in the same office. Now and then we went out together. There wasn't anything more to it than that. Then one day she burst into tears because I didn't love her. Her tears got me with my back to the wall. I couldn't be a cad. Don't I wish to hell I had been? To comfort her, to please her—oh, damn it all, to make her stop crying—I said I did love her. And that was that. At first, she wasn't quite what she turned into later. She was only dull and drab and selfish. I thought, as you do, that we'd get along somehow. Well, you know just how we *did* get along."

"But, Dad," said John patiently, "it'll be different with Gladys and me."

"It won't be a damned bit different. You blasted young fool. You infernal idiot. Go ahead and marry the girl. Go ahead and find out for yourself. If you can't see her exactly as she is, I can. She's another Cora. You'll find out you've married your mother—the mother you fought to get away from only a year or so ago."

"What can I do? I've promised."

"You can break your promise."

"I can't. I can't. Only a swine would do that."

"It'll be a fat lot of help to you in the years to come to reflect on your past nobility. God, you'll go through it! I did. Your mother took me down into hell. She poisoned every day of my life with her."

But John was not convinced. He could not see himself in Philip's shoes and Gladys in Cora's. He couldn't see himself middle-aged and tied to the wrong woman. How could he? John was young.

Philip was desperate. By hook or by crook he had make John understand. It seemed there was only one way to do it. He played his last card.

"If I'd had any guts," he said hoarsely, "I'd have killed myself long ago. Instead, I—I killed her."

The horror he had expected did not dawn in John's eyes. The boy still didn't understand. He thought that what Philip had said was only a dramatic piece of rhetoric.

"That's a—a silly thing to say."

"As God's my witness, it's the truth. Her death was no accident. She made my life unbearable and at last— I murdered her."

Their eyes wrestled and fell, exhausted, apart. John's face was white, his mouth flabbily quivering.

"My God!" A sweat broke out on him. "It's true. You did kill her."

Suddenly, he was on his feet, sick and trembling with horror.

"It wasn't because she nagged. That wasn't why you did it. I see now. It was this other woman. The one you were in such a hurry to marry. You killed Mother for her. And the money—you killed her for the money. How can you sit there? A murderer. Oh, my God! You're foul, foul, foul!"

Chapter 16

Night after night for a week Mary lay in bed until the small hours, listening to the creak of bedsprings from the adjoining room, where Philip tossed and turned. Sometimes he cried out in the brief periods when, exhausted, he dozed off and was plunged into a nightmare. "John!" he would cry. "John!" A frantic plea for help from one sinking in mire; a soul's cry of despair from the engulfing bowels of hell. And then Mary would hear him muttering dementedly and know he was reliving horrors which for sanity's sake he must forget.

He had come home, weak with misery from the meeting with John, and sagged into a chair like a thing of sacking and straw. He felt sure he had lost his son for ever. Losing him, he hoped he had saved him from a damning blunder. But even the saving of the boy, so vital to him, had not relieved the bleak emptiness of his mind and spirit. The following evening had come a terse note from John. The handwriting was all that identified its origin. It began without salutation, ended without signature:

"I never want to see you again. Don't be afraid that I shall give you away, but from now on you are dead to me."

Better for Philip in that long week had he in truth been dead. Dead, he would have known no pain. Dead, he would have known no hunger of the soul. It was his punishment to be alive to taste to the dregs his cup of bitterness.

For seven nights Mary lay awake and listened to his grief, hushed when he tossed sleepless, frenziedly voiced when he sank into slumber. With him she suffered every pang. And on the eighth morning she knew it could be borne no longer.

John worked in an insurance office. That morning a messenger came and told him there was a woman in the waiting-room who wished to see him. Her name, scribbled on a form, was Mrs. Philip Marshall. John swore. His first impulse was to tell the man to send her away; and then he thought of the gossip it would cause in the office if he did so. Cursing the woman inwardly, he rose and followed the messenger.

The sort of creature he expected to see was not sharply defined in his imagination, but she would be bold and hard of eye, her hair dyed some bizarre colour, her brows plucked to resemble those of a vulture, her fingernails sharp and red as though dripping blood. The sort of glorified harlot one would expect to lure a man from his wife and turn his thoughts to lust and murder. The woman he expected was not in the waiting-room.

In a corner sat a quietly-dressed girl who looked worried (a widow, calling on the insurance company on a sad, inevitable errand?) That could not be she. With this girl one would be at rest, there would be no wild leaping of the pulse, no mad propulsion to lust and murder. No, this could not be the woman. But there was no one else. "You are not Mrs. Philip Marshall?" It was less a question than a statement.

"Yes, I am." Mary rose and submitted herself to a long, appraising scrutiny.

"You're not—not quite what I expected," said John. "But"—he hardened his jaw— "that doesn't alter the fact that I have nothing to say to you. You can get out of here as fast as you like."

Her voice was low but very firm. "I can't go until I have said what I came to say."

"I won't listen to you."

"Please don't think I want to thrust myself on you. Try to forget me. I don't matter. Think of me as a voice to which you must in decency listen."

"In decency? That's a good one. You have your nerve coming here. I suppose my father sent you."

"How little you know of him, if that is what you think."

"I don't know him at all—but I've only lately found that out."

"I know what you mean," said Mary gently.

John gave her a sharp look. "Oh, you do, do you? You know about…about my mother. How she died. The truth, I mean."

"Yes, I know."

"Of course. He did it for you."

"I deserve that. But it's not quite true. He did it mostly to escape from a sort of prison."

"There were no bars. He could have walked out."

"Could he? Would she have let him?"

"Perhaps not. But he needn't... My God! He needn't have killed her!"

"I know. It's hard to look that in the face."

It was impossible to be angry with her. She was only a girl.

"Aren't you afraid," John asked, in wonder.

"Afraid of what? Of Philip? Why should I be?"

"Because of what he's done."

"No, I'm not afraid. I'm sorry for him."

"Sorry! Do you think he deserves pity?"

"Oh, so much."

"But why? You know what he is. A murderer. That's the worst a man can be."

"Is it?"

Oh, why need her voice be so gentle, so patient?

"Of course, it is."

But, was it? He could not be sure. In his heart, he could not reconcile this murderer, the worst a man could be, with Philip the kind, the good, the loving father of his young boyhood.

"To murder a body," said Mary, "what is that, compared to murdering a soul?"

"You're speaking of my mother, accusing her. I shan't let you do that."

"Forgive me. You loved her?"

John turned his head away. "What right have you to ask me that?"

"Please. I'm only a voice, pleading for your father."

"What my father did was unforgivable. The fact that I didn't love my mother does not alter that."

"She made you unhappy, too."

"Unhappy? That isn't the half of it. Endless bloody misery, that was my life at home."

"Do you think your father suffered less?"

"He suffered a hundred times more. But he needn't have killed her. You can't talk round that. He killed her. Murdered her brutally. That was foul."

"The guilt is not all his. That is something you must share. As though with a sharp knife, you cut him out of your life. The law would not call that murder—but what do you call it? If you had not deserted him, if you had lightened his burden with your love, is it not likely that this would never have happened?"

John could not answer. With a groan, he covered his face.

"You were so fortunate, John. When life became unbearable you were able to clear out, without once looking back. But supposing you hadn't been able do that, what then? If you had been tied, as Philip was tied, tied to your mother and her bitterness all—all your life."

"Don't," he said sharply. "It's too ghastly to think about."

"That was how it was for him. There was but one means of getting away. She was holding on to him grimly, wrapping him round like an octopus, dragging him down, down…"

"You love him, don't you?" said John, raising his head and

looking at her as if for the first time. There was much more to this girl than he had dreamed.

"As a daughter loves a kind father, I love him. As a father loves his daughter, he loves me. Whatever life has made of him, Philip is lovable, you know."

"I know. My God, don't I know? I grew up knowing it. But for that, I might feel less harsh toward him now. But—that is not the kind of love I meant. After all, you married each other."

"Your father married me because I am going to have a baby by a man who won't acknowledge it." Mary brought out the words cleanly, laying herself bare.

For a moment, John stared at her and then, "I'm terribly sorry," he said.

There were tears in his eyes.

"Oh, my God," he said shakily, "I don't know anything. Not anything."

Mary took his hand and she gripped his fingers tight. You are so young, she thought, not thinking that she herself was no older. Now they were both moist of eye, tremulous of mouth and trying, because there was nothing to say, to smile at each other. Nothing came of their poor attempts to smile except a warming sympathy. For a time, they sat like that, holding each other's hands as though something precious would be lost when they let go.

At last, John said: "I don't think I can face him just yet. There is more thinking I must do."

"Too much thought," said Mary, "is not for humans."

"How true that is. It is only in my brain that I have hated him, never in my heart."

"May I tell him that the hate is gone?"

"Yes, tell him that. Tell him I'll try to come to him soon."

When Mary was leaving John frowned and added:

"If it will help, tell him I've seen the force of what he said to me that night. It didn't come to me by reason or by thought. I looked at Gladys with his eyes and knew I could not go on. There was a scene, of course. It proved him right, if proof was needed. The next day I moved on, but I have a lot to go through yet before I am free." He frowned again and said, awkwardly:

"They found out where you live. I don't know how. I didn't tell them. They may make trouble for my father. Tell him this is my affair. I'll settle it myself."

"I can tell him that," said Mary, "but I can't promise he will agree with you."

*

One evening, a day or two later, Philip answered a knock to find Gladys Lemon and a stout, scowling, middle-aged woman standing at the door of the flat. The older woman planted herself in front of him, her hands on ample hips.

"So, you're 'is father. Well, I might 'ave known it. A man oo'd bust up a romance between two lovin' 'earts—"

"Be good enough," said Philip curtly, "to wait a minute."

He shut the door on them and went into the living-room.

"Mary," he said, "will you go to your room and wait until I call?"

Without a word, Mary rose and departed. Philip went back to the front door and opened it.

"Please come in," he said.

There was a lot in Mrs. Lemon that had to come out. She kept it corked up until she was seated in the living room and then she took out the cork and let it gush. She'd never heard of such a thing in all her born days. Who was Philip, she'd like to know, to sit in judgement on her daughter? Who was John, to turn up his nose at the poor lamb? Maybe they thought they could do as they liked with the poor defenceless child. Well, they'd soon learn different. As long as there was breath in her body, Gladys's mother would make it her business to see that Gladys had her rights.

"She's a 'uman bein' same as 'e is, ain't she? She got feelin's, 'asn't she? You wait. You just wait. You'll see. We'll drag that snooty son of yours through every court in the land. We'll show 'im up for wot 'e is, a—a snake in the grass—a—a—"

"A wolf in sheep's clothing?" suggested Philip.

Mrs. Lemon glared at him.

"Funny, ain't ya? You'll laugh on the other side of your face w'en my Gladys gets 'eavy damages."

"I expect my son's savings amount to about twenty pounds. You can't wring heavy damages out of that."

"We'll drag you in, too. We'll see wot the judge 'as to say about you comin' between 'em."

"I'm afraid you can't do much to me for advising my son to the best of my ability."

"That's right, sneer. Go on, sneer at 'er. You don't care wot you do to the poor child. Look at 'er. Just look at 'er. Broken-'earted, that's wot she is—broken-'earted, and it's all your fault. Wot call 'ad you to stick in your interferin' nose?"

Philip looked at Gladys. She returned his look brazenly.

"She'll live, I think," he said dryly. "Let's come to the point. You want money. Well, you won't get much."

"If you think money can mend a broken 'eart. If you imagine for one moment—" Mrs. Lemon broke off. "'Ow much?" she asked.

"Fifty pounds."

"It's an insult."

"I shan't make it a bigger insult. Fifty pounds. Take it or leave it. You'll get no more. If that isn't enough, I'll use it to help my son fight you to the limit."

"I'll take it," said Gladys quickly. Until that moment she had not opened her mouth.

"An insult," mourned her mother, "that's wot it is."

Philip made out a cheque and a form of release for Gladys to sign. Gladys scrawled her name on the paper and thrust the cheque into her bag.

"You can tell your sheep-faced son from me that I wouldn't marry him, not if he was the last man on earth, I wouldn't. Tell him he made me sick with his everlastin' jaw about honour and decency and keeping fit. Tell him from me—"

"I'll tell him," said Philip.

When they left, he washed his hands very thoroughly.

He put the paper Gladys had signed into an envelope and posted it, without comment, to John.

And then, on another evening, there was a knock. The caller was John.

"Hello, Dad," he said, when Philip opened the door.

"Hello, son."

There was only a fragmentary pause before they shook hands.

"Hello, Mary," said John, coming into the living-room where Mary sat knitting.

"Hello, John," she answered, smiling.

It was as simple as that. As banal as that. But they did not see the banality, only the divine simplicity.

Chapter 17

Autumn evening, washed by a waning sun, hushed by the ageing of the year, ringing with the clear voices of boys playing last games of cricket on the Green... Philip walked down the narrow alley leading to the 'The Hole in the Wall.' Outside the public-house stood a dilapidated touring car, as much a part of the place as the sign above the door. Belonging to the landlord, who was secretly as proud of it as another man might be of an old coat, when not in use it was parked in the alley, night and day, in all weathers.

Since his marriage to Mary, Philip had not been in the place. There had been so many things to do more interesting than standing at a bar with a glass in one's hand. This evening he had an hour or two to kill. Mary had gone driving in the country with the Ramsdens and would not be back until around eight. She was bringing the Ramsdens home with her; John was coming to the flat at about the same time and they were going to have a party.

The place had not changed, public-houses rarely do. The same warm, smoky, friendly atmosphere; the same cheerful faces reflected in the bar mirror; the same tankards in the same hands; the same involved discussions; even the same old jokes. A group of the regulars were pulling the landlord's leg about his car. They had been doing that for years.

"Ain't you afraid some one'll pinch it, Charley?"

"Don't worry, Charley. If it was pinched, the thief would bring it back. He'd have to, to keep his self-respect."

"You'll catch it, Charley, if you're pulled up by cops. That old crock has tuberculosis in the cylinders and cancer of the brake lining. Cor, blimey, you ain't even got safety glass in the windscreen."

"I've driven it a hundred thousand miles without accident. Unless you hit something, what do you with safety glass?"

"Tell that to the cops, Charley, when they pull you up."

Philip ordered a half-pint of bitter and stood listening. A voice at his elbow said:

"Hello, stranger."

It was Simmons, looking shabbier and more down-at-heel than ever. His hands were dirty, the fingers nicotine-stained to a deep mahogany, the nails rimmed with black. His face was grey and marked with lines of dissipation and bitterness. He gave Philip an odd, sly side-glance.

"Haven't seen you since your second marriage."

"How did you know I'd married again?"

"Oh, I get to know things."

"We kept it quiet," said Philip awkwardly. He was hanged if he knew why he should feel uncomfortable but he did. "We didn't want a lot of talk. People might have thought I was remarrying in indecent haste. It wasn't any one's business but my own, but you know how it is."

"Yes," said Simmons. "I know how it is. I know exactly how it is." He glanced at the tankard in Philip hand. "That looks good. Since you press me, I'll have a pint of it."

Philip laughed. "Still the same old Simmons."

"Only more so," said Simmons wryly.

When the pint of bitter was placed before him he waited for Philip to pay, then said:

"Let's sit over there in the corner."

Although Philip had no wish for intimacy with Simmons, he could see no way to avoid it without being rude, so they crossed the lounge together. The novelist took a deep gulp at his tankard, eyeing Philip queerly, furtively, over the rim. He set it down. Picked it up. Drank again. His hands were shaking, beneath one of his eyes a nerve twitched. He opened his mouth to speak and closed it again without saying anything. Suddenly in a hoarse whisper, his lips scarcely moving, he said: "Lend me five pounds."

"You mean, give you five pounds. I've lent you quite a lot in the past but I've never had a penny back."

"Alright, give me five pounds."

"Don't be so damned silly."

"I mean it."

"It's early in the evening to be so drunk."

"I'm not drunk."

"Then you've the nerve of the devil."

"Maybe I have. What about the fiver?"

"In the first place, there's no earthly reason why I should give you money. In the second—"

For a moment Philip thought that Simmons was going to burst into tears. His face was working convulsively.

In a hoarse voice he said: "Don't tell me you can't afford it. You came in for a packet of money when you murdered your wife."

It was as though the floor had risen and hit Philip in the face. His mouth fell open. He gaped at Simmons. There was a roaring in his ears, a choking in his lungs. Simmons rose and walked to the bar. He returned with a glass of brandy.

"Here. Drink this."

Philip stared at the glass.

"Funny," he muttered—and he almost laughed. "That's the first drink you've ever bought me."

"I didn't pay for it. I said you'd pay later. Drink it."

They stared at each other and they were both afraid, but the fear in Philip's face made the other man bolder. His lips parted in a slight, unsavoury smile. In Philip's brain a small voice was saying: *What does he know? He doesn't know anything. He's bluffing, he must be.* But the smile made his flesh crawl. He would have risen and walked away but his legs refused to function.

"You dirty little rat," he said in a strained, unnatural tone. "What filthy game are you trying to play with me?"

"Blackmail, I believe they call it. Not a nice word but we might as well be frank and use it. I can see it trembling on your lips."

"You must be mad. What makes you think you can blackmail me?"

"I don't think it, I know it. I know it as surely as know that you murdered your wife."

"You've said that twice. I don't know how you got the idea that I did anything of the sort—"

"Come off it," said Simmons impatiently. "Playing for time won't do you any good. Do we come to terms—or do I go to the police?"

"Go to the police by all means. You've nothing to tell them that they'd be interested in hearing."

"Haven't I?" There was a pause during which the novelist's eyes nibbled like mice at Philip's face "Perhaps you've forgotten a night some months ago…a night when I was plastered. Perhaps you thought I was too drunk to remember; but drunkenness is my natural condition."

"I don't know what you're talking about."

"I think you do. We discussed the perfect murder that night."

"You're referring to one of your dipsomaniacal monologues, I expect," said Philip, trying to speak calmly. "Good Lord, man, you don't suppose I can remember all the nonsense you used to babble in my ear? I never listened."

"Didn't you? You wound me deeply. Try to recall it. I said the perfect murder must look like an accident. That if, for instance, one wished to rid oneself of an unwanted wife, it couldn't be done better than by pushing her downstairs."

"That's a lie. You talked of guns going off by accident and a lot of rot about Underground trains."

"I thought you couldn't remember the occasion? You weren't even listening."

"I remember now. You must be mad if you imagine I paid any attention to you."

"That's as may be. But supposing I went to the police and told them about that night...about how we talked of killing a woman by pushing her downstairs?"

There could only be one answer to that. Philip would hang. It would be the evidence the police needed to complete the case against him. Philip knew it and his blood ran cold. "But we didn't."

"I could tell them we did," said Simmons quietly.

"You're a filthy swine."

"Do you think I don't know it?"

"Simmons," said Philip urgently, desperately, "if I swear to you that I didn't kill her, if I give you my sacred word of honour that it was an accident—"

"I'm no moralist. I don't care a hang whether you killed her or not. That isn't the point. The point is that I can make the police believe you did, which is all that matters to me. When you come to think of it, that's all that matters to you, too."

"Tell the police anything you like. They're not such fools as to believe you."

"You say that almost as though you meant it."

For a time, they were silent, watching each other warily.

"Call me names, if it will make you feel better," Simmons at last. "I shan't mind. You can't think of a name for me that I haven't already used on myself. Maybe you think I like doing this. I don't. I've got to have money, that's all."

"I suppose the idea of working for it hasn't occurred to you?"

"Don't talk like a damned fool," retorted Simmons angrily. "I can't work. I'm less capable of working than if I'd lost an arm and both legs. It's my own fault, I know that. I've schooled myself in mental and physical laziness. But there it is. If my life depended on it, I couldn't do an honest day's work and I need money as badly as the next man, so I have to get it how I can."

"You used to live on your wife. What's happened her?"

"I still live on her. But it isn't a fat living. Food and bed, that's the best she can do. A man needs more. That's why I'm tapping you for five pounds."

"Five pounds today," said Philip, "and you'll want another five pounds next week. And still another five pounds a couple of days after that."

"Or perhaps ten," replied Simmons, completely ashamed. "I'm new at this game. I'll grow more ambitious in time. Well, do I get it?"

"I haven't that much money with me."

"That's all right. I don't mind a little trouble. I'll walk round to your flat with you."

Philip rose, leaving the glass of brandy untouched on the table. They walked to the bar. "I've got to take home some drinks. My wife and I are giving a little party tonight."

"That's fine. I'll help carry the bottles. Maybe I'll even stay to the party. I like parties."

They stood at the counter while the barman wrapped the bottles. Suddenly, Simmons said harshly: "Don't look at me like that. As if you were sorry for me. It won't do you any good to be sorry for me. Save your sorrow for yourself."

Philip did not answer. It was true, he was sorry for Simmons and sorry, damned sorry, for himself. He realized with dismay that he would have to kill the man who was standing at his side.

Chapter 18

Putting down his liquid cargo, Philip groped for his latchkey. He glanced at his wristwatch. Almost seven. An hour at most, probably less, in which to dispose of Simmons. At about eight Mary and her friends and John would come and before that Simmons must be out the way. How to dispose of him was a problem, for Philip dared not kill him—yet. Nor could he let him leave the flat alive.

The key skated all-round the lock.

"Nerves," said Simmons. "You needn't be like that. The worst is over. Pay up and look pleasant and everything will be all right."

You fool, thought Philip, you poor, self-deluded fool…All you think of is the power you hold over me. You apparently haven't considered what I might do to you. If you knew what's in my mind, you'd go clattering down those stairs as though all the hounds of hell were baying at your heels. Steadying his hand, Philip unlocked the door and they went into the flat and put their burdens on the living-room table.

"I could do with a drink," said Simmons, unwrapping a bottle of Haig.

"I'll fetch glasses."

In the kitchen Philip stood by the window, sick and faint, clinging to the back of a chair. At first his rage at Simmons for doing this to both of them was too great to permit him to think, and then his brain cleared and into it came the image of a small bottle standing on a shelf in his medicine cupboard. Mr. Simmons could do with a drink. Mr. Simmons should have a drink. Bracing himself, he found two glasses, carried them to the bathroom, and poured into one of them half an inch of colourless liquid. It was many times the amount Philip usually took when he couldn't sleep. Would it be enough to knock out Simmons and keep him quiet for a few hours? He wondered whether to increase it but, after a moment's hesitation, decided he had better not. It was too powerful a drug with which to take risks. He didn't want to kill Simmons—just yet.

"You took your time," said Simmons, when Philip returned to the living-room.

"I felt sick." Philip was holding the loaded glass so that his fingers concealed the liquid.

"You look bloody awful. I'm a bit shaken-up myself."

"If you knew what you are doing to both of us—" began Philip fiercely.

"I know what I'm doing, all right, and perhaps I'm taking a hell of a chance being here alone with you. If you bumped me off, you'd spare yourself a lot of headaches, that's what you're thinking, isn't it? But I think I'm safe enough. What could you do with the body? You couldn't leave it lying around, not when you're going to have a party, and you couldn't carry it out in broad daylight and dump it somewhere. Besides, we were seen leaving 'The Hole in the Wall' together. Yes, I think I'm safe—for the present. Later on, when you've had time to think up a juicy scheme for murder, I'll have to watch my step."

"If I could convince you that I didn't kill her—"

"Oh, shut up and pour me a drink. We've had enough talk."

Philip poured him a drink and handed it over with fingers that scarcely trembled. Simmons downed it quickly and handed back the glass.

"Fill it up. Make it a good one."

Philip obeyed. He made it a good one. He poured one for himself as well. He needed it.

Glass in hand, Simmons strolled to a chair and sat down.

"Cosy little place. You're a lucky fellow, Marshall. You did a good thing for yourself when you killed your wife and married a younger one."

"I didn't kill her."

"All right, you didn't kill her. Just the same, I'd take a leaf from your book and get rid of my own wife—if she didn't happen to be worth more to me alive than dead."

The clock on the mantelpiece ticked away the seconds with disconcerting rapidity. Philip watched the other man's face but it told him nothing. His own breathing began to sound loudly in his ears. The room seemed be filled with the beating of his heart, magnified by his tense nerves to the pitch of sledgehammer blows. Odd how chilly it was becoming although the evening had been warm when they came in and the windows were shut. It was chilly and at the same time so stuffy that breathing was difficult. Philip felt his skin rising in little pimples. His head seemed to be swollen to the size of a pumpkin. His scalp prickled, as though with the touch of icy fingers.

Calmly, almost nonchalantly, Simmons sipped his drink.

"I'm no good. Never have been. It's a pity, Marshall, a great, great pity. There's a lot of stuff in me that I ought to give to the world to enjoy. I could write a hell of a fine book—if I was any good. But I'm no good. I told you that, didn't I?"

"You're damned right, you're no good. You're a swine, Simmons, if ever there was one."

"That's what I'm telling you. I'm a swine. And that's a tragedy, don't you go making any mistakes about that. D'you think a man starts life wanting to be the kind of perisher I am? If you do, you're crazy. When I was a kid, I was chockfull of high ambition. God, I was going to amount to something in this world. I was going to show them. And the stuff's in me, all right. I *could* have shown them. Sometimes I get choked up inside with the wonderful things that are in me, just waiting to be written down. A lot of stillborn literary babies. It's a tragedy, Marshall, a goddamned tragedy."

Closing one eye, he squinted at Philip. "We're forgetting something."

"What?"

"The five pounds."

"Of course. The five pounds."

"I *thought* you'd forgotten. Well, I haven't. You'd better cough it up now."

There was money in a bureau drawer. Philip counted notes into the novelist's grubby palm. One. Two. Three. Four. Five.

"Make it ten. You oughtn't to keep so much in the house."

Without counting, Philip thrust the rest of the notes into the outstretched hand.

Time was flying and his fate balanced on the seconds. Around eight...that might be ten past but was as likely to be ten to... the minutes rushed away like leaves in the wind, and Simmons sat there, his legs crossed, a little smile on his face, talking, talking, talking. Rustling the notes between his stained fingers as though he loved the feel of them. By this time, he ought to be drowsy, but he wasn't. He was wide awake. Looking forward to the party. The sweat broke out on Philip like water from a squeezed sponge. God, would the drug never take effect?

He should have made the dose larger. That was it. In order to do any good, the drug must knock out Simmonds quickly, and it wasn't doing that. What an inglorious fiasco this would be if Simmonds stayed awake until the others came and then fell asleep—quite safely—in the middle of the party. Philip would never have another chance to get rid of him. If Philip failed this time, Simmons would be on his back, like an Old Man of the Sea, until his last penny was gone. The clock on the mantelpiece mocked Philip. Tick. Tick. Tick. Surely the damned thing was accelerating, ticking faster and faster like an engine warming up?

With a smug look on his face, and a smile that boasted his power over Philip, Simmons sat there, talking…He had finished the drink which should have robbed him of his senses; he had drained it to the last drop, rolling it on his tongue; and he was as wide awake as ever.

Simmons held out his glass. "I'll have another, old boy."

Philip took it but made no move to pour the whisky. Perhaps that was what was wrong. Perhaps the liquid Simmons had consumed was nullifying the drug. Damn him in hell. If he didn't go under…but that though was not to be faced. He must go under. He must.

"You're sweating like a ruddy pig," remarked Simmons. "What's up?"

"It's nothing. Nothing."

"Scared of me, huh?" The idea tickled Simmons. "Hell, you needn't be. We're pals, old boy, pals. You see me right and I'll do right by you." He blinked his eyes rapidly. "God, I feel queer. There's a numbness in the pit of my stomach. Must be something I ate. Only, I haven't eaten anything."

He looked up and their eyes met.

The short hairs bristled at the nape of Philip's neck. He wanted to look away, but he couldn't.

Time stood still while they stared at each other in suffocating silence, their faces drained of colour, their lips twitching.

"You bastard. You bastard. You've poisoned me. The whisky… you put something in it…"

As Simmons struggled to rise, Philip hit him with a bottle. There was an awful moment while Simmons, open-mouthed, goggling, swayed between chair and floor, then he sank to his knees and fell slowly forward on to his face.

Putting out a hand, Philip leant on the table. His limbs shook, his guts caved, his spine crawled moist and chill. He could not have stood without support. Despairing, he derided himself for a fool. What he had done was stupid, futile. What he planned to do was absurdly involved, infinitely dangerous. He had but one thread-slender chance; that the drug would keep Simmons under when the effect of the blow wore off; keep him under for hours, until the party was over. What chance was that? None. Worse than none. Better, he told himself hopelessly, to have paid and gone on paying, closing his eyes to the day when he could no longer pay and to what would happen then. Instead, he had taken a step down a path that led by ninety-nine ways to the gallows and by only one to freedom.

Well, it was now too late to draw back. He must go on. One chance in a hundred? He had no option but to take it.

Hauling Simmons across the room, he pushed him under a draped divan which stood against a wall.

On a sudden inspiration, he gathered up the drinkables he had brought in and went through the flat, hiding the bottles under beds, under cupboards, in every out-of-the-way corner.

Back in the living-room, he picked up the notes which had fluttered to the floor when Simmons fell, stuffed them into his pocket and went round the room, tidying it. Where he had dragged Simmons over the carpet, the pile was rubbed the wrong way leaving an unmistakable track that ran from chair to divan. Barely had he finished smoothing it than a key grated in the front-door lock.

"We're all here," said Mary, kissing him. "We met John on the stairs coming up."

Thank you all, thought Philip, for not coming sooner...

Almost fiercely, he returned the pressure of her lips.

"My goodness, what passion!" giggled little Mrs. Ramsden. "I wish Fred would put as much feeling to it when he kisses me."

"You know what you always say," her husband objected, "when I do."

"Now, Fred, don't be disgusting."

"Yes," grinned Fred. "That's it."

"Philip," said Mary—her tone was uncertain, "you're alright?"

"Right as rain, dear."

Blessed interlude, while they rid themselves of outdoor apparel.

"If you want a drink," said Philip, trying to speak lightly, "you'll have to find it. I thought we'd start the party off with a Treasure Hunt, so I hid the drinks. The living-room is Home Base. I'll wait there with glasses and corkscrew. The first to strike lucky gets a bonus."

In a few minutes they trooped in to join him, flushed and smiling, hugging bottles.

Fred sprawled on the divan and told a story about a pal of his whose wife was a temperance crusader and who had to hide his Scotch to keep her from pouring it down the sink. Then he told another about nothing in particular but the look on his face made them all helpless with laughter. He gave his time-honoured impression of a Jew trying to borrow money from a Scot, followed by another impression of two cats on a wall, which the boys in his office had voted a riot. Fred was a card, there was no denying that. Ask Fred to a party and all the others had to do was sit back with glasses in their hands and enjoy the fun.

"Nothing wrong, is there, Dad?" whispered John, who was sitting close to his father.

Philip's mind came back with a jerk from a dark journey.

"What? Oh. No, there's nothing wrong. I wish you and Mary would stop fretting about me. What would be wrong?"

"Well, you needn't bite my head off. I only asked."

"Sorry."

"That's all right. This chap Ramsden's a scream, isn't he?"

"Yes," said Philip, "he's a scream."

He was listening to Simmons breathing under the divan. Above the laughter, above the talk, he heard it plainly. No one else seemed to, not even Fred, who was practically sitting on the unconscious man.

It was torture facing the others, afraid that at any moment a hidden voice would start muttering hoarsely or a hand come groping out. Afraid someone would drop a pencil or a coin and it would roll, maliciously, under the divan, putting a sensational end to everything. Fred Ramsden made the most of his jolliest evening in weeks, Philip Marshall died a thousand grisly deaths.

They ate sandwiches. They ate cake. They drank Scotch, sherry, ale. And at times, it seemed to Philip's agonized mind that they were having a game with him, that all the time they heard the breathing—how could they help hearing it? —and knew perfectly well what lay under the divan and were only biding their time before making an end of the game and of him.

Perspiration beaded his brow, salted his lips. He took a couple of drinks to pull himself together. All of a sudden, he found himself talking out loud, although he had not meant to do anything of the sort. Talking a lot of nonsense, which he tried to stop but couldn't. Words poured out of him; absurd jokes, half-forgotten limericks, doggerel of his schooldays. It was as though he had condemned to recite Joe Miller's Joke Book by heart.

They must think he'd gone mad. What else could they think? They were laughing, it was true, but surely it was forced hysterical laughter? Shut in with a madman, all they could do was humour him. That was it. That must be it. It would not be necessary for the hoarse voice to start muttering or the hand to come groping out. Philip was giving himself away, behaving like a halfwit. Every frantic word was nailing his coffin tightly. He knew that, but he couldn't stop.

Why didn't they make some excuse and go? It was as though they'd taken root. Shaking with mirth. Humouring him. They would never go. They'd sit on and on and on. This crazy party was doomed to last for ever.

And then, when he was geared to eternity, the party shifted to the hall, concerned itself with hats and coats and goodnights.

"You were marvellous, darling," said Mary, when the last goodnights rang on the stairs. "You were so funny, I thought I'd die. Fred says he'll have to take a back seat when you're around. And John told me he'd never seen you in such good form. The party woke up when you came out of your shell and got going."

Philip gaped at her. She meant it. It was incredible, preposterous, but she really meant it!

"It can't be that time already," she said, glancing at the clock. "I'm not a bit tired. I think I'll do the dishes before I turn in."

"No, you don't," he said, pushing her gently toward her room. "You know you'll insist on getting up in the morning to see me off. To bed with you, woman. I'll bring you a hot drink."

He poured into the hot drink some of the fluid from the bottle in the medicine cupboard and put the bottle in his pocket, intending to get rid of it at the first opportunity. He carried the hot drink to Mary, kissed her good night and started to leave the room.

"Philip," said Mary.

He turned from the door.

"Philip," she said again, and he came back to the bed.

She took his hand and placed it on her body. He felt life stirring within her.

"It will be soon, now, Philip. It's going to be a boy. He'll look like you. I've set my heart on him looking like you, so he will, won't he?"

"He's got to amount to something, Mary. You must see to that."

"I'll have you to help me."

"Forget about me. This is a solemn charge I lay upon you. Make something of him, something good, worthwhile. Promise me."

"I'll do my best, Philip."

She drained the steaming cup to the last drop and he took it from her, switched off the light and went out. Taking pains to do it quietly, he locked her door and put the key in his pocket.

Chapter 19

Opening the door of the darkened living-room, Philip listened. No sound. Not even the breathing he had so plainly heard before. His heart skipped a beat. Had the drug and the breaking bottle killed Simmons too soon? Turning on the light, he walked unsteadily to the divan, bent over it, and heard a grumbling sigh. Every muscle tensed, he waited, but nothing happened. He could hear the breathing now, deep and somnolent. The drug was holding Simmons.

From a bureau drawer he took a box of odd keys, whose use for the most part he had forgotten, which he still kept because a key—no matter how useless—is something one is reluctant to throw away. Fumbling in the box, he fished up in turn practically all but the one he sought. Impatiently, he tipped the lot out onto the bureau top and spread them. Almost the last he turned over was the one he was looking for, a car ignition key. Putting it in his pocket, he bundled the others into the box and replaced it in the bureau drawer.

He put his ear to Mary's door to make sure she was asleep, then went to his own room for gloves, hat and an old raincoat. On stockinged feet he went downstairs and out of the building, putting on his shoes when he reached the pavement. Half-past one in the morning. Night lay upon the district like a purple drape. Deserted streets. Hushed dwellings. Walking along the High Road, collar up, hat-brim down, Philip passed but one solitary night farer; a policeman trying the handle of a door on the opposite pavement, who did not look round as he went by. On his toes, Philip went down the alley leading to 'The Hole in the Wall.' The public-house and neighbouring buildings were wrapped in silence. Shut eyes, the dark-gleaming windows. Open mouths, the cavernous black doorways.

Opening the door of the dilapidated car, Philip released the brake. Tiptoeing to the back, he put his shoulder to it. The car rolled slowly down the alley. Out of earshot of the public-house, he climbed in and tried his key in the ignition. He pressed the starter. After a fit of asthmatic wheezing, the engine responded with noisy life. Turning on the sidelights, Philip drove off.

Fifty yards from the block of flats in which he lived, he killed the engine and let the car coast the rest of the way. Knowing that the brakes would scream like cats, he turned the wheels in towards the pavement and let the rubbing of the tyres on the kerb bring them to a stop. A tyre-lever lay on the floor at his feet. He wrapped it in a rag and took it up with him to the flat, leaving his shoes on the steps outside the building.

He opened the door of the living-room and his veins froze. A leg stuck out from under the divan. It twisted this way and that, the heel scraping the carpet. The hoarse voice of Simmons was muttering: "What the hell? What the hell?" over and over again.

The leg went in. The divan heaved up and subsided. The leg came out again. Philip gripped it and hauled Simmons out to the light. With the wrapped tool he struck him on the head.

The blow didn't stun Simmons. He glared up with fear-flooded eyes. Simmons knew what was happening. Dumb beasts in slaughter-houses know. Knowing, he tried desperately to rise, his fingers scrabbled on the floor. Philip struck him again. Struck him hard. It was hell and damnation, hitting down with those frenzied, dumb-beast eyes staring up, but he had to do it. The second blow did its work. Simmons gave up the struggle to rise, to live. His eyes glazed.

Although Simmons was puny and light, it was all Philip could do to carry him down to the car.

He put on his shoes and started the engine again.

They drove through drowsy streets together, clammy-handed murderer, unconscious victim. Side by side, in the publican's ramshackle car. And while they drove, Death scrounged a lift. Without fuss, without the last breath-rattle of tradition, Simmons surrendered the spark that made him alive. It was the sort of dirty trick Simmons had played all his life; dying before the accident that was to kill him took place. Philip did not know. That was as well. What could he have done if he had known? He could not have breathed life back into the corpse until the right moment came for him to die.

In a side-turning where there were no houses, Philip slowed the car to twenty and deliberately drove it into a telegraph pole. That he might be hurt himself was a chance he had to take. But he was not hurt. Simmons sprawled on him, making his heart leap with fright. There was a tooth-jarring crash, a pattering as water drained from the buckled radiator, a jolt as the car bounced back from the pole and sank sideways on a broken spring. The engine panted on, no more asthmatically than before.

Thrusting Simmons aside with a hand-flutter like an old maid warding off a drunkard, Philip climbed into the back and covered himself with a rug he found there.

He took Simmons by the shoulders, pushed him over to the driving-seat, then drove his head up against the screen.

It made a ragged hole and stuck there; the neck impaled on jagged spears of shattered glass.

Tossing the rug aside, Philip jumped out.

Suddenly he became a child scared in the dark.

Whimpering, he took to his heels and ran.

His lungs were bursting, he was streets away, before he slowed to a walk. A policeman stopping him then could have had a confession for the asking. But no policeman stopped him. In the mile or so that lay between the wrecked car and his flat he met no living soul. Safe in his room, he inspected his clothing for bloodstains and found none. In one way that was reassuring, in another it wasn't.

His face, haggard, twisted, livid, stared at him from a mirror.

"You're not me," he said to it in horror. "God knows who you are, but you're not me."

Before he went to bed, he unlocked Mary's door. He wanted to go in. Touching her warm, soft, sleeping body, might bring him comfort and make him feel less terribly alone; might in some way cleanse him as the body of a virgin is supposed to cleanse the diseased. He tore himself from the door. He did not know how he was to face her when the hour of waking came.

For a long time, he lay in bed staring at the darkness.

Simmons lay on one side of him, Cora on the other.

"What makes you think you're alone?" they whispered almost lovingly. "We're with you. We'll always be with you. You'll never be alone again."

He had killed Cora for his freedom and Simmons to make him safe, but he knew that he was neither safe nor free.

Chapter 20

Nose-teasing, tantalizing, a blend of odours crept through the flat, tickling like slim fingers into every corner. Browning toast. Sizzling bacon. Kidneys dribbling their red juices. Coffee brewing, hot and black. From the deepest caverns of sleep, Philip groped his way back to consciousness. Fumbling across the bedside table, he found the red tin alarm clock and brought it to his nose. The hands pointed accusingly to eight. He jumped out of bed and put on his dressing-gown. Opening the door of his room, he heard Mary humming as she went about her work.

"I'm late," he called. "I must have forgotten to set the alarm."

"You didn't forget," said Mary cheerfully, coming to the kitchen door. "I turned it off. You were so fast asleep when I looked in on you, I thought an extra half-hour would do you good."

"I'll be late at the office for the first time in twenty years."

"So what?" said Mary, going back to the stove and shaking the frying pan.

"So what?" echoed Philip to himself as he stepped into a cold bath, his warm flesh goosing. So what? Last night he had killed a man, this morning he was worrying about being late at the office. That was funny. That was very, very funny. But he did not laugh.

He ducked under; came up spluttering; climbed out dripping on the bath mat; towelled himself vigorously. Working up a bubbling lather, he tried to shut out of his mind the memory of the night before. But the face reflected in the mirror, across which he guided his razor, was as often the face of Simmons as his own. Simmons, the drunken author. Simmons the scrounger, the blackmailer who had got what he asked for, who had been the victim of the kind of murder he himself suggested.

At breakfast, Mary chatted eagerly about the party. "You were in wonderful form, darling. I've never known you quite like that before." She hesitated. "You—you're a lot—a lot easier in your mind than you have been, aren't you?"

Philip smiled at her, and she did not perceive the irony in his smile. "Yes," he lied.

"I'm glad of that. So glad."

On his way to the station, he put a casual hand into his pocket and discovered, with horror, that he was still carrying the bottle of sleeping medicine. There was no suitable means of disposal at hand, so he left it where it was, with a mental note—urgently underlined—to get rid of it as soon as he safely could.

When he came out of the office for lunch, he bought a noon edition of an evening newspaper. Although itching to search there and then for mention of a fatal car accident, he forced himself to tuck it under his arm and walk in his usual unhurried style to his customary resting-place. He ordered a chop and spinach, and unfolded the paper with an everyday air. He took time to peruse the front page, although the first glance told him that the story he sought was not there. He turned the page as though there were no hurry, no hurry at all.

A headline caught his eye:

NOVELIST DIES IN ACCIDENT

In simple language, the news item described a milk-roundsman's discovery of the dead body in the wreck of the publican's car. There was no suggestion that the death had been anything but accidental. Mrs. Simmons had identified the body and told the police that on previous occasions her husband had borrowed cars for joyrides without permission and that once before he had been involved in an accident in a car thus acquired. It was all very matter-of-fact and reassuring.

Philip heaved a sigh of relief. That was that. He attacked his food with relish.

"That looks good, Mr. Marshall," said a dispassionate voice.

Philip looked up and the knife and fork clattered from his limp hands to the plate. His face ashen-grey, his stomach turning over, he stared at the stout, ox-eyed man who sat opposite, picking his teeth with a sharpened matchstick. It was Sergeant Huxley of the Criminal Investigation Department.

"Finish your chop," said the Sergeant, with an airy wave of his hand. "There's no hurry."

"What do you mean? What do you want?"

"I don't want anything. It's Inspector Haddow. He'd like a few words with you."

"About what?"

"I'd better let him tell you that. Finish your chop. Looks like a nice piece of meat. Pity to waste it."

Pushing his plate aside, Philip rose and reached for his hat. Eyeing the chop regretfully, Sergeant Huxley followed without haste. On the pavement outside, he said mildly: "We'll take a cab, if you care to pay for it."

Philip nodded dumbly and the C.I.D. man hailed a passing taxi.

In the taxi, Philip put a hand in his pocket and touched the bottle. If they searched him and found that it would be all up with him. Should he throw it out of the window? Should he bury it in the cushions? He missed both ideas as wild and suicidal. His fingers were still clutching the bottle—it was cold, but it seemed to burn—when he followed the Sergeant into New Scotland Yard. They went straight upstairs to Inspector

Haddow's room. The Inspector was bent over a pile of papers. His face was stern. Without preamble, he said to Philip:

"I intend to put some questions to you. Regulations require me to inform you that you can refuse to answer. If you decide to answer, what you say will be written down and may be used in evidence."

"Let me get this straight," said Philip, taking his hand from his pocket. "Am I under arrest?"

"Not yet. It is possible that I may arrest you."

"What am I supposed to have done?"

The Inspector motioned Philip to a chair. It was so placed that the light from the window fell full upon Philip's face.

"You knew a man named Gilbert Simmons?"

"Yes, I knew him fairly well."

"You're aware he is dead?"

"I was reading about the accident when Sergeant Huxley came for me."

"It was not an accident," retorted the Inspector, watching Philip's face keenly.

Philip took a deep breath. To his surprise, now that his worst fears were realized, he felt quite calm. "Not an accident? But according to the newspaper—"

"At the time of the car smash," said Haddow coldly, his eyes boring like gimlets into Philip's head, "Simmons was dead. We know that definitely. There are a number of factors that prove it, including the fact that although badly cut about the face and neck by broken glass, the body had scarcely bled. The accident was faked, to cover a murder, Mr. Marshall."

"Well, you needn't look at me like that. I don't know anything about it."

"You were in the dead man's company last night. You left 'The Hole in the Wall' together shortly after seven."

"That is so."

"Where did you go?"

"Simmons walked with me as far as my flat."

"For what reason?"

"He had asked for the loan of a pound. I hadn't that much on me but told him I'd let him have it if he came home with me."

"There was no money on the body when it was found."

"Simmons could do a lot to a pound in a few hours."

"Why should you lend him money?"

"I really don't know. I'd done it before. Perhaps I was sorry for him. Must there be a reason for everything one does?"

"When you reached the flat did he go in?"

"Yes, for a short while."

"How long exactly?"

"Ten minutes, I suppose. Not longer."

"Was there anyone else in the flat?"

"No. My wife was out with some friends in their car."

"Ah," said Inspector Haddow. The fact that Philip and Simmons had been alone seemed to please him.

"Do you know if anyone saw him coming out?"

"No," snapped Philip, "I don't. I don't even know if any one saw him going in. I'm telling you the truth, not what I think you'll be able to find out from other people."

"You're sure he was not in the flat longer than minutes?"

"Dead sure. Simmons was more than willing to stay—he had helped me carry home a load of drinks and he couldn't keep his eyes off the bottles—but my wife was giving a party, so I got rid of him."

"A party?" echoed Inspector Haddow sharply. "Last night?"

Philip almost laughed at the crestfallen expression the Inspector's face. "Yes," he said, "last night. Quite a small party, Inspector. It began about eight and went on until after one."

"Who was present?"

Philip gave the names and addresses of the Ramsdens and John, which Sergeant Huxley carefully wrote down.

"You won't mind waiting in another room for a while," said Inspector Haddow, his tone making it plain that he didn't care whether Philip minded or not. "I'll want to see you again later."

"I don't mind in the least. I suppose I may smoke?"

"You can do what you damned well please," retorted Inspector Haddow irritably, "as long as you don't try to leave."

On his way out of the room, Philip paused and turned back. "By the way," he said, with a frown, "why on earth should I murder Simmons?"

"If I knew that," retorted the Inspector harshly, "I'd arrest you this minute."

A policeman kept Philip company in the detention room to make certain that he remained. The constable was used to that sort of duty. Under his breath he softly whistled the refrain of a popular song.

Nerves on edge, hands clammy, Philip sat by the window smoking his pipe. Just sitting there, just keeping still, took all the self-control of which he was capable. He wanted to rise and pace the floor. He wanted to hit the policeman on the head and run. He wanted to yell. Instead, with a forced air of coolness, he sat waiting. Waiting for what? For the Inspector to make up his mind about arresting him. For more evidence to be uncovered that would point to his guilt. For a search of his person to reveal the drug he had used on Simmons. It was all Philip could do to keep his hand out of the pocket that contained the bottle. Incredible that the Inspector had not noticed the bulge it made and said, ever so quietly: "What have you got there?" That would have settled everything, once and for all. And in a way, the result would have been more bearable than this damned waiting, waiting, waiting...

"Nice day, ain't it?" said the policeman, glancing over Philip's shoulder at the patch of clear blue visible through window.

"Eh?" Philip goggled at the man. "What did you say?"

"I said it's a nice day."

"Oh," said Philip. "Yes. Yes, it's a nice day."

He started to laugh.

The policeman was shocked. He looked at Philip as reprovingly as an undertaker might look at someone who laughed at a funeral.

*

"What did we do at the party?" repeated Fred Ramsden, wrinkling his brow. "Well, Inspector, what does one do at parties? We talked a lot and told some stories. We had a few drinks. About half-time Mrs. Marshall brought in some grub—sandwiches, cakes, the usual sort of stuff. Nothing wrong in that, is there?"

"No," said Inspector Haddow. "There's nothing wrong in that."

"Well, then, what's all this about?"

"Did you notice anything odd in your host's manner?"

"Nothing whatever. He was as happy as a lark."

"Oh, he was, was he?"

"Yes, he was. And, while we're on the subject, I don't know that I care much for your manner."

"At a more suitable time," said the Inspector blandly, "I'll listen to any personal criticisms you may care to make. For the present, let's keep to the party. You talked. You told stories. You ate and drank. Is that all you did? No cards? No parlour games?"

"No cards," snapped Fred. "No parlour games. It was just like I've told you. Wait a bit, though. We have a Treasure Hunt. Phil hid the drinks and made us look for them. Is that against the law?"

"Where did you look?"

"All over the place. Under beds. In cupboards. Everywhere you could hide a bottle."

...Or a body, the Inspector added silently.

"You searched the whole flat? None of the rooms were locked?"

"I just told you we searched the whole flat. That ought to be good enough."

"Yes," said the Inspector thoughtfully, "That ought to be good enough."

Reflectively, he tapped his desk with a pencil.

"With me," remarked Fred pointedly, "time is money."

"You may go. I'll see Mrs. Ramsden now, Sergeant."

"She can't tell you any more than I have," objected Fred.

"Be good enough," said the Inspector curtly, "to let her tell me so herself."

*

"Why, no," said Mrs. Ramsden, opening her eyes wide, "Mr. Marshall didn't seem the least upset. He was the life and soul of the party."

"About this Treasure Hunt. Did you take part in it?"

"Yes." She giggled. "I found the Scotch."

"Where was it hidden?"

"In Mr. Marshall's wardrobe."

"I see." The Inspector stared at the ceiling. "Now, Mrs.

Ramsden, you're a housewife. You women have your little domestic secrets—private belongings you wouldn't want even your best friends prying into. You know the sort of thing I mean?"

"I think so."

"I thought you might. And naturally, if you were having a Treasure Hunt in your house, you'd warn your guests to keep away from any special preserves. I suppose that's what Mr. Marshall did. Told you that you were free of the place, except for—except for—"

"But he didn't. Oh, dear no. We went everywhere. But absolutely everywhere. It was great fun."

"I'm sure it was. Good afternoon, Mrs. Ramsden."

"Good afternoon, Inspector."

*

"I don't know what you want me to say," exploded John impatiently. "I've told you over and over again every single thing that happened last night. A handful of friends having a good time together, that's all there was to it. What more do you want of me? What on earth is all this about, anyway?"

"Did your father leave the flat, even for a few minutes, during this party?"

"I've answered that already. The answer is still no. And he didn't seem to have anything on his mind. And there wasn't anything on his mind. If there had been, could he have sat there telling stories? Damned good stories, too. What's he supposed to have done? Are you holding him?"

"And you and the Ramsdens searched the whole flat—the *whole* flat?"

"That's what I said. The whole flat. There's only three rooms and a bathroom and kitchenette. Good Lord, man, what more do you want? Do you think there was a body hidden in it, or something?"

"If I did," said the Inspector quietly, "I don't any longer."

*

"No, he didn't go out again after I went to bed," said Mary positively. Her hands were clasping and unclasping on her lap. "I am a very light sleeper. I should have heard him. Inspector, won't you please tell me the meaning of all these questions? Where is my husband? What do you want with him?"

"He is waiting in another room," said the Inspector gently. "You can leave together now. I shan't require him any longer."

*

A few minutes later, to his amazement, Philip was walking away from New Scotland Yard with Mary on his arm. Free. He could hardly believe it. The bottle—the ice-cold red-hot bottle that could have hanged him—was still in his pocket.

*

"What could I do but let him go?" asked Inspector Haddow crossly. "He didn't do it. He couldn't have done it. We know Simmons was kept somewhere in a drugged condition for hours before he was murdered. With the flat full of people, where could Marshall have hidden him? And that Treasure Hunt. That clinches it."

"Almost too neatly," murmured Sergeant Huxley. "As though he knew he'd be suspected and arranged the Treasure Hunt to prove himself innocent."

"Yes, it does look a bit like that. But the fact remains, Simmons could not have been hidden in that flat. And that being so, Marshall didn't kill him."

"Which brings us," said Sergeant Huxley, in a slow, lingering, almost affectionate tone, "to the other suspect."

Chapter 21

Walking along Holborn one evening a week or so later, on his way home from the office, Philip noticed a woman coming toward him whose appearance struck a chord in his memory. She was tall and carried herself like a queen but her face was an alabaster tomb in which two demented eyes were buried alive. To avert his gaze and go quickly by was his first impulse but something within him too strong to be denied made him halt and raise his hat. The woman looked at him as dispassionately as if he were one of the lines on the pavement. Plainly, she did not know who he was; as plainly, she did not care.

"My name is Marshall." The words crushed in his throat and came out flat. "I knew your husband, Mrs. Simmons."

One lifted eyebrow asked a question—*what is that to me*? —and at the same time rejected an answer. For seconds that felt like hours they stood looking at each other and then, in a tone which had been through the frustration of impatience, the futility of anger, and had come to know but one emotion, indifference. She said: "I remember now. One night you brought him home. I couldn't make out why you bothered."

Philip tried again. "I was sorry to hear of his death."

She said: "Were you?"

Desperately, Philip blurted out: "Please forgive me for stopping you. I wouldn't have, only—only, I couldn't help it. I felt you were in trouble. If you are and I can help you have only to say so."

"Now I know why you brought him home. It's the Good Samaritan in you. A sort of complex."

"It isn't that at all. It's only—only—"

"I'm in trouble, all right," said Mrs. Simmons, with a laugh that was not pleasant to hear, "but there's nothing you could do about it."

"Won't you tell me what's wrong?"

"Why should I?"

"If you put it like that, I'm afraid I don't know."

Again, she laughed, with a frantic urgency. For a moment the mask dropped and she was neither cold, nor dead, nor aloof, but only frightened and on edge with worry.

"God knows I've got to tell someone or go mad," she said, more to herself than to Philip.

"Is it as bad as that?"

"It's worse than that. Worse than you could imagine."

"There's a little teashop round the corner where we could talk in peace."

"Where the atmosphere is so quiet and sane and normal that a poor woman who's going crazy couldn't possibly be such a cad as to make a scene? Very well, Mr. Marshall. Let's go there. Perhaps it'll help me keep my feet on the ground. But I warn you, you may get more than you bargain for."

At a table with an orange-checked cloth Philip ordered tea. Mrs. Simmons watched him with an ironic glint in her eyes. When the waitress left them, she remarked almost casually: "The police think I murdered Gilbert."

"Good God!" exclaimed Philip. His eyes opened wide.

"I knew you'd say that. But the police theory is perfectly logical. Someone murdered him—and I had every reason to."

"But you didn't."

"No, I didn't. I can't for the life of me think why not."

"They can't really suspect you. Probably they've asked a lot of searching questions and seemed to doubt the answers, but that's only the official manner."

"I'm not quite a fool, Mr. Marshall. They suspect me. I'm

quite certain of that. A plain-clothes man follows me wherever I go. He's hovering around when I come out in the morning and he sees me home at night. I only got rid of him today by going where he couldn't follow and leaving in haste by another door."

"But it—it's absurd. It's ridiculous."

"Not so absurd. Not so ridiculous. I've wished Gilbert dead a hundred times—and said as much, to people who turn out to have inconveniently long memories. And the police caught me in a lie at the start. I told them I was at home in bed at the time Gilbert was murdered. When they found out I wasn't, there was nothing else I could tell them."

"A lie isn't as serious as all that, even when told to the police. You can put matters right by telling them the truth."

"No, I can't. The truth is the last thing I shall tell them."

"Why not?"

"Never mind why not."

"In a matter of life and death—"

"They can hang me," she replied fiercely. "Do you think I should care? Gilbert strangled my soul; they might as well finish his work."

"They won't hang you," said Philip soberly, "but they'll find a way to make you tell the truth."

"I'll never tell them that," she retorted, and he did not for a moment doubt that she meant it.

Philip stared at her in silence for a while. At first, she met his gaze defiantly and then she averted her eyes.

"As long as the police think you are guilty, they aren't likely to discover the truth," he said slowly. "But when one starts with the premise that you're innocent, the answer is fairly simple. You'll forgive me, but there's a man in this, isn't there?"

"You think you're damned clever, don't you?" she jeered—but her mask had broken into a thousand pieces. "The clear logic of the masculine mind—not to mention its vanity—produces the inevitable solution. There's always got to be a man in everything, hasn't there? Well, this time there isn't. There's no man in this, so get the idea out of your head."

"I'm sorry," said Philip humbly.

Mrs. Simmons sat glaring at a point in mid-air above his head. "Why should I tell you anything?" Her mouth was quivering.

"You've got to tell someone," said Philip gently. "And you can trust me. I'd tear out my tongue before I betrayed your confidence."

The fires of hell burned in her eyes. Her finger-nails, blood-red and pointed, dug into the palms of her hands.

"I can't let him in for this," she said; and her tears were none the less bitter because they were unshed. "It wouldn't be fair. It isn't only that he's married and has children he adores. It's his work. That's great and important, greater than human issues, too important to be jeopardized. He means something to the world, something noble and fine."

"And yet he's willing to let you shoulder the blame for something you didn't do, when a word from him would clear you."

"He doesn't know I'm suspected," she said angrily. "Do you think I'd tell him?"

"There needn't be a scandal. He could go to the police, satisfy them that you were with him at the time of the murder, and that would be the end of it."

"And the end of everything for me. I'd lose him. If that happened, I wouldn't want to live."

"He wouldn't blame you for something you couldn't help."

"You think not? How innocent you are. He's no hero. For all his importance, he's a man, like other men. Since Adam and Eve, men have been blaming women for things they couldn't help. And, even if he didn't blame me, he'd never want to see me again. It would be all over between us and I'd have no right to complain. It would hurt him as well as me, but he'd cut me out of his life and heart without hesitation.

"In the beginning, we were honest with each other. We laid our cards on the table, every single one. There was his work. His home. His family. All these had come first. Nothing could be allowed to touch them. If our—our friendship so much as threatened them, it must end. . .just like that...

"That's the way it had to be. I agreed to it. What else could I do? I love him more than I can say; more than you'd understand even if I were able to express it. No matter how little of himself he could spare me, I needed that little so very much. Well, we made a bargain and I'm keeping it. If I broke faith with him, I'd have nothing—not even the last poor tattered remnant of my self-respect. Don't bother to tell me he isn't worth it. I know that. No man is. But there you are. I've taken a stand and I'm going to dig in and hold to it while there's a breath left in my body.

"Don't look like that," she added, with the wan ghost of a smile. "Poor little man, I've made you miserable."

Philip did not speak. There was nothing he could say. Nothing unless he confessed to her the truth about her husband's death. Any other words would reek of sham and hypocrisy.

"If it came to a trial," she said, her lips taut, "he'd have to know. He'd come forward. Thinking of that is what drives me frantic. As long as the police merely suspect me, I can bear it. But if it came to a trial—Well, it won't. I'll see to that."

"What do you mean?"

He knew perfectly well what she meant.

"There are such things as emergency exits," she said quietly.

Reaching out convulsively, Philip gripped her hand in fingers that shook. "Don't talk like that. Don't even think like that.

In a little while this burden will be lifted from your shoulders. I promise you."

"You sound as though you were quite certain of it."

"I am," he told her positively.

Sceptically, her tired eyes searched his face. "I don't see how you can be. But—it's funny, I'm half inclined to believe you."

Chapter 22

This is where I was born, thought Philip, this little shop in the Finchley Road. Surely it was not always so very small? He had not been near it for almost thirty years. He did not quite know why he had come to look at it now, on the heels of his meeting with Mrs. Simmons. The shop had a hangdog air. Much taller and more modern buildings shouldered it arrogantly on either side, emphasizing its shabbiness and decay. It had a hot, stale, malodorous breath. It was a fried-fish shop now.

In my time, thought Philip, it was a drapery establishment, presided over by my father, a small harassed man in a black coat which he inked at the seams where it showed its age the most. He sold reels of cotton and lengths of elastic during the day and worried about bills half the night. Always, day and night, the spectre of impending bankruptcy peered over his shoulder and gibbered in his ear. His head was inclined a little to one side, as if he were listening to it, and his face wore a perpetual nervous frown. On his desk in a gloomy corner at the rear of the shop stood a spindle on which a sheaf of urgent demands was spiked. Rent. Rates. Overdue accounts from wholesalers. The bills of the grocer, the butcher, the baker, the milkman. He paid a little here and a little there but the sheaf grew perceptibly thicker. He was like a man shovelling for dear life to hold back an avalanche.

He employed a no-longer-young woman in a shiny black blouse buttoned to the throat, a long black dress, black cotton stockings and white collar and cuffs. He could have supplied the wants of his few customers without her help, and her meagre wages were a severe drain on him, but he never for a moment considered dispensing with her services. It would not have been in keeping with his dignity as a tradesman to stand alone behind his counter. For the sake of appearances, it was necessary for him to have an assistant.

Respectability was the altar on which he and my faded, resigned mother sacrificed themselves to the God of shabby gentility. For the sake of appearances, my mother had a servant girl, although we never had quite enough to eat. For the sake of appearances, I was sent as a small boy to a private school that boasted a smart cap and blazer, although the fees were paid in drops of my father's anaemic blood. None of the masters was properly qualified, but they made up for that by wearing mortarboards and gowns. The council school offered a sounder grounding in the essentials but it was open to the poorest of the poor, which rendered it out of the question for the son of a respectable tradesman. Besides, the private school held an annual Speech Day at which prizes were presented by the stout wife of a suburban mayor and parents in their Sunday best took tea in a striped marquee and were at liberty to imagine that their sons attended a minor Eton or a lesser Harrow.

We lived above the shop in five dark rooms with snowy lace curtains on the windows. My mother's life was one long fight against dirt. No matter how tired she might be, she was always ready to seize a duster and fly at a speck of dust as ferociously as if it were a mortal enemy. The parlour was full of very solid, very ugly mahogany furniture on which a high polish was kept by the sweat of the servant girl's brow and it contained ninety-two china ornaments—I once counted them—which my mother washed in ammonia and water once a week with fanatical regularity. Cleansing the ornaments and keeping the curtains so beautifully white gave her the hands of an overworked charwoman but when she went out, she invariably wore gloves.

When I was eight, I found a stray mongrel and pleaded and

wept to be allowed to keep him. My parents loved me and were kind, but they refused and whipped me when I insisted. He would have brought in mud on his small paws and my mother already had more to do than she could manage. He would be one more mouth to feed and, in our house, there were no leftovers. The few shillings to be paid every year for his licence would be a strain on our budget, we were as poor as that.

For the most part, bread and butter and tea was our staple diet. The butter might have been painted on with a camel-hair brush. When we had company a huge Dundee cake was brought out and I used to plot and scheme for an extra slice before the callers left and the cake was returned to its tightly-lidded tin. On Sundays we had one of the cheaper joints of beef and mutton but there were no second helpings, for it had to last the first three days of the following week. With the deftness of long practise, my father carved it paper-thin.

On Sunday mornings my father donned his frockcoat, laid away in mothballs through the week, and his striped trousers, which kept their crease between sheets of brown paper under the mattress of his bed, and his glossy silk hat, of which the brushing took him a good half-hour, and my mother put on her lavender silk dress and her feather boa and her grey silk toque and her grey gloves, and I, who had been scrubbed standing up in a zinc tub the night before, was dressed by the servant girl in my sailor suit and button boots, and we sallied forth to church. There we worshipped our genteel gods and took approving note of our worthy neighbours who did likewise and were approved by them. After the service we walked home slowly by the longest way, bowing in the prescribed manner to acquaintances and stopping here and there to exchange small courtesies with the families of other local tradesmen. This half-hour was my parents' Sunday reward for the scraping and pinching and working and worrying that was their lot throughout the week.

Sometimes on the homeward stroll we passed a Salvation Army band, its members, in hideous blue and red uniforms, blowing cornets and pounding drums and shaking tambourines and chanting hymns un-melodiously. After they had blown and banged and sung one of them— a middle-aged man with a thin red nose, spectacles, and hair ragged at the back, or a worn pallid woman with no bosom and her hair done in a bun at the nape of the neck—would step into the middle of the circle and shout and exhort in a hoarse voice while the other Salvationists stood round, shivering in winter with their coat collars turned up and drips on the ends of their noses or sweating in Summer.

My father and mother always walked on stiffly, pretending that the band had no existence, but I used to screw my head round to stare and it absorbed me so much that sometimes I walked into a lamppost and went on with a bump on my forehead. When I tried to dally my father would jerk me on by the hand and say in a tone of annoyance that he really did not know why the Salvation Army came into our neighbourhood disturbing the peace with their infernal row; nobody wanted to listen to them, except the ragged children who followed their brassy procession, and they, too, let down the tone of the district.

After Sunday dinner, which we had at two in the afternoon, my parents settled themselves in the parlour in front of a fire that was seldom more than one coal and a wisp of smoke and I was despatched to Sunday School with a penny for the collection in my moist palm. Quite often I stopped at a sweetshop, run by an Italian who kept open on Sundays (to the horror of all right-minded people), and spent the collection penny.

At the beginning of the afternoon, you sat with your class on one of the long wooden benches which were placed one behind the other down the length of a large hall. The pupils were graded by ages; the toddlers occupying the front benches and the largest children those at the rear. First you sang a hymn, accompanied by a hesitant organ, played by a young lady with a pigtail, and the superintendent, a very clean, pink man with a large moustache, conducted with a stump of pencil. After that you listened or not while the superintendent addressed you in vague terms on Being Good, read a passage from the Bible, and sometimes made a few remarks about Boys Who Went Out Noisily Last Sunday. The guilty parties were older boys, sitting at the rear of the room, and they did not hear his remarks because they were kicking each other, exchanging dubious jokes and giggling, to the despair of their teacher. A teacher sat at the end of each bench and mouthed threats and shook fingers at the bad boys but, if two or three others were between the culprits and the teacher, they paid no attention.

Afterwards, each class trooped with its teacher into one of the alcoves that lined the hall and there we had a Bible Lesson which started with the teacher asking how much was remembered from the previous week. One or two children could rattle off the previous lesson from beginning to end but I could never remember even what it was about. The teacher was a prim young lady and when I could not answer the simplest of questions she would turn fondly to a little girl with long golden ringlets and say, "I'm sure you know, dear." The little girl always did know and she imparted her knowledge with glib superiority. The teacher would say, "There, aren't you ashamed of yourself, a big boy like you letting a little girl beat you." I was not in the least ashamed but longed to smack the little girl's head.

Then an envelope was passed round for the collection pennies and the teacher had her eye on me, so I did not get away with my pretence of dropping in an imaginary penny. No use telling her I had lost my penny on the way from home, since I had been chewing caramels all afternoon. Her eyes made me feel as if I had robbed a blind man's cup, and I kicked any boy who laughed at my discomfiture.

After the Bible Lesson we clattered back to the benches and sang more hymns, this time in louder voice, for the dusk was drawing in and we felt the spirit of them more; and the superintendent read out some announcements. I seldom listened, for I felt guilty when the amount of the collection was read, and the other announcements were dry stuff about the Church Lads' Brigade and the Missions to foreign lands. But once the superintendent made an announcement that gave me the most poignant hour of my life.

He spoke about a boy of eight, a pupil of the Sunday School, who had died, and he asked us to pray for his soul. He touched on the boy's goodness and purity and on the lingering illness that had carried him off. I had not known the boy, had never seen him that I could recall, but I have never felt a death more keenly. With the dusk creeping in to darken the long hall, I could almost feel the dead boy's presence at my side. He was more real to me than the children whose elbows rubbed mine. I could see his smiling face and straight, well-formed body. I knew we should have been friends if this dead boy had only lived. I should have liked him and he would have liked me. I was filled with a sense of irretrievable loss.

If anyone had spoken to me on the way home, I should have burst into tears.

All my life I have been hungry for friendship. You could call it a complex, I suppose. Did it have its roots in the creeping dusk of that unforgettable Sunday afternoon when I mourned for a dead boy I had never known?

I was, of course, very small and thin and undernourished.

At school I was nearly a dunce but got good reports because the headmaster, who was also the proprietor, feared my parents would take me away if they realized how poorly I was progressing. He could not afford to lose the fees for even one small boy for he, too, lived on the brink of insolvency. All the boys in the school took home good reports. On Speech Day there were almost as many prizes as pupils and it was proof the ingenuity of the headmaster that he was never at loss for a pretext on which to award one to even the biggest dullard. The prizes were always books from a publisher's remaindered stock which he bought for next to nothing. They were unreadable but the bindings looked expensive and that, after all, was what counted.

Coming in from school one evening at the age of eleven I was met by my father, who rubbed his hands together and asked me how I would like a baby brother or sister. I said I'd like one very much, for preference a brother. My father tried hard to appear elated over the coming addition to the family but there was a scared look in his eyes. The thought of the expense involved in childbirth must have frightened him like the devil. Not to mention another mouth to feed.

We told each other how glad we were about this baby that was on the way (it was only a day or so off when my father thought it not indecent to tell me) but, of the three members of the family, I was the only one who was genuinely happy about it. Now that I was to have a brother—for, of course, it would be a boy—I would no longer be so sadly often alone.

The next evening when I came home my father was absent from the shop for the first time on a weekday that I could remember. On one side of the counter his no-longer-young assistant was in a flood of tears and on the other a customer stood gaping at her in bewilderment. "I only asked for a yard and a half of percale," said the customer, when I came into the shop.

The assistant looked at me and then at the stairs leading to the living quarters and wept more copiously than before. I went up the stairs two at a time. My father met me at the top. For a moment I thought he was going to box my ears for coming up with such a clatter. I asked him about my baby brother. In the despairing but resigned tone he always used when speaking of money to my mother, he told me I was not to have a brother. In sudden fright, I begged him not to look like that. I didn't mind, at least, not very much.

And then he told me I no longer had a mother.

I cried a lot that night. Dry-eyed, he nursed me in his arms. His world must have been shattered about him but he showed no emotion. The agony he felt burned, hidden, inside him. It would have been easier if he had been able to go out and get drunk. But he could not do that. It would not have been respectable, and respectability was all he had left.

Before the funeral, a couple of days later, he asked if I wanted to see my mother for the last time. I had loved her but the suggestion frightened me. He saw my fear and said no more about it.

I had a new black suit for the funeral; there were six carriages for the mourners; the headstone for the grave cost fifteen pounds. All this expense almost pushed the little shop into the hands of the receiver then and there, but my father felt that these things were necessary and important, that he owed them to the wife he had loved.

When we returned from the cemetery, he took me upon his knee once more. He was far from being a demonstrative man and until my mother's death I had not been on his knee for years.

"We have only each other now, Philip," he said.

I felt closer to him than ever before, closer than I have been since to anyone but John. It is wonderful and rarely lovely to be completely in tune with another being.

From then on, his hopes were centred on me. I was to be the vindication of the two drab and frustrated lives. I was to grow up to be someone of importance in the world. Most of the professions were barred to me because of the cost of training for them, but there was the Civil Service. I could enter it by passing an examination at the age of fifteen, and once in I could work hard and study and apply myself and pass more examinations. There was no reason why I should not go right to the top and become one of those exalted beings who guide the destiny of the Empire. For services rendered to a grateful country I might even receive the accolade of respectability; a knighthood.

"Sir Philip Marshall," my father said, rolling title and name lovingly on his tongue. That sounded all right, didn't it?

He called on my headmaster, told him the more modest of his plans for me and inquired whether the private school could undertake to equip me for passing the initial examination, on which so much depended, when the time came. Most solemnly, the proprietor assured him that it could, indeed. I was progressing excellently, he said. True, I was not a quick boy, but mental nimbleness was not everything, nor even greatly to be desired. Slow but sure was the thing. My father need have no misgivings. When the time came I would be ready. St. Mark's School for the Sons of Gentlemen would see to that...

During the next four years my little father seemed to shrink into himself. Sitting at his desk at the cavernous rear of the shop, he looked like a gnome. He was a dying man these four years, but his determination to see me launched on the world kept him, miraculously, alive.

Meanwhile, the proprietor of the private school sweated, to stuff into me the required knowledge for passing the Civil Service examination. He swotted up the subjects as we went along, but he was a slow-witted man and never more than a page or two ahead of me in any of the textbooks. We tried hard, but it was as if we had entered three-legged in a marathon.

On the day I went up for the examination my father fainted behind his counter and a doctor was called in. Until then he had refused to have medical advice because of the expense it would entail. It was now too late. The growth destroying him had almost finished its work. That night, when I went to see him in hospital, I was shocked at how ill he looked. He asked me eagerly how I thought I had done. I told him I thought I had done pretty well.

Every day I went to the hospital. At each visit he realized that a little more life had ebbed out of him since the last, but on the day when the examination results were out, I found him sitting up in bed, with feverish impatience. All he could say was:

"Well?"

I told him I had passed. He fell back on the pillow and a sigh fluttered through his bloodless lips. "Thank God for that," he whispered.

He need not hold on any longer. It was obvious relief.

After his funeral the executors sold the shop, lock stock and barrel, for what it would fetch, and another bloodless little man took up the struggle with bankruptcy. My father's creditors received a few shillings in the pound of their claims. All his life my father considered it almost the least respectable thing one could do was to die insolvent, but there are limits to what a harassed little man can accomplish.

The executors made overtures on my behalf to one the wholesalers who had supplied my father and I was given a junior clerkship in the counting-house of this firm; for, of course, I had not come anywhere near passing the Civil Service examination.

If I thought I had been lonely before, the six or seven years immediately following, taught me what loneliness really is.

There was no one in the world who cared a button for me and I had no facility for making friends. There was nothing about me to attract the liking of others. I was dull; I was insignificant; I could do nothing well; and I had precious little money.

Because time lay heavily on my hands, I concentrated on my work and became, as much to my surprise as anyone's, efficient at it.

I met Cora, who worked in the same office. She had no friends either. It seemed natural for us to drift together. I took her to one or two theatres, in the gallery. We walked in Hyde Park on Sunday afternoons. One drizzling wet evening she made the occasion even more moist by bursting into tears because I didn't love her. I had no experience in coping with a woman in tears. It was the most embarrassing incident of my life. In a panic, to make her stop crying, I did the only thing I could think of; I told her I did love her.

We became engaged on the spot. I tried hard to love her. I did my best to clothe her in glamour for me, at least. For a time, I almost succeeded. It isn't really hard to fool yourself when you are young and lonely. And then came the chance of a better job with Sturgis & Mathews and I took it and we were married.

It was not long before I realized what a fool I had made of myself, but it was then too late. I had made my bed and I must lie in it.

When John came, a couple of years later, he made up to me for everything. For the poor thing I was; for the stunted thing my life was and had always been. He made me realize that all one needs for happiness is someone to love.

And then... And then... Oh, hell, why did I come here? Why am I walking along this suburban thoroughfare in which I was born? Why must I remember and go on remembering?

*

While Philip was deep in thought, his feet of their own volition had carried him to within a stone throw of a cemetery. He turned to go back and then, as if a hand tugged at his sleeve, he went on again and through an open gate. He walked between the rows of white crosses and headstones, to one on which was inscribed:

MARY ELIZABETH MARSHALL
1868-1903
EDWARD MARSHALL
1865-1907
R.I.P.

The stillborn baby was buried in the same grave but not mentioned on the headstone. For a long time, Philip stood there, looking at the inscription, thinking and remembering.

He was disturbed by a bent old man with toothless gums and a wispy white beard who shuffled to his side.

"You'll 'ave to think about goin'," the old man mumbled. "I'm lockin' up in a minute."

Philip read the dates on the headstone. "They were young to die," he said to himself, but the old man heard him.

"Lor' love you, we get 'em 'ere all ages. All ages, from little mites of babies to old uns like me. There's no set age for dyin'. You come 'ere when it's time for you to come, no sooner, no later."

"Would there be room for another in this grave?"

The old man stooped with painful slowness to peer at the stone. "There's only two buried 'ere. Lor' love you, there's room for a lot more. Who might it be? One of the same family?"

"Their son," said Philip.

Chapter 23

John said explosively: "But if there's no danger that they'll hang this woman, if she may not even come to trial. I don't see why you must—"

"Do you think hanging's the worst thing that can happen to her?" asked Philip. "If she isn't cleared, this thing will ruin her whole life. I can't do that to her."

"If you give yourself up and they hang you," said Mary, in a voice wrung dry, "it will kill me, too."

"Do you imagine I haven't thought of that? All the way home I've been hag-ridden by worry. Do you think I don't know that I'm breaking your hearts? It would be so much easier to spare you, at the expense of this woman. But how can I do that? She's straight and decent and she's harmed no one. Can I let her go through hell to save my skin and your sorrow?"

"God!" said John, staring at him, "I don't understand you. You've done...done things I daren't even mention and yet... yet you want to surrender your life to spare the suffering of a woman you hardly know. You say yourself that the police can never prove she did it. She'll go free."

"If you call it free."

"All right," said John angrily, "let's look at her side of it. The police will worry her guts for a while and then another case will crop up and they'll leave her alone. Maybe she'll lose this man she loves—"

"Is that a small thing? To lose the one you love?"

"It's on the cards she'll lose him sooner or later. A married man. A hole-in-the-corner romance. That can't last."

"No, it can't last, but while it does, it makes up to her for the misery she's suffered in the past five years. I haven't the right to take a moment of happiness from her."

"Alright, so you rob her of perhaps a few years of happiness. But she doesn't die. Probably, in time, she meets some other man. Look at the reverse side of the picture. You give yourself up. They hang you."

"I've already forfeited my life twice over. Oh, I'll admit that until today my debt to society has not weighed heavily on me. It's funny but I've never thought of myself as a murderer. I wonder if one who kills ever does. There are always reasons—excuses—for killing and in one's mind it is not hard to make them plausible. Yes, the name 'murderer' must always be a shock to the one to whom it is applied. To oneself, you see, one isn't that at all. One has only done something to solve a problem that could be solved in no other way. Killing made me ill, but it was with self-disgust, not remorse. Even now, I am not truly sorry for what I did. It was done in self-preservation. I killed Cora because she would not let me go and Simmons because it was his life or mine. Neither of them mattered to a soul in the world except themselves, that made it easy. But my mind can't squirm its way round the vile thing I shall be doing if I let this woman shoulder my guilt. That's something else again, something fouler than murder, something I cannot do."

"What about John and me," said Mary quietly, "don't we count in this?"

"Mary, for God's sake don't make it harder for me. I know that when I give myself up, I shall be doing something dreadful to both of you. But don't you see, your hurt has come out of something I did a long time ago, something I can't undo."

"There must be another way," said John desperately. "We could clear out of the country. There are places in South America from which they couldn't extradite you. Once out of reach of the law, you could send back a confession to clear this woman."

Philip had already thought of that and rejected the idea as hopelessly impractical.

"You could change your name," said John, and then the light that had dawned in his eyes died out. "No, that's no good. I'm forgetting, you'd need a passport. Oh, hell, surely there's something we could do."

"The passport might be arranged," said Philip thoughtfully. "My firm employs a commercial traveller named Muir, Peter Muir. Some time ago there was talk of sending him abroad to open up new markets. We prepared the necessary papers to obtain a passport for him but the application wasn't made because the idea fell through. The papers are still on file at the office. I could substitute my photograph for his on the application form—"

"That's it," said John eagerly. "That's it."

"The police are no longer bothering about me," Philip went on, displaying more enthusiasm. "It might be weeks before they found out that I'd disappeared. By that time, we could be thousands of miles away."

"Philip," said Mary doubtfully, "don't raise our hopes only to dash them again."

"My dear, I really think it could be done. The *Ascania* sails from Southampton three days from now. It takes ten days to reach Brazil. We could leave some small coastal vessel as soon as we landed. A couple of weeks' grace is all we need, and I don't think the police are likely to check up on me within that time. After all, at the moment, their attention is riveted on the woman I told you about."

"Three days," said John. "That doesn't give us much time."

"So much the better. A long delay might be dangerous. I've

had no holiday this year and this is a slack time at the office. I could have a couple of weeks off at as short notice as I chose. That would lull suspicion as far as the firm is concerned, and it's all the neighbours need know as well—that we've gone on holiday."

"It wouldn't be safe for all three of us to go at once," objected Mary. "If this really can be done, if it isn't a wild impossible dream, you'll have to go alone. Later, when you're safe, we can join you."

"Nonsense," said Philip, sounding enormously self-confident. We'll go together or not at all. We'll have to do it discreetly, but it can be done. Remember the passport you told me you took out when you holidayed abroad with your father? It's in the name of Mary Grey. All you need do is renew it tomorrow. There won't difficulty about that. You, John, can obtain one in your own name. The police aren't in the least interested in your activities. There isn't much to it. A couple of photographs, a form to fill in, a character reference from some person of substance who's known you for a while, that's all. You can have your passport by the day after tomorrow at the latest."

"Sounds easy," said John, with a tinge of apprehension.

"Too easy," said Mary soberly.

"It *is* easy," insisted Philip. "A certain amount of caution is all it will take. Each of us will book passage individually, from different travel agencies. We'll travel to Southampton separately, by different trains. Once on board the ship we'll go to our own cabins and stay there until she is well out at sea. Then we'll meet in my cabin and have a mild celebration—for it will be the beginning of a new life. Three days from now we'll all be born again."

All night they talked, and gradually Philip's enthusiasm infected Mary. For every doubtful question he had an answer, and both Mary and John were sufficiently young and inexperienced to accept what he told them. A new life, a fresh start, were the themes on which he harped, and he made them sound immensely attractive. They wanted to believe in this rosy picture and that made the persuading the simpler. But all the time he knew, only too well he knew, in heart and soul and brain he knew that there could be no fresh start for him.

Chapter 24

An old man exhausted by the journey, the train groaned and grunted into the station. No need for haste, this was Southampton and the last stop, but passengers fell over each other in a scramble for hats and coats and luggage. (Those who had been standing in the corridor, all gathered up and ready, for twenty weary minutes told themselves how right they had been.) John was as eagerly impatient as anyone. A troupe of dancers inside him were doing the Highland Fling. This was exciting, this was too much, there was no room in one body to hold it all. Going away. Going abroad. Throwing off chains. Escaping. Making a fresh start, with a clean sheet, leaving dirty, smoky London for a sun-washed land where the air was worth breathing and there was room to expand. A suitcase barely missing his head and grazed his shoulder, but he hardly felt it.

"It's all right," he babbled. "Quite all right. Please don't mention it."

The owner of the case, a red-faced oldster with a bleached moustache, who hadn't intended to mention it, gave him a glare and mumbled: "Infernal young idiot."

That didn't worry John. Nothing worried John. With salt air in his lungs, sea breeze on his face, what did anything matter but the enormous fact that he was free—no longer a wage-slave—and setting out with those he loved on a grand adventure.

On the dock, waiting in line to show passport and ticket, there was still that gleeful leaping in him. There she was, the towering ship that would carry them away. White paint glistening in the sun. Brass work gleaming. Above her funnels, a gull wheeling and crying.

The formalities were soon over. In a few minutes he was

walking up the sloping gangway and a steward was reaching for his bags.

"Your cabin number, sir?"

John knew it by heart: "B.29." Had he not happily filled it in on a dozen exciting labels?

"Yes, sir. This way, sir."

A glimpse of white sails in a sparkling blue sea, of seagulls exquisite in flight, made John yearn to linger on the deck, feasting his eyes; but he remembered Philip's instructions and followed the man down a companionway and along a corridor. The steward threw open a door, revealing rivet-studded white walls, two prim white berths and, through an open porthole, the dancing sea. There was another man in the cabin already, hanging bright-coloured ties on a hook beside the washstand. His presence made John resentful, although he knew that was foolish. B.29, John's B.29, was as much this other man's as his.

"Forty minutes before we sail, sir," said the steward. "You'll find it pleasant on deck."

John gave him a coin and the steward went out, shutting the door. The cabin-mates looked at each other.

"My name's Forsyth. I see they've given me the lower berth. Hope you're a good sailor."

"Mine's Marshall. About being a good sailor, I don't know."

"Well, you'll find out soon enough."

They shook hands. "Coming on deck?" suggested Forsyth, opening the door. "You'll find the bustle interesting if you've never seen it before."

"I may be up later."

"Oh. Right." Forsyth went out. John crossed the cabin to the porthole and put his head out. The deck and its commotion were on the other side of the ship, which was a pity. On this side, though, there was the sunbathed sea, dimpled, ruffled, always on the move with restless impatience. Little boats with tall white sails heeling in the breeze. Big ships straining at anchor like greyhounds on the leash. Fleecy clouds chasing each other across the sky. Everything in motion, or itching to be.

This period of waiting brought back John's reluctant mind to the reason for their departure from England. If the departure was glorious, the reason was not. He sat on the lower bunk and thought of his father, trying to see through the man Philip appeared to be, to the man he must be. But, somehow, he could not do it. All he could see was the father he had always known and loved. The awful crimes Philip had committed had no more reality for John than bad dreams, soon to be forgotten. They would go away, John and Philip and Mary; they would come to a new land; they would start life all over again; and England and the grimacing horrors they were leaving behind would exist no longer.

Time dragged slowly. Now and then he rose and looked out of the port-hole. Sea. Little boats. Big ships. Gulls wheeling, dipping, screaming. Forever changing, everlastingly the same. And then, when the Highland Fling in him had dwindled to a nervous fluttering, the steel walls began to reverberate to the labouring of the engines, a slow but quickening rhythm pulsed beneath his feet, twin giant screws began to churn the water. The tall ship backed into its own foam, swung slowly from its moorings.

Through the porthole, John watched the sea slipping away beneath, slipping faster and faster and faster. Craning his neck, he was rewarded by a glimpse of the dock and then the ship had its back to shore and he could see the pygmy land-tied figures waving, the wharfs, the still-imprisoned hulls of other ships, the rattling derricks, the swinging bales in mid-air and upward-jutting skeletons of steel that were he knew not what.

He glanced at his watch, mentally noting the time. In an hour he was to go to the cabin of Mr. Peter Muir, the Mr. Muir who was Philip. To kill time, he started to unpack but he was so jumpy that he abandoned the task before it was fairly started. Stretching himself on a bunk, he tried to read a magazine but the printed lines meant nothing. Flutter in his breast. Every nerve tense. An uneasiness was growing in him, a fear that everything might not have been so easy as Philip had predicted. This and that and the next thing, all nagging at him as time crawled by snail-slow.

Before the hour was up, he could wait no longer. He left the cabin and raced upstairs. A large sheet of paper, on which the passengers were listed, was pinned to a noticeboard on an upper deck. He ran his eye down it, looking for the cabin number of Mr. Peter Muir. It was not listed. Bewildered, he scanned the list again, looking not only at the M's but at every name. He saw the name of Mary Grey and his own name, John Marshall, but no Philip Marshall, no Peter Muir. Of course, the omission was a mistake, it must be a mistake.

He went to the purser's office and, in a tight-throated voice, said: "Can you tell me the cabin number, please, of Mr. Peter Muir?"

The purser glanced at an index and shook his head. "Sorry, sir. There's no one of that name on board."

"But I know there is. There must be."

"I'm quite certain there isn't."

"You see," John mumbled, scarcely knowing what he was saying, "he's—he's just got to be on board."

The purser looked at John as though thinking that must be mad. "We haven't a Mr. Muir," he said sharply. "What is your name, sir?"

"My name's Marshall."

"Mr. John Marshall?"

John nodded silently. The purser went on looking him up and down. "May I see your passport, sir?"

In a daze, John handed it over. The purser examined it carefully, raised his brows, and handed it back. From his desk he took a bulky envelope, registered and heavily sealed. "This is for you, Mr. Marshall. Sign here, please."

Numbly, without glancing at the envelope, John took it and scrawled his name on the receipt.

"I've got to get back to land. It's a matter of life and death. I've got to get back to land."

"I don't know how, Mr. Marshall, unless you swim. We're about ten miles out and Rio de Janeiro is the first stop."

There was nothing more to say. John stumbled away. He went downstairs and along a corridor, gaping mistily at the numbers on the cabin doors. He had to put his eyes up close before he could read the numbers. Without knocking, he turned a handle and went into a cabin. Mary was looking out of a porthole. She turned eagerly.

"He isn't on board," said John, without preamble.

Her mouth fell open. "You mean Philip? But he must be."

"He isn't," said John angrily. "I tell you he isn't."

"No," she said, throwing up her hands as though to ward off a menace. "No. You've made a mistake." But in her heart, she knew there was no mistake. At the back of her mind from the start had been a foreboding that something like this would happen. "Oh, my God! John..."

"We've been fools. He made it sound so easy. He isn't on board, Mary. He isn't on board."

"What's that in your hand?"

He looked down stupidly at the registered envelope. "The purser gave it to me."

"Open it. Don't you see, it's from Philip."

John ripped apart the stout parchment and a sheaf of bank-notes fell out. They scattered across the cabin floor. Fifty-pound notes, almost a score of them. Neither Mary nor John spared the money a glance. It wasn't money that mattered, it was Philip.

"Forgive me for the trick I have played. I had to lie to you because you would not have left me if I had told you the truth and the most important thing in the world to me was for you to go. It was a lovely dream, that of us three setting out together to a new life—but there is a radio in every ship to halt a guilty flight and no country left in all the world from which a hunted man cannot be brought back. Don't be afraid for me, for I am not afraid. Don't be unhappy, for as I write this, I know real peace for the first time in many months. Think of me, if you can, with pity, as a squirrel who has been running round and round in a cage for a long time and is at last to be let out. Be glad of my release: I am taking it in the only way I can. It is only when I think of you, the two people I love, that I am unhappy, for I know only too well the misery I have caused you and am causing you now. But you are young and life stretches before you. I know your wounds are deep but time will heal them. Be kind to each other. Of all human qualities that is the loveliest: kindness. I love you so very much.

"Philip."

Mary uttered a cry and fell, senseless, to the floor.

*

Hours later, John paced the deck outside the ship's hospital. He had aged, in that handful of hours. Suffering had ironed the weakness out of his face and replaced it with maturity.

The hospital door opened and a man in white came out. John grasped his arm. "How is she?"

The doctor looked at him gravely.

"Are you the husband? I am sorry to say the child was still-born. There is every hope that we shall save your wife."

"You must save her," cried John frantically, shaking the doctor's arm. "You must, do you hear? My God, she's all I have."

Chapter 25

Alone in the flat, Philip sat in the dark with a glass in his hand, waiting for the police. They were coming at ten. He had made the appointment on the telephone that morning. He had not told them why he wanted them to come, he had said simply: "I shall have something to say to you. No, I can't say it sooner than that."

The intervening hours between morning and night he had needed to make his peace with the hereafter, and to give his mind the pain and pleasure of dwelling lovingly, for the last time, on the two people who alone mattered to him. By this time, they would have read his letter and the hurt of it would be like a sword twisted in them. There had been no way to avoid hurting them; their pain was rooted in the things he had done which no efforts of his could undo. Alone in the flat, in the dark, he shared their wounds and felt their agony. There was but one comforting thought to which he could cling, they were young. Young enough to absorb the hurt, if not forget it.

It would help now, he thought, if I could believe in a personal God. But it was a long time since religion had had any meaning for him. His first and last real impression of a God had been derived at the age of three from a servant girl who planted in his mind a picture of an old man in a nightshirt who wore a long white beard; a prying tyrant who spent his time lurking about in the hope of catching little boys red-handed in mischief. It had taken Philip many years to conquer his fear of this bogey and he had never been able to replace the old man in the nightshirt with a kindlier deity.

Ten o'clock came all too soon and with it Inspector Haddow

and Sergeant Huxley, twin heralds of a finale which, when you thought of it, was only the overture to a new first act.

"A drink?" suggested Philip, indicating decanter, siphon, and glasses on the sideboard.

Inspector Haddow shook his head. He had an idea that shortly he would have to arrest this man and in those circumstances it was not in accordance with etiquette to accept his hospitality.

Philip motioned them to chairs. They perched, stiff-legged, on edge. He lowered himself into a comfortable chair and gazed reflectively at the glass of amber liquid in his hand.

"You have something to say to us?"

"I wish to confess to the murder of Cora Marsh and to that of Gilbert Simmons."

For a moment the police officers were too stunned for speech and then Inspector Haddow stammered: "It is my duty to warn you that anything you say will be taken down and may be used in evidence at your trial."

"I want to tell you about it," said Philip calmly. He told them, very simply and in complete detail and, such was their amazement, he had uttered several sentences before Sergeant Huxley remembered to take out his notebook and write it all down.

After he finished there was silence for a while. And then Inspector Haddow rose slowly to his feet. "Do you know—it's funny—I've wanted all along to get you, and now that I'm arresting you there isn't the least satisfaction in it. Why, damn it all, I'm almost sorry."

"You needn't be sorry, Inspector," said Philip quietly. "You aren't going to arrest me."

He raised his glass and drained it to the last drop. Into the whisky and soda, earlier that evening, he had stirred some of the crystals John had used for killing butterflies.

THE END

DIAMONDS OF DEATH

The Battered Butler

"Cold night," said Constable Green.

"Perishin' cold," agreed Constable Harkness. The wind that blew in Rothernor Square seemed to muster forces and with trebled fury blast the mews behind. Even through their heavy uniform coats it chilled the two policemen. They would have been warmer had they been wearing their helmets. But they were smoking cigarettes into their helmets. Their sergeant was a nosy sort with an eagle eye for the faintest red glow in the darkest alleys. They were taking no chances. The watery moon which rode high above the roof peaks gleamed faintly on the black puddles which dotted the cobblestones. The dark outline of the garages and stables which lined the narrow lane was gaunt and forbidding.

Constable Green nicked the glowing end of his cigarette, put on his helmet, and secreted the stump in an inner pocket. "Got to be movin'," he growled.

The other policeman flipped his cigarette into a puddle. "So long," he said, turning away. "See you later."

Constable Green moved along the lane with slow, ponderous strides, avoiding the oily puddles by instinct and long practice. The ray of his lamp cut the darkness now and then, as he examined a door and tried a handle.

Towards the other end of the mews, he spotted a dark bundle huddled against the wall. He plodded over and directed his light downwards. It was a man, lying face downwards on the cobblestones. His breathing was hoarse, guttural.

Drunk! Thought Constable Green. He tapped the sole of the prostrate man's boot with his toe. "Come on, my lad," he said gruffly, "you can't lie there."

The limp figure did not stir.

Constable Green had a short way with drunks. Bending down, he rolled the man over on his back and jerked his head up with a firm hand on his collar. His light revealed a white face with waxen eyelids and an ugly wound on the forehead.

He dropped on one knee and slid a beefy hand under the unconscious man's waistcoat. Then he rose to his feet, tilted his helmet forward, and scratched his head. He threw a doubtful glance over his shoulder at the back garden gate of a large house which faced Rothenor Square, then turned and ran heavily down the mews in the direction from which he had come.

He found his mate a few hundred yards away.

"There's an unconscious man lying against the wall back there," he grunted breathlessly. "It's Jakes, Count Victor de la Fontaine's butler. There's a nasty bruise on his forehead. He smells of drink, but I never knew the butler who didn't at this time o'night."

Together they went back and stooped over the motionless figure.

"Sergeant told me when I went on duty that the Count and Countess are away for a few days, so p'raps he's been celebratin'," ruminated Constable Green. "Maybe he's fallen downstairs, or he might have had a row with his missis. They don't get along too well. You stay with him while I go and see what's in the wind."

He opened a garden gate and disappeared into the darkness beyond. Following the wavering light of his electric torch, he picked his way across a lawn dotted with shrubbery to the back door of a tall house. The door opened to his touch and he went cautiously into a passage leading from it.

Suddenly he stopped. His light illuminated a tall man in dark clothes standing at the foot of the stairs which led upwards from the passage. A foreign-looking man with a thin, pale face, high cheekbones, arched eyebrows, fringed with a moustache which was hardly more than a dark line on his upper lip, and eyes which seemed to glow oddly. A man who stood quite still, saying nothing, peering unblinkingly into the light...

"Who the blazes are you?" demanded the policeman, growing a shade uncomfortable at the stare of those unfathomable eyes. There was a trace of accent in the voice which replied:

"I am the valet to Count de la Fontaine."

"Never seen you before."

"I have not been here long."

"Um." Constable Green turned his light on the passage walls, found the electric light switch, and turned it on. "Jakes," he began.

"I was looking for him."

"I thought you might be," said Constable Green curtly. He jerked his thumb over his shoulder. "He's out there. Broken head. My mate's with him."

"I see." The foreign-looking gentleman raised his eyebrows. "Monsieur le Count is away. Jakes was a leetle drunk..." He spread his hands expressively.

"And had an accident, eh? Where's his missis?"

"Mees' Jakes is upstairs." There was a momentary pause. "Eef you care to come up—"

"I intend to." The policeman walked to the foot of the stairs. "After you," he said.

The 'valet' smiled and preceded him upstairs. On the ground floor landing, Constable Green halted at the door of a room. The pleasant odour of a good cigar came to his nostrils.

"Who's in there?" he demanded suspiciously.

"Friends of Monsieur le Count."

"Friends? But he's away."

The 'valet' shrugged his shoulders. "Monsieur le Count went

away quite suddenly. He was unable to postpone the visit of a lady and gentleman who were coming to stay with him for a few days. They came. They are to be made comfortable until Monsieur and Madame return."

"Sounds alright," said Constable Green. He scratched the back of his head. "I'll have a word with them."

"But certainly!" The other threw open the door.

Constable Green instinctively took off his helmet as he entered a wide, lofty room, with panelled walls and a parquet floor. In armchairs on either side of a roaring fire a man and a woman in evening dress were sitting.

The woman was young—about twenty-four or five—and had a delicate oval face, exquisitively curved red lips, and curling golden hair. She was expensively gowned, but she had on rather too much make-up. It was applied with artistry, but the fact remained that her pencilled eyebrows, rouged cheeks, and carmined lips struck a note of artificiality, robbing her of really striking beauty.

The man was about forty, tall and broad, with a shrewd, strong face, a dominant nose, and full lips. His hair was lightly powdered with grey at the temples.

"Beg pardon, sir," said Constable Green awkwardly. "I don't mean to intrude, but the fact is...er...the butler..."

"Jakes," interposed the 'valet' smoothly, "has been unwise. He has consumed too much alcoholic refreshment. It is a matter of which Monsieur le Count has frequently spoken. There has been a leetle accident."

A keen glance passed between the 'valet' and the man who smoked a choice cigar in the comfortable chair before the fire.

"I see," said the man in dress clothes. He looked at the woman. "Servants, my dear," he said, shaking his head, with a humorous twinkle in his eye.

The woman uttered a rippling laugh, like the tinkling of silver bells. "I told you his manner was odd while he was serving dinner," she drawled, producing a jade case and selecting a cigarette.

Her companion leaned towards her with a lighted match. "You were perfectly right, my dear," he chuckled. He glanced over his shoulder at the policeman. "I hope he isn't seriously hurt?"

"I don't know, sir. He's unconscious."

"That sounds bad. He'd better be brought in at once."

"Yes, sir. I'll—" Constable Green broke off sharply. He had heard a muffled, but unmistakeable sneeze. It had come from behind an ornamental screen which partitioned off a corner of the room.

"Poor Toto!" said the woman softly. "He has such a dreadful cold in the head!" She smiled at the policeman. "My Pekinese, you know," she added.

"I see, Mum."

But Constable Green was vaguely uneasy. It hadn't sounded like a canine sneeze. It had sounded remarkable human. And in the corner of the room which the screen hid was the safe in which Count Victor de la Fontaine kept his wife's famous diamonds. Constable Green knew that. He had it on the excellent authority of his sergeant, who had bidden him to be extremely watchful of this particular house.

The man in dress clothes rose to his feet and crossed to a table on which stood a decanter of whisky and a soda syphon. The gurgling of liquid and the swishing of soda reassured the policeman. There was something about a man pouring himself such a drink which made everything seem alright. His eye met the forceful gaze of the man in dress clothes, and he fumbled uncomfortably with the strap of his helmet. He turned towards the door. "Sorry to disturb you, sir. I'll help my mate bring in Jakes at once."

"Thanks, Constable."

There it was again! This time it was unmistakeable. A man had sneezed; a man who must be crouching behind the screen which hid the safe! With startling agility for one so heavy, the policeman strode across the room and pushed aside the screen.

His startled gaze took in the picture of a short, burly man in dark clothes kneeling on the floor; of a mattress pressed against the door of the safe; of spilt grey powder on the floor…then instinct warned him of danger.

He wheeled, and for an instant saw the man in dress clothes behind him with one arm raised. Then something heavy crashed on his skull and oblivion overwhelmed him.

The man in dress clothes replaced the leather-covered black-jack in his hip pocket. "That was an uncomfortable moment," he said lightly, dropping into his chair again with his cigar in one hand and the whisky-and-soda in the other. "Everything is ready, Mike?"

"Sure."

"Then get on with it!"

The match flared in the calloused hands of the man behind the safe. He drew back and watched the puff of smoke and flame which ran along the floor and under the mattress.

There was tense moment of silence, then a muffled explosion.

The mattress was thrown back, one side blackened and torn, the feathers strewing the floor, as the door of the safe was wrenched violently from its hinges.

"Good work, Mike!" exclaimed the man in dress clothes, as he knelt beside the safe and tugged open a drawer.

The beautiful woman with golden hair placidly puffed at her cigarette before the fire. When the man in dress clothes left the safe, placing a package in his pocket, she rose from her chair and drew an ermine wrap about her rounded shoulders.

She stepped over the limp body of the unconscious policeman and went out of the room, followed by the three men.

As casually as though they were leaving their own house, they went down the front steps of No. 14 Rothenor Square and entered a sleek, shining limousine which stood at the kerb.

The car glided off into the night...

A few minutes later the shrill blast of a police whistle shattered the silence of the sleeping square.

£5000 for Lost Gems

Bill Peters made his father's letter into a paper boat and floated it on the steaming water. He lay back in the bath with his muscular brown arms behind his head and stared reflectively at the ceiling.

So that was that! Not only had dad refused to advance him two thousand pounds to buy a partnership in a thriving motor agency, he had also stated emphatically that he would not allow Bill another penny unless he went home to Newcastle and went to work in the modern, hygienic soap factory which was William Peters', senior's, pride and joy.

Except to wash him, Bill had no interest in soap. His line was cars. But Dad's letter said: 'Not another penny unless you come home and learn the business.' So that was that!

The paper boat became sodden and sunk. Bill's plans were sunk as well. He had spent all afternoon tinkering with the powerful engine of his car. That was work he knew, work he loved. Making soap wasn't. But unless a miracle happened, he would be in Newcastle making soap within a day or two.

Bill was a square-chinned young man, with broad, muscular shoulders, a face which might have been chiselled out of granite, and blue eyes which could be penetrating and shrewd, or surprisingly mild and friendly. His hands were rough, the hands of a mechanic, with a sure touch for the steering wheel of a car.

When he had rinsed away the grime of a long afternoon, he massaged himself with a Turkish towel until his skin glowed. He dressed and went into his tiny sitting room, where his landlady had already served his dinner. Propping a copy of the *London Evening Herald* against the cruet, he applied himself to nourishment and the day's news.

GIGANTIC DIAMOND ROBBERY

THIEVES ESCAPE WITH £100,000 LOOT!

£5,000 OFFERED FOR RETURN OF GEMS.

"£5,000 reward!" he murmured speculatively. "No soap-making for you, Bill, my boy, if you could get your fingers on those diamonds!"

With five thousand pounds he could buy a partnership, a new car, if he liked, and still have something over for a rainy day…Five thousand pounds! It would put him properly on his feet. He sighed. What was the use of daydreaming? He had less than one chance in a million of earning the reward.

Nevertheless, he read with interest the first few paragraphs which followed the headlines.

In the absence of his master and mistress the previous night, the butler of a wealthy French nobleman living in London had admitted to the house a man and woman of prepossessing appearance who claimed to be friends of his master, desirous of leaving a note to be given to him on his return. The butler had closed the front door and turned to lead the visitors into the drawing room and had known no more until he awoke in hospital with a splitting headache some hours later.

It was obvious from the story of a policeman who found the butler's unconscious body lying in the mews behind the house that the butler had been struck down with a blunt instrument and rendered senseless. Probably he had regained consciousness later, had attempted to give the alarm, but had collapsed just outside the back garden of the house. The policeman who found him…

Bill read no further. He had too much on his mind to be concerned about Count Victor de la Fontaine's vanished diamonds. And the reward was almost as far out of his reach as the moon. His immediate concern was his landlady.

She entered the room as he was finishing his meal. She stood beside the table with her arms folded, looking down at him with a severe expression on her thin face.

"You've had a letter from your father, Mr. Peters?"

"Yes, but…"

"Then you'll be able to pay me?"

Bill reddened. "I'm afraid not, just yet. You see…"

Mrs. Haigh nodded grimly. "I see alright. I haven't lived fifty years with my eyes shut. I shall have to ask you for your room. I'm sorry."

She didn't look sorry. She just looked grim.

"Alright," said Bill wearily. "I'll go."

"If you could let me have a bit on account…"

Bill dug his hands into his trouser pockets and produced his entire resources: a crumpled pound note, a few silver coins, and two coppers. Mrs. Haigh calmly took all but the coppers from his outstretched hand.

"If you could go today…" she suggested.

"I will," said Bill. "At once. I'll send you the balance from Newcastle."

He threw his shaving things and a toothbrush into a bag, put on a hat and raincoat, and left the house. On the pavement he drew a deep breath, then, shrugging his shoulders, fumbled for a cigarette. The case was empty. He crossed the road and entered a tobacconist's, feeling in his pockets for a stray shilling. There was none. His fingers closed on two solitary coppers.

"A packet of Woodbines, please," he said.

The girl stared, but handed him the cigarettes without comment. Bill went down the street and through the wide-open doors of the garage where he kept his car. A grimy mechanic grinned and waved a hand. Bill went over to his shining sports car and looked at it ruefully.

"Shorty," he said to the mechanic, "if you had a choice of parting with this buggy or making soap, which would you do?"

"Mr. Peters," grinned Shorty, "if that car was mine, I'd sweep the streets rather than sell it."

Bill nodded.

"That's the way I feel. How's my credit rating here, Shorty?"

"Good for anything you like Mr. Peters."

"Good for ten gallons of petrol and a couple of quarts of oil?"

Shorty nodded emphatically.

"Thanks," said Bill gratefully. "Fill her up, will you?"

"O.K.," grinned Shorty.

Death in the Car

Leaning from the driving seat of his sports car, Bill Peters cast a gloomy eye over the deserted main street of Brindley. It was almost midnight and the rain was pouring down. The little industrial town, shrouded in darkness, relieved only by the yellow flicker of antiquated gas street lamps, was slumbering peacefully. But for the smooth hum of the car's progress through the town, the place was as silent as a country churchyard. The exhaust's full-throated purr echoed down sleeping streets and cobblestone passages.

At the end of the handful of grimy houses and factories which was Brindley, a dark figure lurched into the rain-swept road. Bill pulled up. In the bright light of his headlamps stood a tramp, ragged and unkept, with a bundle done up in a bandana handkerchief in his hand.

"What's the idea?" shouted Bill. "Suicide?"

The tramp blinked and shaded his eyes. "Going far?" he asked huskily, walking forward.

"Newcastle," growled Bill.

"Gimme a lift?"

Bill hesitated. He had seldom seen a less prepossessing individual than the ragged man who stood at his elbow. But it was a foul night—and Bill could take care of himself. "Alright," he snapped. "Get in."

As he pressed the clutch pedal, he noticed a new-looking motorcycle partially dismantled, leaning against the wall from which the tramp had slouched. "Yours?" he asked doubtfully.

"Is it likely?" grunted the tramp. Settling himself on the front seat.

The retort did not make for conversation. Bill snicked the

gear lever across and the car moved on. The motorbike might be stolen property, he reflected, but in that case it was now out of the tramp's possession.

As he took his hand from the gear lever it brushed against the tramp's shabby jacket, and he felt something which felt ominously like a revolver. Bill glanced sideways at the man beside him, but the tramp dropped his shaggy head on his breast and dozed off.

The rain was clearing a little, and the pale moon transformed the road into a faint silver ribbon threaded through a dark blanket. The powerful car hurtled up the road, its headlights cleaving a path through the darkness, its tyres sucking and swishing on the wet surface, its engine humming smoothly.

Bill kept his eyes glued on the road. It was almost deserted—an occasional glare of headlights looming out of the darkness and a muffled roar as a car travelling towards London went past were the only signs of life—but he hugged his side of the road as though it were teeming with traffic.

He slowed down for a corner, and, as he rounded it, his mouth tightened into a hard line. Out of the dripping mist two glaring headlights leapt at his car. It was a nasty moment. The road was like glass. The oncoming car was heading straight for him. His teeth bit into his lower lip as he braked furiously. His car skidded, then slithered forward, broadside on.

A collision seemed inevitable, but at the last moment the other car swerved off the road and crashed into a telegraph post with a rending of metal and shattering of glass.

Bill pulled up and mopped his damp forehead. The tramp slumbered peacefully.

Out of the wreckage a girl ran toward him. An ermine evening wrap accentuated her tall, slim figure and emphasised the golden beauty of her bare head.

Bill leaned out of the driving seat and she clutched his arm. He switched on his spotlight and shone it on her face. Her eyes were wide with horror.

"Will you help me?" she gasped breathlessly. "You *must* help me!"

For a moment Bill was silent. He was stunned into silence by her beauty. An odd feeling swept over him as he looked at her, an emotion no other girl had ever aroused in him.

She had on too much make-up. She was fragrant with expensive perfume. Her wrap, falling open, revealed a shimmering white dress, cut daringly low. She was exactly the exotic, butterfly type of woman he had always faintly despised.

But as he stared at her numbly, he realised that she was the first woman to come into his life who really mattered. Why, he could not have explained. She was beautiful, but the attraction was more than that. Character was expressed in her face, but even that did not explain the elusive emotion she evoked in him.

"Help you? Of course, I'll help you," he stammered. "I'll do anything..."

"Turn your car, please," she urged. "Take me to London."

Bill laughed unsteadily. "I'll take you anywhere in the world!"

There was something unreal about the whole scene: the girl, the smashed car in the shadows across the road, the raindrops that spattered fitfully on the windscreen; it was like a wild dream from which he would shortly awake.

He climbed out of the driving seat. "I'll take a look at your car," he said. "You'll want to send back for it. I'll find out if it's badly smashed, or if it can be towed or driven in."

The girl grasped his arm and drew him back. "Please don't!" she exclaimed huskily. "Don't go near that car!"

Bill stared. "Good Lord! Why not?"

She shook her head. "I can't tell you."

Bill looked at her thoughtfully.

"There's something about this that I don't understand," he said slowly. "I don't want to appear ungracious, but I'm afraid..."

He walked towards the tangled wreckage.

"Wait!" cried the girl.

He half-turned and saw a pearl-handled revolver gleaming in her hand, pointing at his heart...

"If you go near that car," she whispered tensely, "I'll shoot!"

Bill looked at her with narrowed eyes. He shrugged his shoulders.

"Go ahead," he said, walking across the road.

The girl dived in front of him and jabbed the revolver against his ribs. "Back!" she cried.

Bill raised his arms slowly and stepped back a pace or two. Then, with lightning speed, he brought a clenched fist down on her wrist.

"Sorry," he said, as the revolver clattered on the muddy road. "But you looked just sufficiently determined to pull the trigger!"

He stooped and retrieved the weapon and stood on the running-board of the wrecked car. For several moments he stood there, looking into the driving seat, then he returned to the girl, his face stern and set.

He broke open the revolver and examined the cartridge chambers. One shot had recently been fired...

"So, you've already used your pretty toy," he said.

Crumpled over the steering-wheel of the wrecked car was a dead man...

And a widening patch of crimson on his chest was mute testimony to the cause of his death.

Hand over the Sparklers

The girl shivered and drew her wrap more closely about her. "What are you going to do?" she asked.

Even at that moment, with a dead man lying in a tangle of twisted metal and splintered glass behind them, Bill was conscious of the silver tone of her voice, achingly conscious of her beauty. "He's dead," he said.

"I know."

"Do you realise what that means?" he demanded roughly. "Murder!"

Tears glistened on her long black lashes. "I didn't do it," she whispered.

"You were with him"—he held up the revolver—"One shot has been fired…"

"I can't explain now," she cried. "I'm in danger. Terrible danger. I've got to get away from here—quickly! I'll tell you everything later, but now, won't you please take me to London?"

Bill reflected for a moment. The obviously safe thing to do was to get away as fast as he could from the whole extraordinary tangle. But he could not resist the appeal of the girl, and though he knew he was acting like a fool, he at last nodded his head. "All right," he said. "I'll take you."

They crossed the road to his car.

"But I won't let you out of my sight," he warned her, "until you clear up everything. Get in."

He was about to tell the tramp that the car was going no further toward the North—but the tramp was gone! Bill looked right and left, but he could see no sign of him.

The car hummed back the way it had come and the man and the girl who sat in it, with their eyes fixed ahead as though they were afraid to meet each other's gaze, were silent. It was as though the dead man, his eyes glazed and staring, his breast dark with his own blood, were sitting between them, an insurmountable barrier.

The car was smoothly climbing a long hill when headlights behind shone on the windscreen. The girl gasped and turned her head. "Faster!" she whispered tensely. "For God's sake, faster! They mustn't catch us."

In his driving mirror, Bill saw the lights coming nearer and nearer. The car behind was eating up the road, careless of the greasy surface. Bill tramped the accelerator to the floorboards, and his engine responded with a burst of speed, but the pursuing car continued to gain on them. The speedometer needle quivered between sixty and seventy—suicidal speed on such a road—but the lights behind crept nearer, until the dazzling reflection on the windscreen made driving hazardous, speed impossible.

He was unable to see the road ahead. The nearside wheel grated on the banking and the car swerved across the road. Bill braked hard and hung on the steering wheel with all his muscle and sinew. He regained control, but as he accelerated again, the pursuing car roared past him. It skidded to a halt a hundred yards in front and swung round to block the road.

Three men jumped out and ran back to where Bill had halted his car. The first to reach it was a tall man in evening clothes, who leaned in and smiled sardonically at the girl. "So, you didn't get clear after all?"

"You're on the wrong track!" the girl protested. "He got the sparklers. I had to go with him to get them back."

The other grinned. "Yes?"

Bill felt a tremor pass through the girl's body.

The man in evening clothes threw open the door of the car. "Get out!" he snapped.

Bill's hand went into his pocket. It came up with the pearl-handled revolver between his fingers.

"You fool!" cried the girl. She struck his hand down savagely. As she did so, powerful arms encircled his neck from behind and his head and shoulders were drawn back, half out of the car. He struggled gamely, but was at last pulled out and flung to the ground.

A face peered down into his; a pale thin face, with high cheekbones, arched eyebrows, thin lips fringed with a slight black moustache, and glowing dark eyes. He distinguished a menacing weapon held in slim tapering fingers.

"Don't move," purred a suave voice. "I shouldn't really, if I were you..."

The girl, who had left the car during the struggle, and the tall man in evening clothes were standing together in the middle of the road. The man was holding the girl's wrist in a savage grasp.

The third man, short, burly, and overdressed, swaggered up to the girl.

"Come across," he snarled, with an accent which had come direct from New York. "Hand over the sparklers, or we'll search you right here on the road and find them ourselves."

"I haven't got them," retorted the girl icily.

"No? Then where are they."

She shrugged her shoulders. "How do I know? He had them. Perhaps they're still in the car."

In the glare of the tangled headlights, Bill saw the short, burly man's face and it was grim and menacing.

"You wouldn't fool us, sister?" he growled. "If you did, it'd be just too bad, the things that'd happen to you..."

"That's enough, Mike!" snapped the man in evening clothes. "We'll go back to the wrecked car and find out. I'll take Sheila." He nodded in Bill's direction. "You two bring him."

Bill in the Toils

He drew the girl after him to the car in which the three had overtaken Bill's car. They climbed in and the car reversed across the road and turned back the way it had come. It drove past swiftly and the man who was covering Bill stood up.

"Get up!" he said. "You're coming with us."

With an automatic against his ribs, Bill got into the rear seat of his car and his captor climbed in beside him. The short, burly man took the steering wheel and urged the car at top speed down the dark road.

They drew up with a squealing of brakes when they came to the wrecked car, which was still standing by the roadside with its nose buried in a telegraph post. The other car was parked on the road beside it.

The man in evening clothes walked across the road and stood on the running-board of Bill's machine. "Got 'em!" he exclaimed jubilantly, displaying a square white package. "They were under the cushion on the front seat."

"That's good," said the man whose automatic was pressed against Bill's side. "Then she wasn't lying after all?"

"No. It was she who found them. By the way, there was someone poking about in the wreckage when we drove up..."

The short, burly man drew in his breath with a hiss. "Who was it? A busy?"

The other laughed. "No, only a tramp. He made himself scarce before I could stop him." He turned away. "I'll go on with Sheila," he said over his shoulder. "You two follow. You can drop your passenger. We won't need him any longer."

He walked away, and a moment later an engine started up.

The man who was covering Bill threw open the rear door

and motioned him into the road. Bill had no course but to obey. He was shepherded at the point of the automatic to the grassy bank which flanked the road.

"Stay here for five minutes," said his captor. "This gun is loaded. It would be—unfortunate, shall we say? —if it went off."

He backed slowly and climbed into the front seat of Bill's car. Bill uttered a hoarse shout, but the automatic was pointed unwaveringly at his head. He could do nothing but stand and watch his car being driven away.

At the last moment a dark figure ran from the shadows which hedged the other side of the road. The car spurted down the road with the tramp clinging to the spare wheel at the rear...

Bill was left alone in the darkness.

He was still dizzy and he sat down again. He lit a cigarette and tried to think, but his thoughts ran in circles.

The girl...the dead man...the car that had overtaken them... the 'sparklers'...the man in evening clothes...the theft of his own car...the tramp...the girl...the girl...

Always his thoughts returned to the girl.

Wearily he rose and walked across the road. A gust of wind threw a handful of rain in his face, and from the trees that lined the road dripped icy globules of water. He turned up his coat collar and leaned wearily against the wrecked car.

He stared down at the body which sprawled over the steering wheel...the answer to the whole riddle...if he could only read it...

But dead men do not speak.

A light flashed on his face suddenly and a hand fell heavily on his arm. "What's all this?" demanded a gruff voice at his ear.

And his eyes became accustomed to the light he distinguished the outline of a burly figure topped with a peaked helmet standing at his side...

Bill Bluffs the Law

The light travelled from Bill's face to the wrecked car. It wobbled suddenly as the policeman who held it saw the wide splash of scarlet which stained the breast of the lifeless man in the driving seat. The corpse was not a pleasant thing to look upon, with its waxen white face and glazed staring eyes...

The policeman drew in his breath with a sharp hiss. "My God! Is 'e...is 'e..."

"Yes," said Bill quietly, "he's dead."

The policeman put a hand on the bonnet of the car to steady himself. "First dead man I've seen," he said hoarsely. "Give me quite a turn."

"I know," said Bill.

Remembering the dignity of his uniform, the policeman pulled himself together by an effort, straightened up, and ran the beam of his lamp along the tangled wreckage, illuminating the shattered windscreen, the crumpled mudguards, and dented radiator. "Smash?" he said.

"He was shot before the smash."

"My God!" breathed the policeman again. "Then it's—murder?"

He was quite young and he had never been further afield than the market town of the county. His short term of service had been spent in the quiet country district in which he had been born.

Drunken men he could cope with, or tramps, or petty thieves, or speeding motorists, but murder was beyond him. It took his breath away. Nothing in his slender experience had taught him how to deal with it.

He thought of his little black-bound notebook, which he

produced with a flourish several times a day, impressing and subduing the minor criminals of the neighbourhood, but of what use was it likely to be in the present emergency?

"'oo is 'e?" he asked.

"I haven't the faintest," said Bill. "I don't know anything about him. You see, I—"

But the policeman wasn't listening. Propping his bicycle against the back of the car, he stood on the running-board, swung open the battered door, and leaned over the dead body. He straightened up with a leather wallet in his hand. Holding it open, he shone his light on a visiting card in a celluloid container on one side.

"Richard Burgess, The Jewellers Protective Association, 9a, Hatton Garden," he read in a husky voice.

Bill started. He was beginning to connect things up. 'The sparklers'...the white packet which the man in evening clothes had taken from the smashed car...the dead man, a detective of the famous Jewellers Protective Association...Were Count de la Fontaine's stolen diamonds the answer to the whole riddle?

The policeman put the wallet in his pocket.

"Look here," said Bill, "I'm beginning to see daylight..."

The policeman peered at him suspiciously. He grasped Bill's shoulder with one hand and ran the other roughly over his clothes.

"Looking for the revolver that killed him?" grunted Bill irritably. "You're wasting your time."

"Thrown it away, eh?"

"I never had it. At least, perhaps I had, but only for a few minutes. You see..."

He paused. He was beginning to realise how difficult it was going to be to explain what had happened to this big country yokel.

"In the first place," he said, "I was driving North in my car..."

The constable jerked a large thumb over his shoulder. "The car's pointing South," he said, "and it looks as though the dead 'un 'ad been driving it."

"That isn't my car," retorted Bill.

"Then where is it? I don't see no other about."

"It was stolen."

"Ah! By the murderer, I s'pose?" The tone was mildly sarcastic.

"I don't know. He..."

"Strikes me there's a lot you do know, though you ain't likely to tell it willin'ly."

"Don't be an ass! I know the circumstances are against me, but there's an explanation for that. Don't run away with the idea that I killed this man. Until half an hour ago, I'd never even seen him."

"Strikes me you'd better tell all that to the sergeant. E'll know 'ow to deal with you better than I do."

"Where is the sergeant?"

"At Brinsley. It's a good five-mile walk, so we'd better be startin'."

"But, look here..." protested Bill.

"And it's my duty to—er—to inform you that anything you say will be—will be—" The correct wording of the warning defied the constable's memory. "Well, it'll all be brought up in court," he finished lamely.

Bill suppressed an angry retort. He could imagine what would happen if he went back to Brinsley with the constable. The sergeant would refuse to believe his story and he would be detained in the cells, probably for days. The crooks, with the diamonds in his car, would be well away—out of the country, perhaps—before he was released.

He was sure that he was right, that 'the sparklers' were the stolen diamonds for which a reward of five thousand pounds was offered. The reward would put him financially on his feet. If he worked fast, he had a bare chance of earning it. He had no chance at all if he let this country policeman take him in charge...

There was another reason why his freedom was essential. The girl. He wanted to see her again. It meant everything in the world to him to see her again. And she was in danger. Only by getting to her quickly would be able to help her.

An idea took shape in his mind.

"Turn your light on the road," he said. "See the track of diamond-treaded tyres on the mud? Those marks were made by my car. They lead, I'm almost certain, to the murderer and to a diamond necklace which was stolen in London last night. But the trail's got to be followed at once. A few hours delay will be fatal. And we've got to have help. You get to Brinsley as quickly as you can—or better still, to the nearest 'phone—and summon the police—all Scotland Yard, if you can. When they arrive, follow the track of the diamond-treaded tyres. And for the love of Pete, hurry!"

"Ah!" said the constable phlegmatically, "and what would you be doing all this time?"

Bill shook himself free. A push with his elbow sent the young policeman staggering back.

"I'll be holding the fort until you bring reinforcements," he shouted over his shoulder as he grabbed the policeman's bicycle and straddled the saddle.

The constable uttered an angry roar, but the darkness swallowed up Bill as he pedalled for dear life down the road.

In a Crooks Retreat

Meanwhile the two cars containing the girl and her confederates were speeding away as fast as they were able, from the scene of Bill's discomfiture.

The first car was a tourer, and at over sixty miles an hour its side-screens were poor protection against the wind which tugged and strained at them. The girl drew her wrap closely about her white throat and huddled down in her seat. She shot a glance at the rock-like figure of the man who controlled the steering wheel.

Without taking his eyes from the road, he smiled. "Feeling nervy?" he suggested.

She shook her head. "Why should I?"

"My dear Sheila, you know perfectly well what's going to happen when we arrive at the house. Mike and Von Arnheim are going to ask awkward questions, which you are going to have difficulty in answering."

"And if I don't answer satisfactorily?"

He shrugged his shoulders. "You know Mike. These American crooks are crude but direct in their methods. He'll probably decide that you and your—er—friend, who is now unhappily dead, were conspiring to double-cross us."

"And if he does?"

"Well...Mike thinks with his gun."

Sheila Lavery looked thoughtful. "And you'll let him?"

The man in evening clothes laughed. "I didn't say that. After all, we've got the diamonds back...and I rather like you, Sheila."

"Thanks," said the girl calmly.

The car turned off the road and lurched down a country lane, its wheels skidding and wobbling on the muddy cart ruts.

Sheila looked back and saw the other car following slowly. They bumped along the narrow roadway for a quarter of a mile, then pulled up beside a pair of ornamental iron gates. Marcus climbed out and swung them open, regained his seat, and drove the car through the gates and up a gravel drive to a low rambling house which was shrouded in darkness. On the wide sweep of the lawn which flanked the house stood a giant aeroplane.

Sheila scrambled out and hurriedly took shelter on the porch from the wind and thinning rain. Marcus joined her and a key grated in the lock of the heavy door.

"After you," he said, with an exaggerated air of politeness.

She went into the house and entered a room to the right of the shadowy hall. Marcus followed at her heels, struck a match, and lit an oil-lamp which stood on a table in the middle of the room. The soft light bathed the long, cobwebbed room and she saw the grim faces of Mike Genarro and Frederic von Arnheim in the doorway. They came in and Mike slammed the door. "Let's get down to business," he growled.

"By all means," said Marcus smoothly.

The girl languidly threw off her ermine wrap and knelt beside the ashes which glowed red in the grate. "A cigarette, Gideon," she murmured.

The man in evening clothes extended his case and struck a match for her.

She exhaled a cloud of fragrant smoke and looked into the heart of the dying fire as though it was the only thing in the world in which she was interested.

"Von Arnheim and me," said the short, burly man, jerking a thumb over his shoulder at the tall thin man who stood with his back to the door, "we want an explanation."

"I rather thought you might," said Marcus smoothly.

"What is there to explain?" retorted the girl. "The man who

is lying dead a few miles up the road held up Gideon and stole the diamonds..."

"Exactly," said the man in evening clothes. "He appeared at the French windows with a gun in his hand and commanded me to cough up. Naturally, I coughed up. Can't argue with a gun."

"...I saw him running through the French windows with the packet of diamonds in his hand," continued Sheila. "He ran across the lawn and someone fired three times."

"Me!" said Mike viciously.

"He was hit, but he staggered through the gates and into a car which was parked a few yards down the lane. I followed and jumped into the car just as he was driving away."

"That's what we want to know," snarled Mike. "Why did you go with him?"

The girl flicked ash from her cigarette into the fire. "What would you have done? Let him get away with the diamonds?"

The short, burly man advanced to the table, with an ugly expression on his broad, flat face. "That's alright," he growled. "But where does the other guy come in? The guy whose car you were in when we caught up with you?"

The girl put another log on the fire and watched the tiny red and orange flames which licked at the gnarled bark. "You badly wounded the man who got away with the diamonds," she said slowly, "and he died at the wheel while trying to avert a collision with the other car. The young man pulled up and jumped out of his car. I climbed from the wreckage and asked him to take me to the next town. What else could I do? It would have queered the whole works if I'd let him stay there until you others came up."

"I don't see why," grumbled Mike.

"What does it matter?" retorted Marcus. "Sheila did what

she thought was right. At any rate, we've got the diamonds back and she found them for us. That's the main thing."

He rose and faced the two men. "What about the 'plane?" he demanded. "How soon will it be ready to start?"

"Within an hour or so," replied Von Arnheim. "I have located the trouble. Now I shall soon put it right."

"Good!" snapped Marcus. "We've got to get away at once. We should have been out of the country last night. It was the devil's own luck that your 'plane broke down. We're in a still bigger hurry now. The young man whose car we took won't stand about cooling his heels. He'll go to the police. Sooner or later, they'll track us here, and when they do, we'd better be gone. Get the 'plane ready to leave as soon as you can, Von Arnheim. Need any help?"

"I think not," said Von Arnheim.

He opened the French windows and stepped out; they heard his footsteps crossing the sodden lawn. Mike looked at the windows thoughtfully. "I can't quite make out that guy," he murmured. "Is he on the level, or isn't he? I've got an idea he's only pretending his 'plane is out of order. Maybe he's watching for a chance to grab the sparklers and leave us flat. If the 'plane's really crocked up, why don't he let one of us help him with it?"

"You're too suspicious, Mike," said Marcus. "It's a bad failing. Go outside and patrol the grounds. Give the alarm if you see anyone coming."

Mike Genarro hesitated, then, with narrowed eyes, he crossed the room and looked menacingly down at the girl.

"I ain't satisfied," he growled, "but I'll close my trap for the present. But get this straight—if anything more happens that don't seem on the level, there won't be no conversation. My gat'll talk—and you won't never hear anythin' else in this world!"

He lumbered across the room and disappeared into the garden.

Double-Cross and Check

Marcus chuckled. "So that's that! You spoke your piece very nicely, Sheila. They almost believed you."

The girl looked up and a whisp of blue smoke curled from her chiselled nostrils. "But you didn't?"

"No. I knew better. You tried to get away with the diamonds. The man Mike shot was your accomplice."

The girl was silent.

"You don't deny it, eh? I thought not!"

She looked up. "I found the diamonds for you," she pointed out.

He chuckled again. "I admit it. But isn't it rather funny that just before you made the discovery, I examined the place where you 'found them'—and they weren't there?"

He lit a cigarette. "That, my dear," he said, "was because you had 'em on you. When we overtook you, you were bolting to London with 'em."

Ruefully, he glanced down at the mud stains and dust on his dress clothes. They had intended to fly to the Continent the previous night and when the 'plane broke down they had been forced to spend the night and following day in the deserted house which they had picked for the first step of their getaway.

None of them had had a change of clothing. There was not even water in the house with which to wash. Only the girl had contrived to keep her appearance presentable—none of the men knew how.

"I have a great admiration for you," he said. "Wonderful is the only adjective which can describe a woman who can look so fresh and beautiful as you do in the present circumstances."

"Why didn't you expose me to the others?" asked Sheila.

"And let Mike shoot you! My dear girl, I have a far better idea than that. You and I are going into partnership. Why should we share the diamonds with Von Arnheim and Mike? If they had the chance, they'd double-cross us. We'll anticipate them. We need Von to take us out of the country, but when the plane takes off, we'll be minus Mike. I'll dispose of him."

He took his leather-covered blackjack from his hip pocket and smacked it gently against his palm.

"A pat with this will keep him quiet for hours. Von won't mind; it will be one less to share the spoils. Later, when the 'plane lands on the Continent, we'll find a way to get rid of Von Arnheim. We'll get fifty thousand in Antwerp for the diamonds. You and I, my dear, will live happily ever after on it!"

Sheila flipped the stub of her cigarette into the fire. "If you dispose of me," she murmured, "that would be one less still to share the spoils."

He smiled. "Yes. I thought of that, but I decided against it. You see, I rather like you, Sheila..."

He took her hand and drew her to her feet. "You are beautiful," he whispered, "very beautiful."

His right arm went about her waist, and his left hand tilted her chin upwards. He bent his head. His lips were about to touch hers...

Marcus wheeled with an oath. Standing within the open French windows was the tramp!

A revolver gleamed in his hand!

Madness of Love

To return to Bill. As he made his escape from the very arms of the law, the policeman dashed forward shouting at the top of his voice; but his shouts soon died away as Bill kept the bicycle wheels spinning at breakneck speed.

The old lamp that bobbed perilously beneath the handlebars cast too faint a light to do more than illuminate the few feet of road directly in front. Every mile or so it was necessary to stop and look for the tyre track which was his only clue to the diamonds—and to the girl who, at first sight, had come to mean so much to him. Her face, pale and beautiful, haunted him every yard of the way. He was aware that the thing at which he had always scoffed had happened to him at last. He had fallen in love. She might be a thief. She might be a cheat. She might be everything that was vile. But he loved her.

As he whizzed past, he glimpsed momentarily a break in the hedge which lined the road. He braked suddenly and almost went head over heels over the handlebars. As it was, the bicycle swung round and he landed in a heap on top of it.

Scrambling up, he shone the light upon the road. The track he was following was gone. He picked up the bicycle and plodded back. He found the trail, leading down a rutted lane. Mounting again, he rode along the lane, slithering perilously on the bumpy surface.

A house loomed up out of the gloom. He rode a couple of hundred yards beyond it and looked for the diamond-shaped track. There was no sign of it. Propping the bicycle against the hedge. He went back cautiously and skirted the high wall which surrounded the grounds of the house. A convenient tree leaned invitingly close to the wall. He swarmed up it, peered into the darkness beyond for a moment, then dropped as lightly as a cat on the other side.

Cautiously he crept through the shrubbery which grew in thick clumps along the wall and slipped stealthily out on the spongy turf. As he did so, a dark shape moved beside him and he felt something hard jabbed against his ribs.

"Up with 'em!" growled a husky voice.

Bill raised his arms and glanced sideways at the short, squat figure of his captor. Recognition was mutual.

"How the hell did you get here so fast?" demanded Mike.

"I..."

"Shut up! Start walkin' towards the house—and watch your step. It wouldn't break my heart to plug you."

Bill took a step forward—and sprang back. His hand fell on the wrist which was holding the automatic and twisted it sideways. His knee came up with terrific force to the pit of the other's stomach. Mike collapsed with a groan. Bill secured the automatic and brought the butt down with a thud on the stricken man's skull. Mike rolled over, incapable of interfering for some minutes at least.

With the automatic in his hand, Bill felt his way carefully across the lawn. There was the aeroplane, with a solitary figure tinkering at its engine. Dodging among the trees and bushes which dotted the lawn, he went round to the other side of the house. An oblong splash of light from the open French windows bathed the lawn and shadowed the outline of a man who was standing just inside a room on the first floor. Creeping nearer, Bill recognised the tramp to whom he had given a lift earlier that night. He was speaking!

"Put your hand in your pocket," he was saying, "and produce the diamonds. No, not that pocket—the other. That's right. Lay them on the table. I wouldn't try any trick, if I were you...

Open the packet so that I can see that the diamonds are in it. Now...stand back!

It was time for Bill to interfere. He dug his weapon against the base of the tramp's spine. The tramp stiffened but did not move. "Step into the room," said Bill sternly.

As Bill followed him into the light, his eyes took in the whole amazing scene; the long, cobweb-festooned room; the man in evening clothes and the pale golden-haired girl standing with their arms raised beside the fireplace; the spilled gems sparkling on the dusty table beneath the oil lamp...

"Keep them covered," he directed the tramp. "Shoot the man if he moves, but don't forget, I'll shoot you if you start anything... Walk forward slowly, keeping well to the right of the table."

With the automatic pressed firmly against the tramp's back he ushered him into the middle of the room. He put out a hand, scooped up the diamonds, and dropped them into his pocket.

"Put your gun on the table," he commanded.

As the tramp obeyed, Bill braced a hand against the shabby back, heaved with all his force, and sent him sprawling into the arms of the man in evening clothes. Almost in the same motion he swept the lamp from the table. It crashed to the floor and went out.

Darting forward, he grasped the girl's arm and hustled her across the room and into the hall. He groped his way through the hall, drawing the girl after him, and opened the front door. His car stood invitingly on the gravel drive outside.

"Good egg!" said Bill, dragging the girl breathlessly down the front steps.

Two figures were coming up the drive. One of them was the tall, thin man who had been tinkering with the aeroplane engine. The other was the squat American whom Bill had left unconscious in the shrubbery; he swayed on his feet as he walked.

They were approaching the house cautiously, holding firearms at an angle which meant business.

"That's torn it," Bill muttered, and dragging the girl back into the hall he closed the door.

"Now, what?" he murmured reflectively.

In the room they had left a battle royal was raging. They could hear the grunts and gasps which followed the impacts of fists upon flesh; the wheezing of a strangling man with the adversary's thumb on his windpipe....

There was a thud as a table went over, a tinkling of broken glass, a metallic clatter. A hoarse oath...

"Make up your mind," gasped the girl, "you've almost rushed me off my feet as it is."

"Sorry."

"You needn't be. I love it. You're the fastest worker I've ever met!"

She was close to him. He could feel the soft warmth of her slender body. Her elusive, tantalising fragrance teased his nostrils and went to his head like wine.

He put out his arms and drew her to him. She clung to him in utter surrender. His lips met hers. For moments he knew nothing, felt nothing, but the ecstasy of a kiss which seemed the beginning and end of all existence.

It was madness.

Trapped with the Loot

A few yards from them, on the other side of the front door, stood two grim, menacing figures. In the room on their right, the tramp and Gideon Marcus struggled and fought for mastery...

All that mattered was the girl he loved.

She shivered, and her arm stole from Bill's neck. Her fingers crept down his jacket and paused at a pocket.

It was as though cold water had been dashed in his face. He drew back from her quickly.

His hand dropped swiftly and imprisoned the fingers which were gently extracting the necklace from his pocket.

"I was forgetting," he said bitterly. He held the diamonds up, and they glittered wickedly in the darkness. "For them a man has died...for them, rogues have cheated and conspired...for them every vileness has been committed...for them, you have drugged me with your kisses..."

The girl shuddered. She was seeing the white face and staring eyes of a man who lay miles away, the man who had died for that gleaming noose of fabulous value, cold and white as ice, hard and lifeless as granite. "You think I'm utterly rotten, don't you?" she whispered hoarsely.

"I don't know what to think of you," he groaned.

"If I explained you wouldn't believe me."

"Probably I wouldn't."

The door creaked as a shoulder was pressed against it. Bill dropped the diamonds into his pocket and glanced about him. He distinguished a door at the rear of the hall. Drawing the girl after him, he turned they key which was in the lock and threw the door open. A large cupboard lay beyond.

"Hell is going to break loose in about five seconds," he declared. "You'll be safest in here until it's over."

"But—if anything happened to you…"

"Would you care?"

There was a sob in her voice as she answered: "It would break my heart!"

"If I could only believe you!"

"But you must. It's true!"

Something leaped within Bill, as though a shout were ringing through his heart. His hands trembled as he urged her into the cupboard. "We'll go into the subject fully later on," he said. "There's no time now."

He shut the door on her, locked it, and put the key in his pocket. As he turned, the front door swung open and two dark figures were silhouetted on the threshold.

Bill sprang for the stairs and took them two at a time. A gun barked behind him and a bullet whistled past his ear, burying itself with a thud in the wall.

From the landing above he peered down the stairs. A flash of red and orange stabbed the darkness and another bullet gouged a hole in the plaster above his head, raining a shower of white dust on his shoulders.

He ducked down and tiptoed across the landing. Opening a door, he found himself in an empty room. Ghostly shapes lurked in the shadows. He struck a match, and they resolved themselves into articles of furniture, enshrouded in dust covers. Cobwebs hung from the ceiling, billowing to and fro in the draught of the open door. As the match flickered out, he noticed an antiquated oil lamp with a battered silk shade trimmed with glass beads standing on a rickety table.

He bent over it. A sudden idea had come to him.

A few moments later he slipped noiselessly out of the room.

The stairs behind him creaked beneath cautious feet. Like a shadow he flitted across the landing and up the next flight of stairs.

He tried the doors which flanked the landing above, but they were all locked. He was on the top floor of the house. His refuge was a bare space about fifteen feet square, without protection from bullets from the stair well. He was trapped. When his cartridges were exhausted, he would be at the mercy of the men who were groping their way up the stairs towards him.

He had the diamonds—but how long was he likely to keep them?

He flattened himself on the floor and a bullet whined above his head.

There was a second flash, and he felt a burning pain in his left shoulder.

Shooting to Kill

Something warm and sticky trickled down his arm and dripped from his fingers. His shoulder ached as though with the searing touch of a red-hot poker. Bill set his teeth and fought back a groan. Perspiration beaded his forehead. For a moment he felt sick and dizzy. He shook his head to clear it.

Raising his hand, he looked dully at the dark streaks which ran down the fingers, gleaming faintly in the pale glimmer from the skylight above. Blood. Drops of it glistened on the dusty boards of the floor.

The men below had shot to kill. It was only luck that the bullet had lodged in his shoulder instead of in his head. It would be luck if he escaped alive from the narrow landing on which he was trapped. He remembered what the girl had said:

"...if anything happened to you...it...it...would break my heart!"

"If I could only believe you!" he had groaned.

"But you must! It's true!"

Suddenly he knew that she had meant it. That a miracle had happened to both of them; she had fallen in love with him, as he had with her. His lips set in a hard line. He must come through alive if only for her.

The silence of the landing on which Bill was flattened against the floor emboldened one of the men below. The stairs creaked as he mounted them slowly and peered upward.

Bill saw the vague outline of a face. Poking the muzzle of his weapon through the supports of the balustrade, he fired.

There was a scream and a curse as Mike Genarro stumbled hastily back with a slug in the fleshy part of his arm. From the landing below he fired two rapid shots upward, but was mocked by the 'thud...thud' as the bullets smashed harmlessly into plaster.

Genarro and Von Arnheim retreated out of range of Bill's fire. Mike uttered a colourful flow of profanity as he rolled up his sleeve and examined the ugly wound in his arm.

"We need reinforcements," said Von Arnheim. "Besides, I don't like all this shooting. He is just as likely to kill one of us as we are to account for him."

"Where's Marcus?" growled Mike.

"How should I know? There were sounds of a fight in the room below. We should have investigated first before pursuing this fellow."

"Cut the cackle," retorted Mike. "Find Marcus and bring him here."

Without another word Von Arnheim went softly down the stairs. At the door of the room to the right of the hall he paused and listened, but heard nothing. He opened the door cautiously, his automatic levelled in his hand.

A groan came out of the darkness... "Who's that?" he whispered. "You, Marcus?"

Again, the groan. He struck a match and advanced slowly into the room. His foot kicked against something which emitted a metallic sound and rolled away across the floor. The match flickered out. He lit another and saw Marcus lying on the floor, struggling to rise.

"Mein Gott!" Von Arnheim exclaimed. "What has happened?"

With a careful glance above him, he hurried forward, knelt beside his leader, and raised him with his arm round his shoulders. Marcus swore and pillowed his throbbing head in his hands.

"The lamp..." he muttered feebly, "...on the floor...light it."

Groping for the lamp, the German barked his shins on the overturned table. He jerked it up with an oath, found the lamp and applied a match to the blackened wick. Blinking about him as the light sprang to life, he saw that the room was in a shambles.

Beside Marcus lay the leather-covered blackjack which was his favourite weapon.

"Der Teufel," breathed Von Arnheim, stooping to pick it up. "What has happened? The diamonds...where are they?"

Shakily, Marcus told him what had happened. The German's eyes narrowed. "This tramp...where did he go?"

Marcus felt his head tenderly. "How the devil do I know? We were fighting. I managed to get my blackjack out of my pocket but he grasped it from me. I don't know...he must have coshed me with it. God! My head hurts like the devil!"

Von Arnheim had no time for sympathy. "I see. Then the young man who is trapped above has the diamonds."

His eyes glowed with an unfathomable light as he turned and left the room. He went upstairs and told Mike what had happened.

"We'll get the diamonds back, then," muttered Mike. "It's only a matter of time. The pup can't get away. But this tramp may queer the game. He mustn't escape. Go back and get Marcus. The pair of you'd better find the tramp and put him out of the way."

Von Arnheim did not move. He glanced quizzically upward to the landing where Bill was crouching. "And leave *you* to obtain the diamonds, hein?"

There was a moment of pregnant silence as they eyed each other suspiciously in the darkness. It was broken by an oath.

"Hell!" cried Mike. "You don't think I'd double-cross you? We're pals, ain't we?"

"*Are* we?" answered Von Arnheim softly.

Each of them had a finger on the trigger of his weapon. The same thoughts were revolving in the minds of both. If there had been a certain means of escape with the plunder neither would have hesitated to shoot the other. But they hesitated. First there was Bill to be disposed of…and the tramp.

"Sure, we're pals. And besides, even if I wanted to, I couldn't get away with the stuff alone. How'd I get out of the country? I need you and the 'plane, don't I?"

"There is something in what you say," admitted the German. "As for Marcus…"

"We'll discuss him later," said Mike grimly. "I'm in favour of declaring him out…but the main thing now is to keep that tramp from going for help. Go and find him…you and Marcus."

Von Arnheim wavered. "Alright," he said at last.

At Deadly Grips

He went down the stairs. Mike tiptoed cautiously to the balustrade and peered over. He saw the German entering the room below. For a few moments he pondered his next move, then he whipped out a handkerchief. He put out his hand warily and waved the white square, to attract the attention of the man who was trapped on the landing above.

Bill saw the signal—but he kept his finger on the trigger of his weapon and waited.

"Hey!" whispered Mike hoarsely.

"Yes?"

"I want to talk to you."

Bill cogitated a moment. "Come halfway up the stairs," he said at last. "But put your gun in your pocket first—and keep your hands in front of you."

"O.K.," whispered Mike. "On the level, now, you won't shoot?"

"Not unless you're up to some trick."

The burly little thug edged cautiously up the stairs.

"That's far enough," said Bill sharply. "Now, what is it?"

The grey half-light from the window in the ceiling shone on the flat, ugly face of the American. His beady black eyes were peering into the gloom where Bill was crouching.

"You've got the diamonds?"

"Well?"

Mike moistened his lips. "Let's do a deal. I'll help you get away, and we'll split 'em—fifty-fifty."

Bill smiled. He could imagine what his share of the spoils would be if he were sufficiently unwary to agree—a lead slug. Probably.

"What about the others?" he replied, playing for time.

"Never mind them. I'll take care of Marcus. We'll need Von Arnheim to get out of the country, but an accident'll happen to him when the 'plane lands on the Continent. What do you say?—half the diamonds and a clean getaway—"

"And the girl?"

"I'll take care of her."

"I see."

"Is it a deal?"

As he spoke, Mike came a step nearer. Bill put the muzzle of his automatic through the railings of the balustrade.

"I shouldn't come any nearer, if I were you."

"Use your head," hissed Mike. "It's a fortune for both of us."

"And more likely a bullet for me!"

"What are you talkin' about?" protested Mike in an injured tone. "I'll split fair with you. On the level I will. Give you my word."

"You touch me deeply," Bill chuckled softly. "But I'm not buying it. The truce is over. "I'll give you ten seconds to get back downstairs."

Mike turned away and took a step downwards. He wheeled suddenly; his hand went to his pocket in a lightning movement; there was a flash and a report. A bullet whistled past Bill's ear. As the American ducked, Bill pulled the trigger of his own weapon. There was a harmless click.

He pulled the trigger again with the same result.

Mike chuckled grimly. He fired again—and again. There was a sudden clatter, and he was up the stairs.

Bill scrambled to his feet, and the kick which had been aimed at his head grazed his knee. The burly little thug had been trained in a hard school. He was used to fighting with his fists, his feet, his teeth; there were no fouls in his code.

A vicious blow smashed to the pit of Bill's stomach. Bill doubled up in agony, and the American followed up his advantage with a punch to the jaw and another to the side of the head, which made Bill rock on his feet. Dazed, he stumbled forward, his arms reaching out blindly.

In spite of the rain of blows which bruised and stunned him, he gripped his adversary's shoulder and hung on like grim death. Mike tripped and fell, dragging Bill down on top of him. They rolled over and over in the dust, arms and legs thrashing wildly.

With a quick twist, Mike manoeuvred himself on top. His fingers fastened on Bill's throat. His lips parted and through is clenched teeth came a sound like the snarl of an angry beast. His fingers squeezed relentlessly, until they seemed to be cutting into Bill's neck. The young man kicked and struggled, but the fingers tightened like the jaws of a steel trap.

There was a roar in his ears and sparks of light stabbed his eyeballs. Through a haze he vaguely saw the face of the man who was throttling him, outlined against the skylight, and it was grim and determined.

Only death could end the struggle. Death…

He was losing consciousness, slipping into the abyss of oblivion, when a wild thrust of his knee found its target in the stomach of his adversary. Mike went limp and collapsed on top of him. Summoning his last reserves of strength, Bill heaved him off, and lay panting for breath.

Mike staggered to his feet and wavered for a moment above his opponent. He swung a kick as Bill's head, but Bill sprawled back out of reach and stumbled shakily to his feet before his enemy could collect himself to aim another blow.

Again, the murderous hands were at his throat. Cold sweat broke out on his forehead, as teeth almost met together on the lobe of his ear. He reeled and staggered, clutching feebly at the other's shoulders. The pain was agonising.

He stumbled to his knees and thrust out blindly. The pressure on his throat relaxed as the American stumbled back. Something cracked like a pistol shot; wood splintered and smashed. Mike howled with terror as he toppled backwards, carry the broken balustrade with him.

A sickening thud echoed up the stair well.

Trapped on the Roof

Bill lay full length on the dusty floor and gulped air into his starved lungs. His head was spinning like a merry-go-round. His wounded shoulder throbbed excruciatingly. His whole body was one vast ache. Gingerly he put up a hand and felt his tortured throat.

"Golly!" he croaked. "One more squeeze and my Adam's apple would have been cider!"

He dragged himself to the broken balustrade and peered down. Two flights below, a limp bundle lay on the floor like a dummy of sawdust and rags, with arms spread out and legs sprawled in a grotesque attitude. He realised suddenly that the man at whom he was looking was dead. But he felt no remorse. Only a dull wonder. It had been Bill's life—or his adversary's! His adversary had lost.

A furtive shadow flitted across the hall and bent over the crumpled form. Bill recognised the ragged tramp to whom he had given a lift a few hours before—it seemed an age ago!—and whom he had catapulted into the arms of the man in evening clothes when he had gained possession of the diamonds.

The diamonds! Bill put a hand in his pocket and felt them, ice-cold to the touch—and hard! If the limp figure below was dead, he was the second to die that night for them. Diamonds of death! Would there be other deaths before the morning came?

Already the grey fingers of the dawn were reaching through the skylight, streaking the dusky floor, outlining the ragged, broken ribs of the balustrade.

The tramp looked up. Bill dodged back. He drew himself up slowly and wavered on his feet. God! He felt weak! It was only by a supreme effort that he managed to remain upright.

He mustn't give way to the lethargy which threatened to overwhelm him. There was much to be done. There was the girl to think of. His own life. And the diamonds—but, compared with the girl, they didn't matter.

He staggered round the landing and tried each of the doors again, but they were locked, and he was unable to summon the strength to force them open. As a means of escape there was only the narrow window above his head. By standing on his toes, he could just reach it with his fingertips.

He put a foot on the rail of the balustrade on one side of the jagged gap through which Mike had fallen. Flattening a hand against the wall, he tried to draw himself up. The rail wobbled; he lost his balance and nearly fell into the yawning pit encircled by the stairs.

Resting for a moment, he saw that the tramp had disappeared. There were two men standing over the lifeless body now, Von Arnheim and Marcus. They looked up. It was a matter of moments only, Bill realised, before they would be at his heels. To gain the roof was his only chance.

He tried again and this time, wobbling perilously on the broken rail, with one hand pressed against the wall, he reached the skylight with the other hand and pushed with all his force. To his relief, it fell back with a clatter. As the rail gave way under his weight, he thrust out both hands and clutched the leaden frame.

For a moment he swung in mid-air, then with a herculean effort, which brought blood in a gushing flow from the wound in his shoulder, he drew himself up until his chin was on a level with the roof. Tired muscles responded for the agonising moment it took to draw his body through the narrow aperture. At last, he lay panting on the slates, worn out by the effort.

A warning creak from the stairs below betrayed the approach

of an enemy. Bill lay still and waited. There was a rustle, a hoarse whisper, the sound of laboured breathing, a grunt...

A head appeared through the skylight...

Bill clubbed his automatic and brought it down as hard as he could. There was a howl, a thump, and the head disappeared. He could hear a burst of Teutonic wrath. Von Arnheim, apparently, had been the owner of the head. He heard another voice whispering urgently.

Two chimney stacks, spaced a few feet apart, offered shelter. He crawled across the slippery slates and crouched between them. There was nothing to do but wait for developments—and hope that the policeman he had encountered earlier that night had had sufficient sense to act on his instructions. Reinforcements would save the situation. Without them, the game was up.

Minutes passed while he lay in suspense.

In the grey dawn he began to distinguish the curves and twists of the lane which passed the house and the spreading fields beyond. There was not the slightest sign of a human being. No sign of approaching help. He grinned ruefully as a scrap of rhyme came into his head. No sign of approaching help. He grinned ruefully as a scrap of rhyme came into his head, *'Sister Ann, Sister Ann, do you see anyone coming?'*

An Aerial Crash

Muffled footsteps moved in the garden. Bill listened intently, and heard a scraping noise, then a ladder grated against the gutter a few yards away. He was too exhausted to manage to scramble across the treacherous slates to repel the man he could hear clambering up the ladder. A head appeared cautiously over the edge of the roof. It was Marcus. He peered about him searchingly, then climbed onto the roof.

Bill worked a slate loose with his fingers and threw it. Marcus ducked and flopped down on his stomach. The weapon in his hand barked and a slug chipped the brickwork behind Bill's head. Bill dug out another slate and balanced it in his hand waiting for Marcus to offer him a target. When the other man started to worm his way forward, he threw the slate and it grazed Marcus's head. Another bullet flattened itself against one of the chimneys.

There was a report behind Bill and a bullet whined across the roof, flying off above Marcus's head.

Bill turned cautiously and peered through a gap in the chimney pots. The tramp was lying on his stomach on the other side of the roof. To Bill's relief, the weapon in his hand was aimed at Marcus. He fired again, and the man in evening clothes dodged back down the ladder until only the top of his head was showing. His hand appeared, holding his automatic, and a bullet whistled towards the tramp.

Bill tore the slates until his fingernails were split and bleeding, but they defied his efforts. He was in the unenviable position, the centre of both fires. Marcus was dividing his attention between Bill and the tramp—and there was every danger of a bullet finding a gap in the chimney pots.

It was like being the only clay pigeon in a shooting gallery on a Bank Holiday.

Something had to be done. He thought of a way to create a diversion.

He took a crumpled wad of tissue paper from his pocket and held it up. His hand appeared above the chimney pots, waving it, and the others ceased firing. They were waiting to see what he was going to do. With a defiant laugh he tossed it into the garden below.

Marcus shouted something, scrambled back to the roof, and clattered across the slates, heedless of the excellent target he made if the tramp cared to fire. He wrenched an electric torch from his pocket and trained the beam downwards. The paper wrapping had burst and the light shone on splashes of sparkling white on the gravel path below.

Marcus turned quickly and ran back across the roof, reckless of the perilous slipperiness of the slates. He reached the ladder just as it was dragged away. He cursed suddenly. The weapon in his hand barked at a tall, thin man who ran round an angle of the house and stooped over the gleaming fragments. The bullet went wide.

Von Arnheim gathered up the scattered sparkling drops and bolted with them to the aeroplane. He clambered in. There was a roar as the mighty engines of the Fokker sprang to life. The aeroplane ran along the grass and swung upward, missing the house by mere feet. With a shrill wail of wires and stays it mounted into the air, its propeller whirring like mammoth wings.

"You double-crossing swine!" roared Marcus.

His face worked convulsively as he watched his former confederate escaping with the plunder for which he had schemed. Three sharp cracks sounded as he swung his weapon up and pulled frenziedly on the trigger.

Two of the bullets buried themselves in the Fokker. The engine faltered, missed a beat, and the aeroplane lurched like a wounded bird. Swerving, it swung its nose earthward and crashed down. It smashed into the turf and buried its nose deep in the earth, throwing up a fountain of soil and small stones. There was an explosion, and red and orange tongues of flame shot high into the air, licking hungrily at the fuselage.

In the cockpit, Von Arnheim struggled madly to free himself, but he was trapped in a raging inferno of smoke and flame.

An Interval for Love

A single scream, blood-curdling and horrible, was the last of Von Arnheim. A cloud of dense black smoke, shot with leaping blades of fire, wrapped and enfolded the aeroplane, and when it lifted nothing was left but a blackened mass of tangled metal and twisted wire. An ear-splitting explosion carried fragments of metal into the air.

The horizon was streaked with crimson and gold. Soon the sun would sail majestically into the sky. Night was over—and with the dawn the dreams of Gideon Marcus melted into nothingness. Marcus could see two cars tearing down the road a quarter of a mile away, to the lane which led to the house. At this hour, who could be in them—excepting the police?

The game was up. No one knew it better than he. The diamonds for which he had risked so much had perished with Von Arnheim in the flames. They could not have escaped the furnace-like heat.

He balanced himself on the roof ridge of the old house and looked at the fire which was consuming his hopes. Clouds of smoke eddied about him, wreathing him with curling tendrils. This was his last stand. He had planned the robbery with painstaking thoroughness. Every detail had been plotted carefully. It had worked like a charm. They had gained possession of the diamonds, had made a clean getaway.

Once on the Continent there would have been a cool fifty thousand to share with the three people who had helped him. More than his fair share would have stuck to his fingers—besides the cached loot of previous robberies which he had committed alone. A roseate future had beckoned. And now—even escape seemed impossible.

The breaking-down of the aeroplane had delayed them in their escape to the Continent. But all would still have been well—but for the intrusion of Bill. With a snarl, Marcus scrambled across the peaked roof to the chimney-stack behind which Bill was sheltering. He levelled his automatic, with a fiendish grin on his face, and pulled the trigger.

As he fired, Bill stood up and threw his empty automatic full in the other's face. Marcus threw up his arms and the shot went wide. His foot slipped and he slid down the side of the roof, clawing desperately at the empty air. He landed with a crash on the lawn below.

Bill wheeled and saw the tramp coming towards him. He scrambled hastily to the skylight and dropped through, landing on all-fours. Down the stairs he clattered, three at a time. In the hall he fumbled in his pocket and found the key to the cupboard in which he had locked Sheila. His quivering fingers inserted it in the lock, turned it, and he threw open the door.

Sheila was sitting on the floor of the cupboard with her back to the wall. He grasped her hand and pulled her to her feet.

"We've got to get away," he stammered breathlessly.

She stared at him. "Have you any idea," she said, "how I've suffered, cramped in this poky little hole for hours? Shooting going on and feet clamping all over the house, and me in the dark, wondering what was happening, hardly able to breathe..."

Her expression changed as she saw the spreading stain on his sleeve. Her eyes widened and she clutched his uninjured shoulder fearfully. "You're hurt!"

He was faint from loss of blood, but he grinned feebly and shook his head. "It's nothing. The police are coming, two carloads of them. I've got to get you away at once. My car...no, we'll take the other, it's faster...it'll beat anything I've ever seen on the road. If we go now, we've just a chance of showing them our dust."

She was looking over his shoulder, her face contorted with horror. He turned and looked in the direction of her gaze. She was looking at the still, lifeless body of Genarro, which lay sprawled out in the shaft of dust-flecked light which was shining down from the skylight.

"Is he…dead?" she whispered.

"I think so. He…" the hopelessness of trying to explain what had happened came home to him. "…Oh, he fell. Hard enough to break his back."

Brushing the limp golden hair from her forehead, Sheila edged past the crumpled body and went into the disordered room to the right of the hall. Bill followed her anxiously.

"We've got to get away," he said again.

Sheila smiled wanly. "Take off your jacket. I want to see your wound."

"What does it matter? Sheila, please come away. The police will be here any moment. I can't bear to think of…of…" His voice trailed away.

She looked at him with misty eyes. "Of what?" she asked.

The words were difficult to utter; "Prison," he said. "You… in prison. I can't bear it."

Her eyes lit up. "Then…"

"What's the use of talking?" he groaned. "I love you. I'm ready to fight for you, die for you. There isn't anything I wouldn't do for you. I love you. You've taken possession of me, utterly caught me and if you are sent to prison it will be the end of everything for me. Don't worry about the others. They're out of the running. Von Arnheim and the other man are dead. Marcus won't be taking an interest in anything for a while. But the police will be here any minute. The *police.* Don't you understand? I've simply got to get you away."

"Yes," she said softly. "I understand."

With a little sob she put her arms about him and held him close to her. Her eyelashes were wet against his cheek.

"Say it again, please."

"I love you."

"It's the most wonderful thing that ever happened," she breathed.

Her lips met his. Nothing mattered but that. It was heaven. He forgot his aching body, his throbbing wound...

Spoof Sparklers

Footsteps sounded in the hall. The tramp stood in the doorway looking in. Sheila thrust Bill aside and faced the intruder as though to guard her lover with her slender body. "Who are you?" she demanded.

The tramp smiled. "Me? I'm Inspector Leet, of the C.I.D. Who are you? I don't seem to have your picture in my album. A transatlantic crook, like Genarro? Or are you a home product who hasn't been pinched yet?"

He looked at Bill with one eyebrow cocked. "Exciting night we've had, eh? But it's all over."

"He isn't in this," said Sheila hotly. "I..."

The Inspector waved a grubby hand. "I know it. I ran into him before you did. But he's been pretty active." He jerked his thumb over his shoulder. "That little Yankee crook, Genarro, for instance. He's dead. Dead as a doorknob. Self-defence, of course. No one's likely to shed any tears, but there will be questions asked and things said. However, I dare say the young man will come out alright. He's been useful. The others would have escaped with the swag if he hadn't butted in. I'm not so sure about you, young lady. You're one of 'em, aren't you?"

Bill came forward. "Leave her alone," he retorted. "She isn't...she..."

"Yes?" challenged the Inspector. "Think up a good story while you're at it."

Suddenly Bill launched himself forward and threw his arms about the Inspector. He clung on, although he felt weak as a kitten. "Run for it!" he shouted over his shoulder to the girl.

There was a squealing of brakes as two cars drew up outside. Feet pounded on the steps outside the front door. The door was forced back on its hinges with a crash. Blue-coated figures filled the hall.

Inspector Leet forced Bill's arms to his sides and imprisoned them in a powerful grip. He shook his head reproachfully. "You shouldn't have done that. It didn't do any good. It's too late for her to escape anyway."

A uniformed Inspector and two constables crowded into the room. "What's this?" demanded the inspector gruffly, clapping a hand on the C.I.D. man's ragged shoulders. "Good Lord! It's Leet!"

Leet grinned and released Bill. "Right in one," he said. "Excuse the get-up. It was I who got the message through to you."

"What's been going on?"

"Plenty!" replied the C.I.D. man. "The Count de la Fontaine's diamonds were at the root of it all. I've been on the track of them ever since the other night and trailed the thieves to this neighbourhood. Did you find an injured man outside?"

"Yes. We put the bracelets on him."

"Good. That's Gideon Marcus, international crook, confidence man, jewel thief, and a lot of other things. He was the ringleader."

"Did you get the diamonds?"

Leet shook his head ruefully. "No such luck. This young man lost his head and threw them from the roof into the garden."

"Wait a moment!" interrupted Bill. He dug a hand into his pocket and drew out the gleaming necklace. The other gaped at it. "In a room upstairs, I found a lampshade trimmed with glass beads." He explained calmly. "I tore off a handful of them..."

"Holy smoke!" gulped Leet. "And it was the beads you threw into the garden?"

"Yes. Something had to be done. Things were getting too hot."

Bliss for Two

Leet took the diamonds and slipped them into his pocket. "Say no more," he said with a grin. "You can go up to the top of the class." He turned to Sheila. "Well, young lady?"

She smiled. "I'm afraid you're going to be disappointed, Inspector. I'm not a transatlantic crook—not even a home product."

She held out a neat little leather case.

Leet glanced at it. Sheila Lavery, The Jewellers Protective Association. "A private detective, eh?"

"Yes. There have been a number of jewel robberies lately—as you know. My chief suspected Marcus. I was assigned to watch him, with poor Dick Burgess. I faked up a criminal record and managed to gain Marcus's confidence. He took me into his gang. Before I could get in touch with Burgess, I was roped in on the theft of the Fontaine diamonds. Dick was on a job, however, and trailed us down here. When he and I were escaping with the diamonds, Dick was shot."

"I see."

Leet turned to Bill. "Well, that's that. I've got the sparklers—and Marcus. I don't think I need take you along as well. You'll have to come to the Yard later, of course, to be scolded by the Chief Commissioner, but I think you'll come out of it alright. If you don't, I'll resign. Going to London?"

Bill nodded.

"Alright. When you've had about twenty-four hours' sleep call round at the Yard. Oh, and you'll get the reward, of course."

Bill grinned. "We'll split it. You and I—and Sheila!"

"That's decent of you. I'm going back to Town, Miss Lavery. Care for a lift?"

Sheila glanced at Bill.

"Miss Lavery's going with me," said Bill.

Leet winked solemnly at the uniformed inspector. They went out to the drive. With a paternal twinkle in his eye, Leet watched the young man and the girl climbing into Bill's car.

Bill pressed the self-starter, moved the gear lever, and let in the clutch. The car moved smoothly down the drive. They bumped and lurched along the rutted lane and turned onto the high road before either of them spoke.

"I thought you were going North?" said Sheila.

"I was. To Newcastle. My father's order. I wanted to go into the motor business, but he disapproved. Of course, the reward changes all that."

The car glided for some minutes.

"You know, Dad isn't a bad sort," said Bill reflectively. "He makes soap."

There was another silence.

"One of his quaint ideas," remarked Bill, "is that everyone should get married young..."

"Yes?"

"Yes. And when you come to think of it, that isn't a bad idea either."

The car swerved slowly to the side of the road and stopped almost in the ditch.

"Your poor arm," cried Sheila, remorsefully. "I had forgotten."

"Blow my arm," said Bill, putting the other arm about her waist...

It was quite a long time before the car moved on.

THE END

RUINED BY WATER

I was enjoying a glass of excellent lager in the Afrikander bar when the swing doors were pushed apart and the Seller of Mousetraps came in. He shuffled up to the bar and ordered the cheapest alcoholic refreshment to be had.

The Seller of Mousetraps was unkempt. His hair was long and untidy, his chin and cheeks were covered with an iron-grey stubble, and he had obviously been a stranger to soap and water for days. His toes peeped out furtively where the sole and upper of his right boot had parted company. The coat, waistcoat, and trousers which he wore had originally belonged to three different suits and were extravagantly dissimilar in pattern and colour; all that they had in common was their advanced state of raggedness.

He was collarless, but he wore a tie of startling design, the blatant newness of which contrasted oddly with the rest of his apparel. Through a hole in the crown of his battered felt hat strayed a fugitive wisp of hair.

I had seen him a few minutes before, standing in the gutter surrounded by a group of idlers, mostly negroes, whom he was haranguing in the rich idiom of the veldt flavoured with the argot of the Jo'burg native boy, with a few words of the Bechuanaland dialect thrown in for good measure. His manner was cheerfully insulting, but bully his potential customers as he might, business in mousetraps was not brisk.

He disposed of his stock-in-trade among his voluminous garments and brought his drink to my table, nodding to me with insolent friendliness. I took no notice of him but he was not at all offended.

"You wouldn't be interested in a mousetrap, I suppose?" he suggested blandly, assuming an accent that was almost Oxford.

I shook my head.

"I was afraid not." He eyed me from head to foot. "Newcomer to Jo'burg, I take it?"

"Yes," I said coldly.

"Where are you stopping?"

"Palmer Hotel," I answered briefly. It was useless to ignore him, for his type are snub-proof.

"Ah! Then you'll need a mousetrap! The Palmer Hotel—better have a package of Bottomley's Champion Bug-and-Flea Exterminator as well. I can recommend it—I wouldn't be without it for a day. Wonderful stuff."

He fumbled in a capacious pocket and produced a bright yellow packet. To save argument I bought it, though I rejected the mouse trap. The Palmer Hotel's mice were not my affair, but I could not maintain an attitude the same indifference to its bugs and fleas.

"Not long out from the old country?" he asked when the transaction was complete, with the trifling omission of giving me my change.

I said that I had been in South Africa for six months, and had drifted up from the Cape, arriving in Johannesburg a few days before.

"I thought so," he nodded sagely. "I am honoured to be among the first to welcome you to our fair city. From London, aren't you?"

I admitted to having lived in London.

"Dear old London! I was born and bred in Hammersmith," he replied. "Until I came to this infernal country, I was never out of London except for holidays, and five years I spent in Dar—Devonshire." He looked at his empty glass. "On an occasion like this—"

Rising to the bait, I ordered two large whiskies.

"Water?" I suggested, balancing the jug above the glass.

With an expression of horror, he put up a shaking hand and brushed the jug aside.

"No water!" he exclaimed vehemently. "No water! Good God, sir! I was ruined by water!"

His bleary eyes and mottled nose belied the statement; but there was obviously a story behind it. With a sigh, I composed myself to listen.

"I was ruined by water!" he reiterated.

He swallowed half of his whisky at gulp before continuing—

"As a boy I was very ambitious," he began, laying down his glass. "Partly through home influence, partly through education. 'Hitch your waggon to a star!' I don't know how many times I wrote that axiom in my copybook. Thousands of times, at least. Ambition! Ambition! Ambition! It was drummed into me, at school and at home. Be ambitious! Hitch your waggon to a star.

"I was taught that to be unsuccessful was a crime. That those who taught me were failures didn't matter. Their lessons took root. There wasn't a lad in the world more chockfull of ambition than I was when I left school.

"My father died about then, leaving a comfortable sum of money—to his creditors, who were none of them entirely satisfied. My uncle undertook the arrangement of my mother's affairs. I was the first affair he arranged. He bunged me into a bank, and, ambition or no, there I stayed for five years. My mother died in the meantime. By that time, I was twenty-three. Still as ambitious as ever.

"I don't mind admitting that it is a moot point whether I was really ambitious or just discontented. I loathed that job. The smiling face of our prosperous-looking manager annoyed me. The eighteen percent dividends we aid to shareholders made me feel sick. My fifteen pounds a month made me sicker. Ever lived a respectable life in London on fifteen pounds a month? Wearing spats to hide the holes in your socks. Examining your socks every morning to see if they'll last another day. Turning your collars. Reversing your cuffs. Letting your hair go without cutting a full week longer than you ought. In debt by the end of the month to every pal who'll lend you a bob.

"You need a safety-valve to prevent you going mad. Mine was my monthly blow-out. Every payday, I'd get gloriously drunk. I'd start with a slap-up dinner at Henrici's. Seven courses, a pint of champagne, liqueur, and a shilling cigar. After dinner, I'd drop in at the Empire—it's gone now, isn't it? —and spend most of the evening in the bar.

"By midnight I'd be gloriously drunk. In the morning I'd have hammers pounding in my head. I'd see what a mug I'd been the night before. I'd swear off for ever; but next pay day I'd repeat the performance.

"I know what you're going to say. Don't say it. A wise fool knows his own folly. I knew mine all right. But I was fed up. Bored to tears. But I had to stick it. That's what used to get me. The same routine, for ever and ever, as long as life lasted. There was no choice; I simply had to stick it.

"But, had I? —that was the question I began to ask myself, the question any ambitious youth was bound to ask himself. And the answer was 'Money.' With money I could do anything I wanted. Without it I was a glorified slave. Money was power, and it lay all around me in piles of crisp notes.

"Banks pay you fifteen pounds a month and trust you with

thousands. From the time we opened in the morning until three o'clock in the afternoon there was hardly a minute when I didn't have the stuff between my fingers. Thousands of pounds at a time. Paying out. Taking in. Checking. Counting.

"I began to plan how I could make some of it stick. Enough to make a free man of me.

Gradually I evolved a plan. It involved half-a-dozen bogus accounts, all sorts of juggling with my ledgers, and a neat bit of work with certain cancelled cheques, but after I got it going it went like clockwork. I didn't waste any time; quick returns was my motto. In three months, I had acquired thirty thousand pounds by my skill at accountancy. Not bad for a beginner, eh?

"It was stowed away under another name, in a box with one of the safe deposit firms, but at last I made an even safer disposition of it. On Sunday I went on a trip to the country, carrying a black leather handbag containing the money in conveniently small notes, done up in sealed, air-tight tins. The spot I'd chosen was about eighty miles from London, and ten miles from a certain manufacturing town of about half a million population—let's call it Branbury, for want of a better name. The spot itself was close to the merest hamlet, nestling in the mouth of a valley; the population was about two men and a boy, a horse, a cow, and a handful of old women. I'd spent a holiday there as a nipper, and it naturally occurred to me when I wanted a quiet spot to hide my—er—professional earnings. I hid the tins three feet under the turf, far up the valley, where no living thing but a browsing sheep was likely to go near them until I wanted them again.

"On Monday morning I was at the bank as usual. Running away was the furthest thing from my mind. I sat tight and took my medicine. They were on to me like a shot, of course, as soon as it was discovered that the books had been submitted to a spot of fancy cooking that wouldn't have discredited a Parisian chef. There was plenty of evidence; enough to convince twelve good men and true and the judge, but they couldn't find the money. They begged me to tell them where it was, nagged, pleaded, stormed, coaxed, insisted; even offered a lightish sentence. To all such persuasion I turned a face streaming with tears, and whimpered that this was what came of drink and cards and backing horses, and what a blessing it was that my poor dear mother hadn't lived to see this day. But I didn't tell them where the money was. I swore that I had spent every blessed farthing.

"The upshot was that I was sent up for five years; the longest years of my life. It seemed endless: a dreary succession of days made horrible by prison food, prison work—and it is work! —prison routine, and prison beds. But I stuck it. There were those tins, you see, containing a fortune in ready money. Thirty thousand pounds to spend, and the rest of my life to spend it; what did prison matter, when I had that to look forward to?

"With remission for good conduct, I was out in a few months over four years. A waiting detective picked up my trail at the prison gates, and followed me to London. You get what he was after; they still believed that I had some, if not all, of the money cashed away, and they hoped that I would lead them to it. What a hope! I led that cop the dance of his life. All over London, back and forward, up and down, doubling on my tracks until finally, I shook him off. Then I streaked for Branbury, and the little village where my money was hidden. All the way from Branbury to the village in the jogging, perspiring local train I was hugging myself with joy.

"But I was in for the shock of my life. They'd moved that village right out of the valley. The station was a good half-mile from where it used to be. And where the village had been, where the deep, wide valley had been, was a smooth, shining plate of blue.

"The town of Branbury had built itself a new reservoir, and forty million gallons of water lay, calm and unruffled, on top of my thirty thousand pounds! It's still there; my thousands in ready money, sealed in airtight cocoa-tins, buried under three feet of soil—and quite a lot of water! And every time I think about it, I just have to curse.

He did curse, with a colour and virility which earned him the respectful admiration of the sleek-haired barman. For a solid five minutes he cursed and never once repeated himself.

"The same again?" I suggested sympathetically, when he paused to drain the remains of his whisky at a gulp.

"Thanks. But no water. I was ruined by water!"

Tactfully I removed the water-jug from the table in front of him, lest its contents should boil away under the red-hot fury of his gaze.

THE END